DreadfulWater Shows Up

DreadfulWater Shows Up

by

Hartley GoodWeather

Harper*Flamingo*Canada

DreadfulWater Shows Up: A Novel
Copyright © 2002 by Dead Dog Café Productions.
All rights reserved. No part of this book may be used
or reproduced in any manner whatsoever without
prior written permission except in the case of brief
quotations embodied in reviews.
For information address
HarperCollins Publishers Ltd,
55 Avenue Road, Suite 2900,
Toronto, Ontario, Canada M5R 3L2

www.harpercanada.com

HarperCollins books may be purchased for educa-
tional, business, or sales promotional use.
For information please write:
Special Markets Department,
HarperCollins Canada,
55 Avenue Road, Suite 2900,
Toronto, Ontario, Canada M5R 3L2

First edition

Canadian Cataloguing in Publication Data

GoodWeather, Hartley
DreadfulWater shows up : a novel

ISBN 0-00-200510-7

I. Title.

PS8563.O83449D74 2002   C813'.6   C2001-902516-5
PR9199.4.G66D74 2002

HC 9 8 7 6 5 4 3 2 1

Printed and bound in the United States
Set in FF Quadraat

for Christian
who knows the joy of sleeping in a pickup
in the middle of nowhere. In the middle of winter.

One

Ora Mae Foreman relaxed on the balcony of the Cascade with her thermos of coffee, a bag of chocolate-coated doughnut holes, and the morning paper, and waited for the sun to light up the eastern face of the Rockies.

"A million-dollar view," Sterling Noseworthy told all the agents. "That's what you're selling."

It was boloney, of course, the kind that Sterling liked to slice and serve when he was trying to be motivational. To be sure, the views at Buffalo Mountain Resort were spectacular—the mountains almost in your living room, the heavy forest of pine and spruce, the river racing down White Goat Canyon and leaping over the edge of the Bozeman Fault, and the vast expanse of prairies stretching out forever under the towering sky.

But the views aside, Ora Mae knew what Buffalo Mountain Resort was really selling—the illusion that you had escaped the rush of the city for the sanctuary of the wilderness, the knowledge that you were among the elite in the vacation retreat game, and the security of the guard at the front gate.

There was wilderness out there, all right. Places to get lost. Cliffs to fall off. Bears. Moose. Maybe even a pack of wolves to brighten your day. But the condominium and casino complex was about as wild as Banff or Lake Tahoe or wherever the rich gathered for an outdoor adventure.

Ora Mae wasn't sure that the Indians had done the right thing, building the complex. Claire Merchant had made Buffalo Mountain the main issue in the tribal election and Claire had come away with enough votes to carry the day. But not without splitting the council, dividing families,

1

and destroying old alliances. Ironically, the most visible casualty was Claire herself, for her son, Stanley—or Stick, as he was known to everyone except his mother—disagreed with her vision of economic independence, formed a mildly militant organization called the Red Hawk Society, and began picketing the project. The protests had interrupted construction from time to time, but aside from the one day someone had bounced a bullet off an idle dump trunk and sent everyone scrambling for cover, there hadn't been any real violence. Just hurt feelings and sore voices. And the bitter taste of having to choose sides.

But that was Indian business and none of Ora Mae's concern. When the complex opened in another week, her job was to move the units as fast as she could.

"Get a feel for the place," Sterling told everyone. "Walk through the models. Stand on the balconies. Imagine what it would be like to own a place like this."

Not that anyone in the office could afford one of the units. Even the cheap one-bedrooms on the north side, where the view included the top of the casino and the parking lot, were going for over a quarter of a million dollars.

Ora Mae was in the middle of the obituaries and working on the last of the doughnut holes when her cellphone went off. When Sterling first passed the phones out to all the agents, Ora Mae thought having a cellphone was the cream on the shortcake. For the first couple of weeks, every time it rang, she couldn't get it out of her purse fast enough. But it didn't take her long to realize that while the phone was cute, even useful, it was also a tether. The longer she dragged it around, the more it reminded her of her sister in Salt Lake City and her four kids. They were cute, too.

Now she hated the damn thing, and every time it rang, she would wait a little longer before she answered it. Most of the time, Sterling was on the other end, and Ora Mae didn't mind making him wait until the pond froze and the geese went south.

"Where are you?"

The man had all the social graces of shag carpet. Ora Mae licked her fingers slowly. They still tasted of warm chocolate.

"At the complex."

"Is everything okay?"

Ever since the models had been furnished and loaded up with all the goodies that rich people required, Sterling had worried about the place being vandalized. So, for the past two weeks, someone from the office had had to drive from Chinook to the complex each day, just to settle Sterling's mind that all of the models still had their potpourri and none of the expensive toys had gone missing.

"Have you seen Clarence?"

"Nope."

Clarence Fellows was Sterling's nephew, a young, muscular man just out of community college who thought of himself as a sports car. Especially when it came to women. When it came to work, however, Clarence was more an old bus with four flat tires and a dead battery.

"He was supposed to check the models yesterday."

"That right?"

"But I didn't hear from him."

"You try his cellphone?"

"Responsibility," said Sterling, his voice wading through warm custard. "The first imperative of a good agent is responsibility."

Ora Mae generally tried to steer clear of other people's business. "Don't worry, Sterling, everything's fine."

"No trouble?"

Trouble was Sterling's noun for anything gone wrong. An unhappy client was trouble. A bounced cheque was trouble. Floods, forest fires, terminal diseases, high interest rates, loose fan belts, tooth decay. Bad haircuts. Sterling liked things that were predictable and organized. Just what he was doing in the real-estate business was a mystery.

"Not a drop."

"Because we don't want trouble, do we?"

It was a rhetorical question, and Ora Mae had given up answering that kind of question even before she left home and headed west to see the sights and make her fortune. That was twenty years ago, and all in all, the sights had been worth it.

"Don't forget to check all the units."

"Maybe Clarence is putting a big deal together." Ora Mae could hear the smile in her voice and wondered whether Sterling could hear it, too.

Probably not, she thought. The only voice Sterling ever listened to was his own.

"And call me back."

Buffalo Mountain Resort had been designed by Douglas Cardinal and had already won several awards for the innovative way Cardinal had combined the demands of an upscale resort with traditional Native motifs and concerns. The most prominent building, the one you saw first as you came off the prairie floor and headed into the foothills, was the casino, a huge copper-plated geodesic dome that glowed and shimmered in the light.

The condominium complex itself was to the south and west of the casino. It was taller than the casino, but the grey concrete walls and the tinted windows made the building all but disappear into the face of the mountains.

Sterling had had an aerial photograph taken of the area and had tacked it to the wall behind his desk. You couldn't see the pattern from the ground, but looking at the buildings from above, it was clear that Cardinal had been both creative and literal. What the cluster of buildings most resembled, if you used your imagination a little, was a buffalo warming itself in the high plains sun.

Ora Mae reluctantly stood up and brushed the crumbs off the patio table. She folded the doughnut bag neatly, slipped it into her purse along with the thermos, and checked her shoes to make sure she wasn't tracking anything across the pale wool rug.

For just a moment, she thought about calling Sterling and telling him that a toilet had backed up and overflowed onto the carpet, or that a large bird had flown into one of the windows and shattered the glass, or that a small electrical fire had damaged a kitchen. She took a moment's pleasure in imagining Sterling's face, but she didn't even think about opening her purse. That was one thing she and Sterling Noseworthy the Fourth or Fifth, whichever he was, had in common. She didn't like trouble any better than he did.

Trouble, Ora Mae's mother had told her and her sisters, was like a man, never in short supply, never too far away.

The Cataract was the smallest of the models, a long, narrow one-bedroom with a kitchen at one end and a living room at the other. Ora

Mae had spent some time trying to find a good adjective for it, something she could use as a selling point. The closest she had come to was "cozy." "Cozy" was almost the right size, but "cozy" also suggested good light and a warm, homey feel.

"Place is so small," she had heard Clarence tell Sterling, "a man can stand at the front door and piss in the toilet with his eyes closed."

It was male grunting. Ora Mae had heard it all before, and she was sure that the attempt wouldn't be worth the watching. If the bathroom at the office was any indicator, Clarence standing across the room from the toilet with his eyes shut wasn't going to be any better or worse than Clarence standing next to the toilet with his eyes open.

When Ora Mae opened the door to the Cataract, she had the distinct feeling that she was not alone. "Clarence?"

She knew about Clarence and Celia Brothers. It was supposed to be a secret, but probably the only two people who didn't know that Clarence and Celia had been touring the motels in the immediate area were Clarence's wife, Barbara, and Sterling. Ora Mae suspected that Barbara did know, in fact, and was just waiting for the right moment to cut Clarence's heart out.

"Clarence! You here?"

Ora Mae stood in the doorway and tested the air. It was heavy and stale. But above the formaldehyde off-gassing from the carpet and particleboard furniture, and the sharp stink of new paint, was an unfamiliar smell, acrid and sweet. An unpleasant smell. A smell that made her anxious and grumpy.

Word was Clarence had run out of motels in the area and had been bringing Celia out to the resort. But the one-bedroom unit? God! The man had no more romance than a Kleenex.

"Give it up, Clarence."

The bedroom was empty, and the bed had not been slept in. Thank God she didn't have to deal with Clarence and Celia naked and hiding in the closet. Ora Mae walked to the living room and looked out the window. Below, the top of the casino was bright gold and red, and all around it, the asphalt parking lot spread out like a lava flow, eating its way through the rocks and the trees and the thick prairie grass. She stood in the light and tried to imagine what she was going to say to prospective buyers to get them to pony up a quarter of a million dollars for a hallway with a designer toilet. Probably something about investment.

It wasn't until she turned around and started for the door that she saw the man.

"Jesus!"

He was slumped in a large wingback chair facing the window. He looked comfortable enough, and if it hadn't been for the way his eyes stared at nothing in particular, Ora Mae might have thought he was relaxing and enjoying the peace and quiet that came with owning a piece of Buffalo Mountain Resort.

As she stood looking at the man, she realized she hadn't taken a breath in the last little while. When she did, it was a long, deep breath, and as she pulled it in, she willed her shoulders to drop and her hands to relax. She had seen bodies before, and it had been a long time since she had let a man, alive or dead, scare her.

Ora Mae walked back to the Cascade. When she got there, she sat down, took the thermos out of her purse, and finished off the last of the coffee. The sun was up now, and as she watched Buffalo Mountain come to life, she realized that she hadn't really noticed the man's face. She didn't think he was anyone she knew, but she was sorry now that she hadn't looked at him more closely or checked for a wallet or a credit card, something that would give the man a name.

Ora Mae dialed Sterling's number first. She didn't want anyone else to give him the good news. Trouble. Ora Mae smiled to herself. That boy didn't know what trouble was.

Then she called the sheriff.

Then she called Thumps DreadfulWater.

Two

When the alarm began ringing, Thumps DreadfulWater went looking for the clock with his elbow. It was one of those old-fashioned clocks that had to be wound. He didn't remember winding it—in fact, hadn't wound it for months. And while he had a vague notion of how to set the alarm, he couldn't think of any reason why he would have done something that stupid. So, he was relieved to discover that the noise that had woken him was the phone and not the clock.

Thumps wrapped the quilt around his head and rolled over on the cat. Freeway didn't yowl or move out of the way as a normal cat would. She simply grunted, stuck her claws into Thumps' stomach, and went back to sleep. As he fumbled for the phone, Thumps reminded himself once again that he needed to get an answering machine and that it was time to clip Freeway's nails.

"I'm not in right now."

"Thumps? It's Ora Mae."

"Leave a message."

"You don't have an answering machine."

"And I'll get back to you."

"Quit fooling around. I'm out at the resort."

"Wait for the tone."

"I found a dead body," said Ora Mae. "Sheriff says to bring your camera."

Thumps held the phone for a moment before he put it back on the cradle. A dead body? At Buffalo Mountain? Maybe Sterling Noseworthy had looked at the prices of the condos and had dropped dead of shock in the lobby. No, Thumps thought to himself, Ora Mae hadn't sounded happy enough for that to have happened. Besides, Sterling had set the prices. The only thing the man would be concerned about at this point were the profits. And what his percentage would be.

Of course, Ora Mae hadn't bothered to say *who* had died at Buffalo Mountain Resort. The woman was truly evil. She knew the hint of a mystery was one of the few ways to get him out of bed on a Sunday morning. The only idea that immediately came to mind was that the Red Hawk Society had had some kind of confrontation with the police. But a death? Not likely. Stick Merchant was young and passionate, but he wasn't stupid. And besides, with the exception of the dump truck incident, all the protests had been peaceful so far, hardly any more contentious than an office picnic.

Freeway stretched and began licking around Thumps' belly button. For some reason, the cat liked this particular spot on his body.

"Knock it off."

As cats go, Freeway was a reasonable sort, and apart from belly buttons, her only other obsession was with anything that resembled string. The first week she was in the house, Thumps had discovered that all the laces on his shoes and boots had been removed at the eyelets. Nice clean cuts, as if someone had come along with a knife or a pair of scissors. He suspected about Freeway, but he didn't really believe she had done it until he began finding the hard ends of the shoelaces in the litter box. After that, he was forced to hide his shoes in the kitchen cupboard along with the cereal and the potatoes.

Thumps fluffed the pillows, straightened the sheets, and arranged the quilt so that it tucked under the pillows and hung over the other three sides of the bed equally. Freeway sat on the floor and watched him as she always did.

"You could help, you know."

Freeway blinked and headed down the hall.

"I get to use it first," Thumps called after the cat, but it was a futile gesture. And he knew it. By the time he got to the bathroom, Freeway was already standing on the seat, her head in the toilet. In addition to her passion for shoelaces, the cat also had a relationship with water that Thumps couldn't quite fathom. He had given her a nice, heavy ceramic bowl for water, a bowl he had made in art-something class during his first year at university. It was a pretty piece, its sides decorated with plump yellow fish trying to swim through a thick blue glaze.

"This is your bowl," he had told the cat with a certain amount of pride and goodwill. "It's handmade."

If Freeway ever used the bowl, Thumps had never caught her at it. Instead, she drank out of the toilet. Thumps found this particularly disgusting and had tried closing the bathroom door. But closed doors drove Freeway crazy. She would scratch and howl and reach under the door with one paw and try to pull herself through.

The mirror over the sink was in a sour mood. Thumps tilted his head to one side to see whether a different angle would help. He was beginning to look like his father. Or, more exactly, he was beginning look like the pictures of his father that his mother had kept. Eugene DreadfulWater had been a tall man with no ass, a long face, and heavy lips that looked as though they had been edged with a razor. He had worn his hair short and cut close against his head. But what people noticed first about him, Thumps' mother had said, were his eyes. They were dead black and so tightly slanted, they appeared to be closed most of the time.

Thumps had his father's face. But he had his mother's hair. His father's hair had been black and straight. His mother's hair had been black and wavy. In the seventies, when he was at university, he had tried wearing his hair long and discovered that if he kept it at his shoulders, he was fine. But if he let the hair go with the idea of working it into a pony-tail or braids, in an effort to keep up with the rest of the Indians who were trying to look like Indians, his hair would simply curl up in unruly twists and ruin the sought-after effect. Now, like his father, he kept his hair short. At least it was still black with no trace of grey.

Thumps checked his teeth. The one real benefit of having skin a little darker than the people around you was that your teeth looked whiter than they were. He tried to remember when he had last had them cleaned. Before he left California? That long ago?

Thumps turned on the shower and stepped in. Okay, he was curious. People in Chinook didn't die all that often, and as he recalled, the condos weren't going on sale until next week, so it was too soon for the Birken-stocks from Los Angeles and Toronto to start shooting each other over the views. Maybe it was a tourist with foresight who had decided to kill himself *before* the casino opened and he lost all his money. But the cop in Thumps, the cop he had tried to leave behind in California, told him that the body at Buffalo Mountain Resort wasn't going to be anything so simple.

Of course the death could be something simple. Something uncomplicated. Something ordinary. A heart attack. A stroke. Out of habit, Thumps had assumed that foul play was involved. Homicide had been his game. Bodies that came his way when he was on the force had not died of their own accord. But Ora Mae hadn't mentioned how the body became dead, had she? Thumps had merely jumped to that particular conclusion.

He padded down the hallway to the kitchen, Freeway weaving her way around his feet, complaining about the late hour and starvation. "You need to lose weight," Thumps mumbled, though it wasn't clear whether he was talking to the cat or to himself.

He opened a cupboard and took out his favourite bowl. One of the heavy water glasses was out of place, and he moved it slightly to the right, so that it lined up with the rest of the set. There was a satisfying feeling to order, Thumps had to admit. Bowls where they should be, glasses in straight lines, flatware in perfect stacks. Cereal boxes arranged by height.

Claire would be up by now, would have already finished her breakfast. If frosted cereal and white toast could be called breakfast. How anyone could face each morning with only sugar and carbohydrates to give them energy and courage was beyond Thumps. Thank heaven for Shredded Wheat. And soy milk.

"Come on," he said to Freeway, and headed for the stairs.

The basement was damp and cool and dark, and the feel and the smell of being underground always reminded him of the eight years he had spent in Eureka on the northern California coast. He had liked the town, had especially liked the weather. Grey. Foggy. Wet. Green. It was an isolated community, to be sure, but you could go up to Clam Beach and walk the two miles from the river to the cliffs and not see another person. Or further on to Trinidad Head and have a sandwich on the pier and watch the ocean run in around the point. San Francisco was six hours to the south when the road was open, but coastal people tended to stay put. Tourists came north, but they were a seasonal occurrence, like migrating birds and mudslides.

Chinook, on the other hand, was high prairies, cold and dry. In the summer, the sweat would fry on your face and leave salt lines around your neck, and every morning you'd have to pry each eye open with your fingers. Winter was worse. You'd spread lotion all over your body to keep the skin from splitting apart and still get smoke simply by rubbing your arms together. Or start a fire by snapping your fingers.

But the weather in Chinook was not why Thumps had moved here, and the weather in Eureka was not why he had left.

Thumps unlocked the door to the darkroom. His nose had been right. The stop bath was dead. He tipped the tray out, washed it, and leaned it against the side of the sink to dry. Freeway loved the darkroom, and she headed straight for the shelves under the sink where Thumps kept the amber bottles of chemistry. Once behind the bottles and buried in the plumbing and the open stud wall, there was no way to get her out until she had had her fill of darkness and mystery.

"We're not staying."

Before he had received Ora Mae's phone call, Thumps had planned to spend the day printing, sitting in the dark in front of the old Omega D-2, sorting through proof sheets and negatives. He hadn't been looking forward to working in the darkroom particularly, but now that he wouldn't be able to hide away in the basement, he found himself feeling resentful for having lost what he now considered to be ... leisure. He sat down in the chair and slid in under the easel. This was his favourite spot. Quiet, dark, private. Sometimes he would work on one negative for days, lose himself in the variations of light, pull print after print until the image was perfect. And then, more times than not, he would decide that the contrast wasn't quite right, or the toner was too strong or too weak, or the paper was too warm or too cold, and he would begin again.

"Come on." Thumps rolled out of the chair, grabbed the Leica and the Vivitar flash, and slipped the seventy-millimetre lens into the bag. "Time for a treat."

"Treat" was one of a handful of words that Freeway knew. Or, rather, it was one of a handful of words she cared about. She loped out the door and up the stairs, and by the time Thumps arrived in the kitchen, she was on top of the scratching post complaining and doing her cat dance.

Thumps hadn't seen Claire for over a week, and he tried to remember whether they were friends again. Claire was a terrific woman, but she tended to be, well, tense. Mostly, it was her job. He understood that. As head of the band council and a single mother, Claire was always under some sort of pressure, and unfortunately, she wasn't the type to delegate responsibility.

Or pain.

And between the council and her teenaged son, she had plenty of both. Not that Stick was a bad kid. He was bright, enthusiastic, and a general pain in the ass. Thumps just wished that Claire could keep her feelings about the two of them separate. If she was angry with Stick, Thumps caught the fallout. If she was annoyed with Thumps, Stick heard about it. Thumps had the distinct feeling that Claire could only manage one man at a time, and he found it confusing trying to remember who was in the doghouse and who was in the yard.

He opened the cupboard, took down the box of Kitty Num-Nums, and placed a tiny brown fishy-smelling biscuit on the scratching post directly under Freeway's nose.

"This is it. Don't ask for more."

Through the window, Thumps could see that it was going to be another bright, high-sky day. He missed the fog and the damp. Sunshine was overrated. Freeway gulped her treat down and began dancing around for another.

"No way." Thumps washed his fingers in the sink.

Dead bodies could be simple affairs. But as he opened the door, Thumps had the distinct feeling that the one at Buffalo Mountain Resort wasn't going to be the easy kind, the distinct feeling that things were about to get complicated. The distinct feeling that this one was going to ruin more than just his morning.

Three

As Thumps drove the twenty miles out to Buffalo Mountain Resort, he realized that if he hadn't wasted time on cereal, he might have been able to enjoy a minor automobile spectacle—Duke Hockney's Ford, Sterling Noseworthy's BMW, and Beth Mooney's Chrysler station wagon flying by him at speeds well over the posted limit. Sterling, who had the fastest car, might have been in the lead. But the sheriff's sport-utility had the lights and the nifty siren, and Thumps wondered what the chances were that Duke would have taken time out of his busy schedule to pull Sterling over and give him a ticket.

All the way out to the turnoff, Thumps kept an eye on the rear-view mirror, half expecting to be chased down by an armada of ambulances, fire trucks, and television vans, hell-bent for the scene of the crime. But by the time his old Volvo had chugged its way up the grade to the new road that the tribe had built to accommodate the flood of cars and tour buses Claire hoped would wash over the tribe's most ambitious economic project, the only vehicle he could see in any direction was his own.

Not that he knew for sure that there was a crime, but when he crossed the river and stopped the car next to the security gate and the guard house, he noticed two things. One, the gate was closed, and two, Cooley Small Elk was smiling so hard, his teeth were beginning to show.

"Hey, Thumps."

Cooley put one arm on the roof of the Volvo and leaned in at the window. The car sagged to one side, and Thumps had to brace his knee against the arm rest to keep from being thrown against the door.

"You're late, cousin."

Cooley had been the perfect choice for the gate guard. Huge and friendly, he was security personified, and he had the one attribute that money couldn't buy. With his dark brown skin, his high cheekbones, his piercing eyes, and his long black hair done up in braids, Cooley looked as though he had just stepped out of an Edward Curtis photograph on his way to a movie set. Not many of the people who were going to visit Buffalo Mountain Resort or were going to buy condominiums at the complex had ever spent any time with Native people. But if they had seen Little Big Man or Dances with Wolves—and who hadn't—they knew Cooley.

"Great-looking uniform."

"Yeah," said Cooley. "You know, they make you buy these things with your own money."

"Hard to find your size?"

"I'll say. Had to send all the way to San Francisco."

The black butt of a pistol hung out of Cooley's holster. Thumps wasn't sure an armed guard was a good idea, especially with a protest lurking at the edges of the complex, that could turn ugly at any time. If it hadn't already.

"I see they're letting you carry."

"Naw," said Cooley. "It's my kid's air gun. They just want me to look like a guard. You'd think that with Stick and his pals playing cowboys and Indians, they'd have me packing."

"Fooled me."

Cooley leaned in farther and dropped his voice. "Got my rifle inside, just in case there's any real action."

"Like today?"

Cooley smiled and stood up. The Volvo lurched back to its feet. "Yeah, today's been great."

"Anybody we know?"

"Nobody's talking," said Cooley. "You going to take pictures?"

"If I can get in." And Thumps let the car roll forward a little.

"Old Nosehairs said nobody gets in without his okay," said Cooley. "As if he's in charge of anything."

"Sterling upsets easy."

"Acted as if this was my fault."

"Can't see how that could be."

"Hell," said Cooley, "they aren't paying me to keep people out."

"People wind up dead in the damnedest places."

"They're paying me to play Indian." Cooley smoothed his braids and hitched his pants. "Soon as they sell most of the units, they'll bring in one of those automated gates, and I'll be history."

"Everybody up at the condos?"

"You got your camera handy?"

"Right here." Thumps pulled the Leica out of the bag.

"How about taking a picture of me? My girlfriend's got a thing for uniforms."

"Sure."

"Wait a minute," said Cooley, and he lumbered over to the guard house. "Let me get my rifle."

From the front gate to the main complex, the road followed the natural curve of the land, so that you had the illusion of winding your way through deep forest. And only after you broke into what Sterling euphemistically called "the clearing," and looked back, did you realize for every tree that had been left standing, twenty had been taken.

Thumps stepped out of the car and slung his camera bag over his shoulder. Even with the sun out, the morning mountain air was sharp, and it caught him by surprise. The hill from the parking lot to the condos was not particularly steep or long, but he paced his breathing so that he wouldn't have to stop and he wouldn't pass out. It was the altitude, he told himself, and the weight of the camera bag, neither of which was the truth. But it was too early in the day to be dealing with personal realities and a corpse.

The lock on the main door was one of those new technical wonders that worked from a computer. If you didn't have the code or a key card, you could spend your lunch hour with a cutting torch trying to get in. Someone had propped it open with a rock. So much for security.

Thumps was surprised at how quiet the building was—dead quiet, he might have said, had he not been out of breath. Given the number of people who were already somewhere inside, he expected to hear voices, see people running back and forth, perhaps even stumble across a sign that said, Dead Body, This Way. But there was nothing. No sound. No activity. Just the echo of silence and the smell of empty places.

The elevators were polished brass, and they glistened in the half-light of the lobby. Thumps checked the indicator. One of the cars on the eighth floor. The body was probably there. And, as luck would have it, so were the models.

As soon as Thumps stepped off the elevator, he knew he was on the right planet. Down the hall and around the corner, he could hear the vague rumour of voices. And they didn't sound particularly happy. No sense in rushing in, Thumps told himself. Not until the dust had settled.

The model across from the elevators was a three-bedroom, two-bath, cathedral-ceilinged affair called the Cascade, and despite Thumps' general objection to anything he could not afford, he had to admit that the place was luxurious. The west wall was glass, floor to ceiling, and the unobstructed view of the mountains made everything feel spacious and airy. The kitchen was right out of an architectural magazine—dark wood cabinets, porcelain sink, six-burner gas stove-top, stainless-steel appliances, and thick dark green granite countertops running off in all directions. With cork floors the colour of warm toast.

Thumps stood in the kitchen and took a deep breath. He could like this. He tried the stove-top. There was a momentary clicking sound as though someone were trying to strike a match on steel, and then the soft blue flame blossomed under the burner.

The refrigerator was a side-by-side cavern built into the wall. Inside, someone had left a large decorator plate of fresh fruit along with a bottle of champagne, two glasses, and a buff card with a gold ribbon that read, "The only true currency is quality."

Thumps ran a hand across the counter. Smooth and cool. He lifted the handle on the tap and watched the water slide effortlessly into the sink, as if it were oiled.

The master bedroom was a long rectangle, painted deep green with a crimson accent. Thick Persian carpets were spread out on the hardwood, and Thumps didn't have to turn up a corner to see that they were handmade. Against the far wall was a king-sized bed, with a carved wooden headboard depicting a forest scene complete with a river, several moose, and a family of beavers. Someone had left a single red silk rose on the duvet next to a small wicker basket of individually wrapped chocolates, a reminder to prospective buyers that luxury was in the details.

Lots of toys, Thumps thought to himself. Lots of toys.

But it was the master bathroom that made him smile—a five-piece, marble-tile ensuite with a deep jacuzzi tub positioned under a greenhouse window so you could lie in the swirling water and see the sky.

The dead body could wait.

The glass door to the shower was etched with dolphins, and the inside walls were wrapped with handmade tiles in an abstract underwater scene. Porcelain and chrome sunflower shower heads bloomed on each of the three walls, while cast-pewter whales near the floor let in fresh steam through their blowholes.

At the back of the enclosure was a stained-glass window with two standing cranes in a marsh done up in blue and green and milk tones. Triangles of clear bevelled glass let in just enough light to nourish the hanging ferns. The cedar bench under the window was a nice touch, Thumps thought. You could stretch out on the aromatic planks and let the water and the warm mist wash over your body, or you could turn the recessed heat lamps on and create your own tropical rainforest at the flip of a switch.

He tried to imagine what it would be like to spend an afternoon stretched out on the bench in the steam and the water, and the more he thought about the water pouring out of the shower heads and mixing with the steam to form a comforting, moist cloud, the more he realized that he had to go to the bathroom.

When Thumps strolled out to the living room, on his way to the balcony and the matched lounge chairs and the white cast-iron table, he found Ora Mae waiting for him in the doorway.

"It was open."

"You got lucky," said Ora Mae. "Locks don't get installed until next week."

Thumps shoved his hands in his pockets and smiled.

"You see anything you like?"

"It's overpriced."

"And you call yourself a detective."

"I'm a photographer."

Ora Mae opened the refrigerator. "You touch anything?"

"Besides the cheap champagne?"

"It's not cheap," said Ora Mae. "And what about this?" She slid the fresh fruit out so Thumps could see the entire plate. "Looks as if someone has helped themselves to some of my apples."

"Not guilty."

"Uh-huh." Ora Mae slid the plate back and closed the door. "You're beginning to remind me of Goldilocks. You didn't mess up the bed, did you?"

Thumps shook his head.

"Use the toilet?"

"So, where's the dead body?"

Ora Mae put her hands on her hips. "Four hundred and fifty thousand," she said. "And that's without the options."

Thumps blinked. "What options?"

"Almost everything you see." Ora Mae looked around the room. "For four-fifty, all you get is formica and broadloom."

Thumps liked Ora Mae, and he was glad that she liked him. "How many have you sold?"

"Why? You thinking of buying?"

"You think it's a good investment?"

"Investment?" Ora Mae smiled her best smile—the one she used on buyers to help them find their cheque books. "Now, what do you think?"

Thumps looked back at the refrigerator. "You think they'd miss a banana?"

Ora Mae turned off the lights and held the door open.

"I didn't have a big breakfast."

"So? Eat a big lunch," she said.

Thumps followed Ora Mae down the hall. In the distance, he could hear Sterling's voice growing louder, more insistent.

"Just get it out of here," Sterling was saying.

"Can't do that." Duke's voice was flat and pitched at an angle, the way a grown-up aims it when talking to a child.

"He's starting to smell."

"Then don't breathe."

Ora Mae stopped just outside an open door that said Cataract and turned back to Thumps.

"Don't go chewing on Sterling," she said. "Poor man's had a hard day."

The apartment was filled with people. Sterling Noseworthy, Duke Hockney, and Hockney's deputy, Andy Hopper, were standing by the window. Sterling was smiling and waving his hands around, as if he were trying to talk Duke and Andy into doing something fun.

Thumps leaned toward Ora Mae. "What's this one cost?"

"You can't afford this one, either." Ora Mae pursed her lips. "We got a body, remember?"

"It's kind of small."

"Then buy the bigger one."

As soon as Sterling saw Thumps, he flew across the room. "Thumps!" he shouted. "Thank God!" Thumps was never prepared for a friendly Sterling. He preferred the man in his natural state, greedy and arrogant. "Did you bring your camera?"

"Right here."

"Look, Duke. Look, Andy." Sterling seized Thumps' arm and began dragging him across the room. "Thumps has his camera."

Andy Hopper was one of those tall, lean young men you see in catalogues, posing in underwear and swimsuits. He had been a football star in high school. He had been prom king. He had been voted the man most likely to succeed. All that was missing from his arsenal was a brain. Which, in some ways, was just as well. So far as Thumps could tell, Andy hadn't yet figured out that high school was probably as good as it was going to get.

The sheriff, on the other hand, was a large man with thin hair, a body that resembled a pile of boulders, and a face that reminded Thumps of a bowl of remorseful oatmeal. But Hockney had a brain, and he knew how to use it.

"Ora Mae get you out of bed?" said the sheriff.

"I was up," said Thumps. "Do I take them now, or do you want me to wait?"

Hockney looked at Sterling, who was shifting from one foot to the other, trying to pretend he was in control of the situation.

"Any time you're ready."

Sterling stopped hopping and dragged Thumps back across the room to where Beth Mooney was squatting by a large wingback chair.

"Hey, Thumps," said Beth. "What do you think?"

"Thumps doesn't do that anymore," said Sterling. "He takes pictures. Isn't that right?"

Beth Mooney was a handsome woman with dark hair and flashing teeth, but what Thumps particularly liked were Beth's muscles. Most doctors whom Thumps had known thought exercise was a golf game once a week. Beth ran and she lifted weights. Even under the baggy sweatshirt and green hospital pants, you could see glimpses of hard flesh.

Thumps sucked his stomach in just a little, so that it lined up with his belt.

"Hi, Beth."

"Looks like you lost some weight."

"Started working out."

"Keep it up," she said, "and you'll be as pretty as me."

Sterling tugged on Thumps' arm. "Can we take the pictures now?"

The man in the chair wasn't going anywhere. Except into the back of Beth's station wagon.

"He looks dead," Thumps said, just for Sterling's benefit.

"Of course he's dead." Sterling's hands were in motion again. "Do you know him?"

The man's face was the colour of stone, the way faces go when circulation stops and the blood settles. His hair was coarse and black and pulled away from his face in a ponytail. Jeans, T-shirt, sports coat. Thumps kneeled next to the chair and looked at the body. He had learned over the years that you couldn't tell much about people from their face. Hands and fingernails were a different matter. The man's hands were soft, and the nails were clean and trimmed. Whatever else he had done in life, he hadn't laid bricks or dug ditches.

"Any identification?"

"Nothing," said Beth.

"Stick Merchant," said Sterling.

Thumps looked at Sterling. "This isn't Stick."

"Of course not," said Sterling. "But this is Stick's fault."

The man had a ring on his right hand. Thumps had seen this kind of ring before. A school ring. The sort of gift that happy parents bought their children when they finished college or moved out of the house. Or both.

"You know him?" Beth was flashing that great smile again, and Thumps made a resolution to do a couple of sets of sit-ups every evening, while he and Freeway were watching television.

"Nope."

"You must know him," said Sterling. "You know everyone from the reservation."

"He's not from the reservation."

"Great," said Sterling, "so now Stick's bringing in Indians from the outside."

Beth looked at Thumps and shook her head. "He's all yours," she said. "Get a good shot of the entry wounds."

"It could be a suicide," said Sterling hopefully. "People do that all the time."

"Not likely," said Beth. "Suicides generally don't shoot themselves more than once."

Thumps spent the next hour photographing the body and everything else in the room. Sterling alternated between giving Beth lessons on the differences between good publicity and bad publicity, and arguing with Duke and Andy about what they should and should not share with the press.

When Thumps had finished, he wandered over to the window and looked out. Unlike the Cascade, the Cataract had no view to speak of. A few trees, the road into the resort, the casino, the parking lot, the top of the computer complex, and the sky. Thumps raised the camera and peered through the rangefinder.

"You ever see any of Ansel Adams' work?" Sheriff Hockney stood next to Thumps with his hands in his pockets.

"He did mountains."

"I was in Tucson a couple of years back, and I saw some of Adams' original prints at that big photography museum, and you know what?"

"What?"

"Adams knew the difference between a mountain and a parking lot."

Hockney's given name was Benjamin, but according to folks on the reserve and in town who kept track of such things, his wife had decided that her husband bore an uncanny resemblance to John Wayne and had begun calling him Duke.

"Sterling ask you if you knew him?"

"He did."

Thumps had to admit that Hockney did look a little like John Wayne. He even sounded like him when he talked, and Thumps wondered whether the sheriff had always talked this way or whether he had taken on the slow, easy drawl to please his wife.

"What'd you tell him?"

"Told him I had no idea who he was."

Duke moved to the window and stood next to Thumps. The sun hadn't hit the copper dome of the casino yet, and the sky was the colour of winter ice.

"Sterling thinks the deceased is one of Stick's bunch." Duke rocked forward on his boots and sighed. "What do you think?"

"You tell him the dead man is Asian?"

"Nope," said Duke. "Not my job to pass out information to idiots."

"He won't be happy when he finds out." Thumps flipped the lever on the camera and rewound the film. "I'll get these to you as soon as they're developed."

"That's great." The sheriff turned back to the small group of people who were standing around waiting for some sign. "Okay," he said. "Let's move it out."

Thumps focused on the mountains. The camera had no film now, but it was reassuring to feel the focusing ring move smoothly and to hear the curtain slide in front of the pressure plate as he squeezed the shutter release.

"Sterling thinks our dead guy is Indian." Ora Mae always seemed larger the closer she stood to you.

"I heard."

"Beth says he wasn't killed here."

"Not enough blood."

"So you're not just another pretty face."

"You ever see him?" Thumps caught himself. Old habits were hard to break.

"You mean, was he a potential buyer?"

"No," he said, trying to back away from being a cop. "I didn't mean anything."

"Don't stop now," said Ora Mae. "Sounds as though you're on a roll."

"I have to get back."

"Is this where you tell me how you're not a cop anymore, just a photographer?"

"That's me."

"So you're not interested in who our friend is, where he came from, and how he got here?"

"Nope."

Ora Mae shook her head and headed for the door. "You're never going to get a woman if you don't learn to lie better than that."

From the picture window, Thumps watched as Beth and Andy loaded the body into the back of the station wagon. Hockney came out of the main entrance behind them and walked to the top of the parking lot. He stood on the edge of the curb, shaded his eyes with a hand, and looked out toward the casino and the computer building. Then he walked back to his car with a purposeful swing to his arms, as though he had found something. But Thumps knew what Hockney was looking for. And from his vantage point, he knew Duke hadn't found it.

Four

It was late morning by the time Thumps got back to Chinook, and the only people at Al's were the usual stragglers left over from breakfast. Normally, quaint local hangouts with a reputation for good food and good prices, in interesting out-of-the-way places such as Chinook, turned into hot spots during the summer months, forcing locals to stand in line behind tangles of tourists bristling with backpacks, guide books, and road maps. But even though Chinook had its fair share of visitors, few of them ever made their way to Al's.

First of all, the café was difficult to find. It was sandwiched in between the Fjord Bakery and Sam's Laundromat, with no sign marking the place except for the turtle shell Preston Wagamese had superglued next to the front door with the word Food painted on it.

And even if tourists found the place—and some did—as soon as they opened the door and stepped inside, they knew, adventure aside, that they were probably better off with the French toast at the Holiday Inn.

Not that the café looked threatening in any way. It was unremarkable, in fact, little more than a long, narrow aisle with plywood booths huddled against one wall and a run of scruffy chrome and red Naugahyde stools wedged tightly against a lime green Formica counter.

To be sure, the place was dark. The only light came in through the screen door and the window next to the grill. And it was damp. With the sweet smells of grease, burnt toast, strong coffee, and sweat forming currents and eddies that ran through the café like tides. Thumps imagined that the main sensation people had who walked in off the street for the first time was that of being shoved underwater.

There was no one at the counter. Thumps headed down the aisle, and when he got to the seventh stool, he sat down. It wasn't superstition. It was experience. Some of the stools wobbled, and some of the stools had sinister lumps lurking just under the Naugahyde. One or two had tears that had been repaired with duct tape and then spray-painted red.

The seventh stool was one of two still intact. Like Al herself. Worn but original.

"Usual?" Al came along the counter, dragging the wet rag across the formica.

"Easy on the sauce."

Alvera Couteau had a love affair with salt. It was the main ingredient in the "secret sauce" that she tossed into the eggs to brighten them up, and it was the backbone of her meatloaf special. In fact, Thumps suspected salt was the only spice—if it actually was a spice—that Al used in any of her dishes. Every so often, someone would remind Al that salt was rough on the heart, and she would point out that smoking would kill you quicker.

Which was another reason Thumps came to Al's. As impossible as it seemed, Al's was a non-smoking establishment. Thumps knew that some restaurants in the east and in places such as California were smoke-free, but, in the west—the real west—where liquor, cigarettes, and guns formed a holy trinity, a non-smoking restaurant was an oddity at best.

For Al, it was a simple matter of taste. "Don't mind if you smoke," she told everyone. "Just don't do it in my café."

Three or four years back, Wutty Youngbeaver had decided to test Al's resolve on this particular matter and lit up at the counter. Al asked him to take it outside. She even smiled. Instead, Wutty sucked the cigarette halfway down and blew a giant smoke ring that floated over the grill and settled on a fresh batch of Al's famous hash browns.

Al didn't say anything. She shovelled the potatoes into the garbage and went about her business as if nothing had happened. Russell Plunket and Jimmy Monroe, who had been sitting on either side of Wutty, got up quickly and moved to a booth. If Wutty hadn't been so busy congratulating himself, he might have seen it coming. But when his breakfast didn't arrive and his coffee cup remained empty, Wutty got the message.

"Can't do this," Wutty told Al. "This is a public building."

Al ignored him. Wutty sat there, determined to wait her out.

"She can't do this," he told the rest of the breakfast crowd, but everyone had already turned away or was reading the newspaper. Wutty stayed on his stool for almost an hour, and then he left in a huff, vowing never to return.

"Sure as hell not the only place in town that'll feed a working man."

And this was true. If you liked your breakfast fried, you could swing over to Dumbo's. Or the Holiday Inn. And if you didn't mind driving out to Shadow Ranch, you could get a chuckwagon breakfast complete with flapjacks from scratch and real sourdough bread.

But you paid for the privilege. Dumbo's was cheap enough, but you didn't get much for your money. Breakfast at the Holiday Inn cost you ten dollars without juice. And the chuckwagon breakfast out at Shadow Ranch was almost twenty dollars, even before you figured in the gas and time. Al's breakfast special—eggs any way you liked them, whole wheat toast, hash browns with cheese and salsa, homemade sausage, and juice—cost three-fifty, rain or shine.

Wutty was gone for a week. Then he showed up at the counter one morning, smiling, as if nothing had happened. Al was a reasonable woman, but she wasn't about to let Wutty come waltzing back, easy as you please, just because he had pretty teeth. There were amends to be made, and to Wutty's credit, he gave up quickly and apologized. Still, it was most of a year before Al filled Wutty's cup as fast as she poured coffee for the rest of her customers, and a while after that before she went back to lavishing salt on Wutty's breakfast or filling his shot glass of salsa right to the rim.

"Haven't seen much of you." Al slid the plate between Thumps' elbows. "You trying to eat your own cooking again?"

"I'm a good cook." Thumps dumped the salsa over the eggs and folded them into the hash browns.

"People are still talking about that macaroni dish of yours."

"Old news." Thumps looked around the café. "Don't see any new faces. You stop feeding tourists altogether?"

"This about the body up at Buffalo Mountain?" Al filled Thumps' cup and put the pot on the counter.

Thumps was always amazed at how fast information could travel. "You know who he was?"

"You been out to Shadow Ranch lately? They're shoving a couple million into the resort. New pool and a mountain slide." Al looked back at the grill to make sure nothing was burning. " 'Course, the casino is going to give Buffalo Mountain the edge."

Most of the time, Al would pounce on conversations. Other times, bringing her around to the topic was like trying to push a boulder up a hill with a spoon. Thumps scooped up the last of the eggs, ran a piece of toast around his plate, and waited.

Al filled Thumps' cup. "Floyd Small Elk's out of jail."

"Cooley's brother?" The last Thumps had heard, Floyd was doing time for assault.

"Got out last month. Rockland gave him a job driving one of those resort taxis."

"The limos?" Thumps tried to imagine Floyd Small Elk behind the wheel of a limo. "Vernon Rockland gave an ex-con a job?"

Five years ago, Vernon Rockland had shown up in Chinook and purchased the old Anderson place. A summer retreat, he told everyone, a getaway from the stress of the city. No one in Chinook thought much about it until an architect arrived the next spring, followed closely by a fleet of bulldozers. And before anyone in town had a chance to think about it, Rockland had turned a modest ranch into an ostentatious resort complete with a championship golf course.

Al settled against the counter and closed her eyes for a moment. "Maybe you should drive out there and talk with him."

"Got nothing to talk to Floyd about."

"Suit yourself. You going out to the reservation?"

"Maybe."

"How's Claire doing?"

"The body at Buffalo Mountain isn't going to make her day."

"Then maybe she should talk to Floyd." Al stood up and straightened her apron. "He's been driving the guy around for the last two weeks."

Thumps used the pay phone at the laundromat. He let it ring until he was sure no one was there. The sun was up and bent on melting the parking meters before lunch. Thumps stood behind the door of the Volvo so that when he opened it, the hot air wouldn't have to knock him down as it toppled out of the car. The newer Volvos came with air conditioning. The year he had bought his, air had been an option. At least the seats were cloth. Claire thought leather smelled nice, and Thumps guessed that it did. But there were drawbacks to sitting on split cowhide. Any temperature above seventy-five degrees, and leather stuck to your back and tore the skin off bare legs. Below forty-five degrees, it turned into plate steel.

As Thumps swung the corner at the 7-Eleven and headed out to the reservation, he began the slow process of asking the kinds of questions that cops ask when they don't have a clue and have to start somewhere. If this were a television movie, Thumps mused, he'd already have two or three good clues and a limited number of suspects.

In the distance, clouds began to pile up against the mountains in a way that reminded him of Ansel Adams. He wasn't a great fan of Adams' landscapes. Or more precisely, he wasn't a fan of the thousands of Ansel Adams' landscape look-alikes, black- and-white photographs of craggy peaks and syrupy mountain streams that cluttered every gallery in the west.

Still, the bright clouds against the darker mountains made a nice picture. And if Thumps had had his field camera with him, he might have been tempted to stop and blow off a couple sheets of film so he'd have something to sell to the collectors and tourists who believed in the concept of abstract art, but who ran back to realism whenever they went looking for their wallets.

He had picked up photography when he was a cop in Northern California. Ron Peat who had done all the crime-scene photographs for the department had retired, and somehow or other Thumps had wound up with the job. He didn't know a thing about photography, but Ron came in a couple of times a week and showed him how to load the camera, how to use the flash, how to develop and print the film. And before long, what had been simply a part of his job became a hobby, and what had become a hobby turned into an avocation. By the time Thumps realized that being a cop was something he could no longer do, photography was his only other good option.

Except for golf. Thumps' secret passion was to play golf. To be sure, golf was an activity that helped explicate the more obvious elements of race and class. Thumps knew that. But the game had a leisure and grace that he loved. You didn't have to rush up and down a court. You didn't have to worry about being sacked in the backfield or cross-checked into the boards. You didn't have to jump. And it was one of the few games involving clubs and balls where you didn't have to sweat. Everything was slow. Everything was civil. Thumps especially liked the rolling, tree-lined fairways, the long walks in the fresh air, the feeling of well-being that came from having nothing better to do with a day.

He had learned golf as a kid growing up in central California. He and his mother had lived in a trailer park that bordered the back side of the Sierra Springs Country Club. And every day on his way to school, if he walked the perimeter of the chain-link fence, he could see the men strolling down the green fairways in the morning light.

But the fastest way to school was not to walk the fence line. It was to cut across the course itself. There was an opening in the wire at the fourteenth hole, just below the No Trespassing sign, and if you timed it right and waited for the gaps in the players, you could work your way across the valley to the tee deck of the fifth hole without being seen. And slip out through the fence on the other side.

Better yet, as you made your way across the fairways, you could find lost golf balls buried in the thick rough, or hidden behind trees, or tangled up in the cattails at the edge of the ponds.

The golf balls were gold. Every Saturday morning at seven, Thumps would take what he had collected to the farmer's market, set up at an empty table, and sell golf balls until the man who collected the table fees came around at nine.

One Saturday, as Thumps was getting ready to walk over to the farmer's market, an old pickup pulled into the park, towing an even older trailer, its sides painted to look like the Grand Canyon. Thumps watched as the man in the pickup manoeuvred the trailer into a spot by a large oak tree and got out.

"Hi."

The man was old, with grey hair, a scruffy grey beard, and skin the colour of dark water. And when he walked, it looked as though he had broken something in his hip and had had to fix it quick with fence wire.

"This a good place, kid?"

"Sure," said Thumps. "You paint your trailer?"

"What you got in the bag?"

"Golf balls."

"You play golf?"

"Sure."

"How many you got?"

"Don't know," said Thumps. "Lots."

The man shoved his hand into his pocket and pulled out a roll of bills. "I'll take them all."

The man's name was Gabriel Garcia, and so far as anyone in the park could tell, he was retired and travelling around. Thumps had seen pictures of the Grand Canyon on postcards, but it was more impressive painted on the side of a trailer.

"What do you think of the new guy?" Thumps asked his mother.

"He seems nice."

"Did you see the side of his trailer?"

"Don't be bothering him."

"It's the Grand Canyon."

"I have to work an extra shift tonight," said his mother.

"Remember that postcard Dad sent us?"

"You'll have to make your own dinner."

"That was the Grand Canyon, too."

The next Saturday, when Thumps came out of the trailer on his way to the farmer's market, Gabriel was waiting for him. "More golf balls?"

Leaning against Gabriel's pickup was a set of golf clubs.

"You want to buy some more balls?"

"Come on," said Gabriel, and he limped out toward the field in back of the trailer park. "Bring the clubs."

By the time Thumps caught up with him, Gabriel had cleared a place in the weeds. "Show me what you got."

Thumps dumped the balls out on the ground. Gabriel pulled a club from the bag and sorted through the balls until he found one he liked. "You see that flag?" he said, gesturing toward the sixteenth green on the other side of the fence. "How far you figure it is?"

"I don't know. Hundred yards."

"One hundred and fifty-five yards." Gabriel rolled the ball to a flat

30

spot, set himself, and swung the club behind his head with a smooth, slow swing that looked as though he wasn't even trying. The ball exploded into the air, climbed over the fence, and landed on the green as soft as butter hitting the floor.

"Neat."

"Show me what you got," said Gabriel, and he handed Thumps his club.

"You want me to hit a ball?"

"That'll be a good start."

The first swing missed the ball completely. The second buried the club face into the dirt. The third sent the ball rattling into the fence. Thumps was lining up a fourth ball when Gabriel held up a hand.

"Wait till they clear the green."

Four golfers in carts emerged out of the trees on the edge of the fairway. Four large men in slacks and polo shirts.

Gabriel squatted down and gestured with his chin. "Watch the big guy in the red shirt," he said. "He's going to hook it right at us."

Sure enough, the ball rocketed off the man's club, took a hard left turn, sailed over the fence, and landed in the thick weeds.

"His alignment was all wrong."

The man in the white shirt got to the green first and picked up the ball Gabriel had hit. He looked at it and showed it to his friends. Then he put it in his pocket.

"Hey," said Thumps. "That's my ball."

"Not anymore," said Gabriel.

"I found it."

"Finding something doesn't necessarily make it yours."

"What about the ball they hit over the fence?"

"You see where it went?"

Thumps got up and searched the weeds. In a matter of minutes, he had found six balls. "Not bad, eh?"

Gabriel looked at each ball in turn. "This one's okay," he said. "This one is cut. This one is shit."

The men were laughing as they marked their balls and lined up their putts. One of them lit a cigar and clamped it in his teeth as he bore down on the putt. Gabriel lay down in the grass.

"Let me know when they finish," he said, and closed his eyes.

The men spent a long time on the green, shouting and laughing, trying to get their balls to go in the hole. When they finally put the flag back and headed to the next tee, Gabriel sat up and tossed a ball to Thumps. "Try it again."

For the rest of the morning, between the foursomes that came and went, Thumps tried to hit golf balls over the fence and onto the green.

"This is the easy part of the game," Gabriel told him.

"Not sure I'm interested in playing golf," said Thumps.

Gabriel got up and took his club. "No point stealing golf balls if you're not going to play."

"I don't steal them. I find them."

"That's private property," Gabriel said quietly, as if he were thinking. "You see that fence?"

"It's not hard to get in," said Thumps. "There's a hole in the wire over by those trees."

"Fence is for show," said Gabriel. "It's just there to remind us." He pulled a longer club out of his bag. "This is the driver." He kicked the dirt into a small mound, put the ball on top if it, and made a couple of lazy practice swings. "The idea isn't to hit the ball."

Thumps had watched golfers hit balls before, but he had never seen anyone strike a ball with such power. And he had never seen a golf ball go so far.

"Wow!"

"The idea is to make the swing." Gabriel walked to the fence and put his fingers through the links. "Next time, don't worry about hitting the ball. Any idiot can hit the ball."

When Thumps got home, his mother was peeling potatoes in the kitchen.

"Dad ever play golf?"

His mother turned and looked at him the way she did when he had done something wrong. "Golf?"

"Yeah."

"No."

"Okay."

That evening, after supper, Thumps went out to the field and found a stick. Gabriel's swing hadn't seemed like a swing at all. Not like baseball or tennis, where the object was to hit the ball as hard as you could. Gabriel's swing had been more like a dance.

Thumps found a flat area beyond the field, down near the creek where no one could see him. The first few tries felt awkward and rushed. The swings had none of Gabriel's smooth, coiling power. By the time it was dark and he came back to the trailer, his neck was sore and his shoulders ached.

"I don't want you messing around on that golf course," his mother told him.

"They don't mind."

"They don't want you there, either."

The next day, when Thumps got up, Gabriel was already in the field. Beside him was a bucket of balls.

"Where'd you get these?" said Thumps.

"These are mine," said Gabriel, and he sent a ball spinning into the green.

For the next few minutes, Thumps watched Gabriel hit balls onto the green. He never missed, and none of the shots landed any farther than twelve feet from the pin.

"You want to collect those before the next group comes along?"

"Sure."

"You know how to repair ball marks?"

Thumps wasn't much better than he had been the day before. Most of the time he'd skip the ball into the fence.

"Something about the club you don't like?" said Gabriel.

"Nope."

"Then why are you trying to choke it to death?" Gabriel rearranged Thumps' hands on the club. "Hold it soft."

Thumps gripped the club again and set his feet.

"Now what are you going to do?"

"Hit the ball."

"Is that right?" Gabriel stepped in front of Thumps and picked the ball off the tee. "How about now?"

"You can't play golf without a ball."

"You can't play golf with a ball." Gabriel took the club from Thumps.

"That little ball's not important. As long as you're looking at it, as long as you're thinking about it, you're never going to play golf. You understand?"

"Sure."

"'Course you do. Smart boy like you understands everything."

"What about the ball?"

"Forget the ball." Gabriel shook his head. "What's important is the swing. Golf balls don't run down the fairway by themselves. Golf balls don't go into the hole by themselves. And they don't go anywhere just because you hit them. They go where they go because of the swing."

Gabriel swung the club and clipped the tee out of the ground. "You want to be a good golfer, you've got to learn to swing as though the ball's not even there." He slid the club back into the bag. "Come on. I'll show you something."

The inside of Gabriel's trailer was small and ordinary. Except for the walls.

"Is that you?"

"I was younger then."

"Who's that?"

"Arnold Palmer."

There were photographs on every wall. Thumps' mother had a few pictures of family in frames on top of the television. Gabriel's photographs were simply stapled to the walls.

"You played with Arnold Palmer?"

"No. I was a caddy."

"You caddied for all these guys?"

Gabriel nodded.

"Did you ever play?"

"This photograph here? This is Lee Trevino."

Thumps followed Gabriel around the trailer. Every so often, he found a golfer he recognized. "You think I could be a professional golfer?"

Gabriel's face softened, and he closed his eyes as though remembering something. "Maybe," he said. "But first, you got to clear the fence."

For the rest of the summer, Thumps hit golf balls. Over the fence. Into the field. Several times, when the weather was bad and there was no one on the course, he and Gabriel would sneak in and play two or three holes.

Woods, irons, wedges. Until Thumps' swing was spring-steel and velvet, and the ball went where his swing took it.

"Not bad," said Gabriel. "You're almost as pretty as me."

"Prettier," said Thumps.

"Maybe you are," said Gabriel, but he said it as if someone close to him had been hurt or had died. "For all the good it's going to do either one of us."

Toward the end of the summer, Thumps' mother took him into town to get clothes for school, and when they got back to the trailer park, Gabriel's trailer was gone. Thumps found Mr. Sullivan, who ran the park.

"What happened to Gabriel?"

"The Mexican?"

"Yeah."

"He left."

"Is he coming back?"

"He left something for you." Mr. Sullivan went into his trailer and came back with Gabriel's clubs and a large cloth bag of balls. "He said you'd know what to do with them."

The rest of that day, Thumps hit balls over the fence. Until each swing was the swing before. Until all the balls were gone. Until the green looked as though a spring storm had come through suddenly and covered the land with hail.

The Ironstone was straight ahead. As soon as Thumps crossed the river, he would be on Indian land. He wondered whether Hockney had found the car yet, or whether there was a car at all. Thumps could think of all sorts of ways that a dead body might have wound up in one of the condos, but most of them involved transportation. The man might have driven himself out to Buffalo Mountain. In that case, there should be an orphan car. This is what Sheriff Hockney had been looking for when Thumps saw him in the parking lot. Thumps hadn't seen a car, and he didn't think Duke was going to find one.

The killer could have brought the man out to Buffalo Mountain, dead or alive, and then driven off. In that case, there would be no car. But if Al was right, and Cooley's brother Floyd had been driving the dead man around, then Floyd could have driven him to the reservation and dropped him off. But then Floyd would have returned at some point to pick him up.

Unless, of course, Floyd has killed him.

Thumps didn't like that option. It raised the nasty possibility that Cooley was involved in a murder. Cooley might scare the hell out of you if he could get that grin off his face, but he was too good-natured to kill anyone. Floyd certainly had a temper, but why would he kill a man he barely knew?

One thing was sure. If Floyd was driving the man back and forth between Shadow Ranch and Buffalo Mountain, then the dead guy had to be doing business with the tribe. And Thumps knew who to ask about that.

It would help to know who the dead man was. A name wouldn't answer all the questions that dead bodies create, but it might go a long way toward explaining why a stranger had wound up sitting in a chair in a condominium, staring out the window at the view.

Five

It was early afternoon when Thumps crossed the river and hit the lease road, a long ribbon of loose gravel and dirt that ran in a straight line from the bridge to the town site. Once a year, the band council would grade out the ruts and oil the gravel. Not that these efforts helped a great deal. At its best, the lease road was a bone-rattling, oil-pan-busting game trail that ruined front ends, split tires, and sent tremors up steering wheels in never-ending shock waves.

Normally, the band office would be closed on a Sunday, but Thumps was betting that today was not an ordinary Sunday. Claire hadn't answered her phone when he had tried her from town, and if she wasn't there, the band office was the next best bet. Of course, she could have gone to the resort to see the situation for herself.

In the distance, as he drove through the ruts and the dust, Thumps could see the water tower on the bluff, and he wondered for the hundredth time why anyone in their right mind would want to suspend tons of water in an enormous metal ball on stilts. If you were determined to keep water locked up in a steel tank, why not bury it? At least the water would stay cool and out of sight.

Thumps knew of a photographer who had published a book containing nothing but photographs of water towers. One hundred and fifty pages, and so far as he could tell, water-tower architecture was not a varied art form. The towers in the book had been uniformly dull. The one on the reservation was uniformly dull. Someone had painted it blue, in an attempt either to brighten it up or to make it disappear into the sky. Not that it really mattered.

The band office sat to one side and was almost as dull as the water tower. The office had started life as a used double-wide trailer, and as more space had been required, single-wides had been added, sending the complex on a short tour of the alphabet. From an I, it became an L. Then a squarish C. And finally an E.

The band office was open. Roxanne Heavy Runner was waiting for him at her desk. An unexpected surprise.

"Hi."

"You're late."

Roxanne was a large, fierce woman who reminded Thumps of a war movie. Some days she charged up hills and blew things to pieces. Other days she lay in wait and ambushed enemy columns. Today Roxanne was making heavy artillery noises under her breath. Thumps smiled and tried to make himself as inconspicuous and non-combative as possible.

"How can I be late?" Now that he was here, Thumps was not sure he wanted to see Claire after all. A dead body dropped into the middle of the band's most ambitious economic project was not going to make her happy. Or reasonable.

Roxanne squeezed her lips together, lowered her eyebrows, and pretended to be a tank. "You better help her or else."

"You still see that guy from Browning?"

"Don't change the subject." Roxanne waved him toward Claire's office. "And don't even think about saying no."

Thumps squeezed by her desk, smiling all the while. As he opened the door, he was aware of a quick metallic sound behind him that could have been Roxanne snapping down on her fillings or pulling the pin on a grenade.

Claire's office was dark and wrapped with simulated wood panelling, the pressboard and textured paper variety that came standard in every trailer. If he were feeling generous, Thumps would have described the room as spartan rather than depressing.

Claire, for all her good qualities, had no decorating sense. The furnishings consisted of a desk, a chair, six four-drawer filing cabinets, a low coffee table, and a blue floral sofa. The walls were bare. No diplomas. No awards. Not even a poster of a famous Indian.

Thumps had given Claire a black-and-white print of Chief Mountain in

Alberta and a photograph of the Tetons he had taken just after a storm. Two of his favourite shots. And he had framed them. For some reason, he had expected that they would show up on the walls of her office, or at least in the reception area. Or in her home. But they had simply disappeared. Thumps was sure the photographs were alive and well somewhere, and he was sure he did not want to ask.

But it was her bookcase that bothered Thumps the most. On the shelves, Claire had stacked everything from government policy papers to books on agriculture to novels, with no regard for order, and whenever he came to her office, he was beset with the overwhelming urge to pull everything down, organize the piles into categories, and arrange each pamphlet and book alphabetically.

Claire was on the phone. She wasn't talking, but Thumps guessed that the voice on the other end was Sheriff Hockney's and that he was giving her a damage report. The death had all the makings of a public-relations disaster. Not that he could read impending disaster on Claire's face. It remained impassive, as if she were listening to a message on an answering machine.

Claire normally wore her hair loose, but today she had pulled it back from her face and wound it in a single braid. Thumps wasn't sure whether she had done this to look severe and formidable, or whether she had done it simply for convenience. He guessed the latter since Claire didn't dress herself any better than she did her office. She didn't wear makeup or jewellery, not even earrings, and she wore a dress only when she had to deal with politicians and bankers. Or when she had to go to a funeral.

Claire was tough and opinionated or pushy and unreasonable, depending on how you felt about strong women. Thumps told himself that he liked assertiveness. But then again, he liked moderation, too. And quiet. In the end, what had attracted him to Claire and what continued to intrigue him was the brooding intelligence that lurked just below the surface.

She put the phone down and looked across the desk at Thumps. For a moment he imagined that he saw her face soften. "Hello, Thumps."

"Hello, Claire."

"Good way to start a week."

Thumps didn't know whether she wanted him to agree or disagree, so he waited to see if she would give him a hint.

"What'd you think of the complex?"

"Looks great."

Claire turned sideways in the chair. The muscles in her jaw and neck were not happy. "Do you know how long it took us to get the resort up and going?"

Thumps did know. Six years. Eight if you counted all the twists and turns that the tribe had been forced to take before the federal government had finally agreed to allow them to do what they should have been able to do without begging permission from anyone.

"Was it murder?"

Duke would certainly have told her that the man had been murdered. There was no doubt about that particular fact.

"Do you know who he was?" The question was disingenuous. Thumps was sure Claire knew.

For many Native groups, it was considered good manners to wait after someone spoke on the off chance that the person needed to catch their breath or might remember something else they wanted to say.

Claire didn't waste any time. "Daniel Takashi."

So, now the dead man had a name. That was a start. Not that the name rang any bells.

"Okay." It was all Thumps could come up with on short notice.

"He's been at the complex for the last three weeks programming and testing the computer."

A computer programmer. Thumps didn't think computer programmers were in the same category as lawyers and bankers and politicians— professionals you might well consider dragging behind your car. And while he had not met many computer programmers, he was reasonably sure that they were an inoffensive bunch. Like bran flakes or vanilla pudding. Why then, would anyone want to kill one? Especially in Chinook. Thumps had seen his share of assholes, but even first-rate assholes would have to break a sweat to make a mortal enemy in three weeks. Unless, of course, the killing had nothing to do with anger or passion and everything to do with politics. He didn't like where this line of thinking was headed and tried to turn it in another direction.

"The sheriff wants to talk to Stanley."

"Stick?" Thumps tried to pretend that he had never even thought of the possibility. "That's crazy."

Claire stood up and walked to the window. Against the bright prairie light, she seemed no more than a dark silhouette.

"Duke just has to touch all the bases." He tried to sound reassuring, but the words came out flat.

Claire opened the sliding door and stepped out on the small porch. Thumps knew he was supposed to follow. She hadn't asked, but there was little doubt what she wanted. It would be hard enough saying no to Claire across her desk, from a safe distance. Standing close to her with nothing but fresh air between them would make it almost impossible.

Thumps compromised and went as far as the sliding door. "It's routine. If I were in charge, I'd want to talk to Stick."

"He went fishing." Thumps could tell when Claire was happy, and he certainly knew what angry sounded like. But the woman talking to him now was neither. She seemed subdued, quiet. If he hadn't known better, he would have said ... desperate.

"Where'd he go?" Thumps didn't know exactly when Takashi had died, but he was betting that the results of the autopsy would set the time of death sometime on Saturday.

"Blackfoot Falls."

Blackfoot Falls was rough country. A perfect place to take a fly rod. A perfect place to get lost. "Good fishing up there."

Claire leaned against the railing and turned away from the wind. Thumps always thought that she went out of her way not to show her emotions. Not to Thumps. Not to anyone.

"Stanley wasn't involved," she said, her voice flat and emotionless. "But I don't want Hockney finding him first."

Thumps knew how many Native people felt about the police. Even in the best of circumstances, there was a deep-seated suspicion that came out of a long history of difficulties. Claire knew better, but old fears are hard to shake. Once Thumps had been stopped in Yellowstone Park for speeding, and he could still remember how he had sat in the car, tense, both hands on the wheel, making sure he didn't make any sudden moves or give the ranger any cause for complaint.

"When did he go?"

"Yesterday." Claire wrapped her arms around her body.

Thumps let his breath out gently. Being Claire's lover could be hard at times. Being her friend and trying to help her son at the same time could prove to be impossible. "I'll see what I can do."

Roxanne was waiting for him when he came out of the office. "Well?"

"Everything's fine."

"Indian people help each other."

This was Roxanne's favourite line. It wasn't particularly true, of course, but Roxanne believed it, even lived it, and she expected that everyone else did, too.

"I'm going to help."

"Then what are you standing around for?"

The car was an oven. Thumps rolled down all the windows and watched the hot air inside the car get pushed out by the hot air outside the car. As he waited for the space to become habitable, he tried to put a positive spin on Stick's situation, without much success. Claire's fears were well-founded. Duke would be looking at Stick because of his involvement with the Red Hawks and the protest. As soon as he discovered that Stick had disappeared at the same time that Takashi had turned up dead in the condo, the sheriff would look at Stick even harder.

It had been difficult for Claire to ask for his help. He knew that. And while he did not relish the prospect of playing police once again, he also knew that he wasn't going to say no.

The good news was that Thumps now had a couple of leads. The dead man's name. His occupation. And why he was at Buffalo Mountain in the first place. Thumps could guess at other bits of information. Al had pointed him in the right direction. If Floyd Small Elk was driving Takashi around, then Takashi had probably been staying at Shadow Ranch, which meant a room and personal effects.

As Thumps slid into his car, he was faced with at least three choices. One, he could go into the mountains and try to find Stick. This wasn't his first choice. If Stick had gone fishing, he could be almost anywhere on the river. If he had gone to the mountains to hide, no one was going to find him.

Two, Thumps could go to Shadow Ranch and nose around. If he was fast enough he might even beat Duke to Takashi's room. This option was potentially dangerous. Even if the sheriff didn't know where Takashi was staying, it wouldn't take him long to find out. And if Duke found Thumps in the room of a dead man, there would be questions that Thumps wouldn't be able to answer.

Or three, he could go back to Buffalo Mountain. After all, it was the scene of the crime. Takashi could have gotten to the resort any number of ways, but almost all of them went through Cooley Small Elk, and the sheriff had no doubt questioned him. Thumps wasn't sure how Cooley felt about the law, but if he had as little love for it as his brother had, there was the chance that he might tell Thumps something he had neglected to share with Hockney.

Thumps could feel his eyes begin to droop as he left the townsite and rumbled onto the lease road. All the clever television shows to the contrary, murder was generally a messy but simple matter. Jealousy, anger, greed. Husbands killed wives. Drunks killed their best friends. Business partners killed each other.

Thumps thought about flipping a coin, but he wasn't really interested in wandering around the mountains, and he certainly wasn't keen to play cat-and-mouse with the sheriff in a dead man's room. Besides the resort was closer.

While the murder at Buffalo Mountain had made a number of people anxious and cranky, Cooley Small Elk seemed to be taking the crisis in stride. When Thumps reached the main gate, he found Cooley propped against a tree, relaxing in the shade of the guard shack. Someone coming upon Cooley for the first time might have wondered about the brown grocery bags next to him. But Thumps had seen Cooley eat before, so it was no mystery. One bag was lunch, the other bag was garbage.

Cooley didn't give any indication that he was going to move, so Thumps pulled the car off the road and got out.

"Hey, Thumps."

"Hi, Cooley."

"You come back to take more photographs?" Cooley fished a banana out of the bag. "You hungry?"

Thumps looked up at the condos. The parking lot in front of the building was empty. "I hear they figured out who the dead guy was."

"Yeah," said Cooley. "Now that was a real surprise. Who would want to kill a computer geek?"

"Beats me."

"You know what?" Cooley polished an apple on his shirt and bit it in half. "They want to blame me."

Thumps squatted down by the guard shack. Inside the grocery bag, he could see several sandwiches in fold-lock bags and what looked to be half a cantaloupe.

"They think I wasn't paying attention."

Thumps did not want to appear too eager. "This was Saturday morning?"

"Right." Cooley dropped what was left of the apple into the garbage bag. "The guy drives in a little after ten. Then, after lunch, he drives away. No big deal."

"He come out here every Saturday?"

"That was a surprise, too," said Cooley. "First time that happened."

Thumps got to his feet and stretched. "Floyd bring him in the limo?"

"Nope. He had one of those camper vans. And that sort of proves I'm telling the truth, right?"

"The camper van wasn't in the parking lot."

"Too straight." Cooley brushed himself off. "If he had snuck back into the building like the sheriff thinks and got himself killed when I wasn't looking, the camper van would still be in the lot."

"So, how'd Takashi wind up in the condo?"

"That's the question old Duke gets paid to ask." Cooley reached into the bag. "You want a sandwich?"

"I'll mention that to the sheriff when I see him."

"No time like the present."

"Hockney?"

"He's at the computer building."

The cop in Thumps was suddenly wide awake. "Thought he was on his way back to town."

"He was," said Cooley, "and then most of New York City showed up."

"What?"

"In a helicopter, no less." Cooley gestured toward the casino. "Corporate types. Old Duke is probably kissing their asses right now."

"You know who they are?"

"Nope. Rich white guy, rich Asian guy, and a good-looking woman." Cooley waved a hand in front of his face. "Smell like they're from France."

"You're doing a great job."

Cooley rattled around in the bag and came up with a sandwich. "Too straight."

The helicopter pad had been built on an elevation at the far side of the casino and the parking lot. The helicopter that currently sat on the pad was one of those small, sleek numbers, black and silver and shiny all over. Thumps had flown in helicopters in California, but they had been the larger, clunkier versions that lumbered through the air, spotting speeders as they raced up Highway 101 on their way to the Oregon border. This one was built for speed and agility. Thumps had always suspected that corporate life was not firmly anchored on moral bedrock, but if you were going to go to hell, riding in your own helicopter was certainly a comfortable way to get there.

Thumps was annoyed to find Duke at the resort. It made snooping all the harder. The sheriff didn't jump through hoops for just anyone, so the new arrivals had to be important. Or at least interesting.

Given the "cost is no object" attitude that marked the condos and the rest of the resort, the inside of the computer building was surprisingly spartan. The walls were painted a middle grey that made the room feel like an overcast day. Thumps would have chosen cheerier colours, pale yellows or Wedgewood blues.

At the far end of the reception area stood a bank of tinted windows, and through the smoky glass, Thumps could see tiny lights flickering and the blue blink of computer monitors. The room looked like a set for a science-fiction movie. Stick was supposed to be a whiz with computers. Thumps had a hard time finding the on switch.

The computer room was heavy with the smell of paint. Duke was standing by one of the monitors, watching information scrolling down the screen. A young Asian man was seated at a keyboard, and a second man, a Caucasian with close-cut blond hair and light blue eyes, was standing behind him. Thumps had always thought that light-skinned people looked somewhat on the sickly and fragile side. But this man was anything but frail. He was lean and angular. His suit was tailored to fit an athlete's body.

The woman was standing out of the lights by a row of squat, metal boxes that Thumps guessed were part of the computer system. She was tall with auburn hair, and the dark suit she wore was expensive. Some people might have been fooled into thinking that she was a secretary or a junior vice-something or other, someone along for the ride, but even though she was standing in the shadows, Thumps could see the steel in her eyes.

The Asian man saw Thumps first and stopped what he was doing, as if he had been caught out in some illegal activity. Duke caught the motion and turned.

"Hey, Thumps," said the sheriff. "Guess it's true what they say."

"What's that?"

"That Indians can sneak up on you without making a sound."

"You've been watching too many movies."

"*Dances With Wolves*. Now there was a movie."

The blond man stepped forward with the assurance that only race and class can provide. "I'm Elliot Beaumont."

Thumps had been right. He could feel both strength and speed in the man's handshake. Duke hitched his belt and ran through the introductions.

"Mr. Beaumont here is the vice-president of Genesis Data Systems." Duke let the name and the title hang in the air, as if he were holding a glass of fine wine up to the light. "And this is his associate, George Chan."

Chan didn't look at Thumps. Instead, he glanced at Beaumont and went back to his keyboard.

"Mr. Beaumont came out to check on his computer."

"Well, it's not really my computer ..."

"I'm Virginia Traynor," said the woman, her voice slicing through Beaumont and cutting him off.

As she stepped out of the shadows, Thumps could see that he had been right. This woman wasn't along for the ride. She was the ride.

"And you would be ... the president of Genesis Data Systems," said Thumps, holding out his hand.

The smile was a quick one, but Thumps could see that he had caught Traynor off guard and that she didn't like it. "Very good, Mr. ..."

"DreadfulWater."

Traynor's hand was cool and smooth. Thumps tried to imagine her standing in front of a stove.

"And you are ..." Beaumont had cocked his head to one side, so he could look at Thumps from an angle. "... a deputy?"

"Evidently," said the sheriff, sliding in, "Mr. Takashi called the company about the possibility of the computer being sabotaged."

"Compromised," said Beaumont.

"Couple of days before he was killed." Hockney lowered his eyes.

Thumps knew that Duke didn't believe in coincidences any more than he did. And right now, the only people who appeared to have anything to gain from "compromising" the computer were the Red Hawks. And the only person with the prerequisite knowledge to keep the computer from going on-line was Stanley Merchant.

"Takashi said someone was trying to sabotage the computer?" Thumps asked.

Beaumont looked at Chan. "He was worried."

"About what?"

Chan turned away from the keyboard. "A virus. Maybe a worm."

"Don't worry." Duke smiled and patted Thumps on the shoulder. "I don't know what the hell he's talking about either."

"Sorry," said Chan. "A virus is a program that ... messes things up. It deletes text. It adds messages to your word files. It's a general pain in the ass. You remember the Michelangelo virus?"

Duke nodded. "Sure, everyone remembers that one."

"It was a time-dated virus. It would get into your system and then go off on a particular date. Michelangelo's birthday, for instance."

Thumps could detect just the trace of a smile around Chan's mouth. All this talk about viruses and worms was making him happy.

"Worms, on the other hand, are more of a problem. They're written to use up the capacity of a computer. They suck up memory exponentially and can bring the whole system down. Nasty pieces of work."

Duke shifted his weight. "So, if a virus or a worm was on the system, someone who knew computers had to put it there."

"Sure." Chan shrugged. "Good viruses aren't that easy to write. Worms are even harder."

Beaumont leaned in and looked at the screen. "You find anything yet?"

"Not yet," said Chan. "It's going to take some time."

Duke turned to Thumps. "How many people we know around here are computer experts?"

"It may be that the system is fine." Beaumont had an earnest tone to his voice that Thumps recognized. "It may be that George was killed because he was in the wrong place at the wrong time."

Thumps did not like being patronized, and he had never liked that particular expression. The danger lay in being in the right place at the wrong time or in the wrong place at the right time. Reason, if not grammar, would argue that being in the wrong place at the wrong time should keep you safe and out of harm's way.

"What Mr. Beaumont is suggesting," said Duke, trying to duplicate Beaumont's condescension with only moderate success, "is that Takashi came out here Saturday and caught someone trying to screw up the computer. Takashi tried to stop him. They fought. Takashi got shot."

Duke was on one of his fishing expeditions. Thumps had seen him play this game before, and the sheriff wasn't bad at it.

Beaumont sighed and spread his hands. "I'm just a computer executive. I'll leave the tricky stuff to you guys."

"Did you know him well?" said Thumps.

"Takashi?"

"Hell," said Duke, "old Takashi was their top computer man."

"Actually, I'm the best." Chan turned away from the monitors. "I'm the company's top computer man."

Thumps could hear the snap in Chan's voice, and he knew that Duke could hear it, too.

"Sure," said Duke, with one of his big, insincere smiles. "But this Takashi guy was good, right?"

"He was very good," said Traynor.

"You knew him personally?"

Beaumont looked at Traynor. "I suppose," he said, "you're wondering why we're not more upset about the murder of an employee."

Traynor moved in between Thumps and Beaumont. Now she was close enough for Thumps to know two things about her. She wore very little makeup, and she didn't wear perfume.

"Takashi came to work for Genesis about a year ago," said Traynor. "He was a brilliant programmer and a pain in the ass. In computer land, that's a common combination. I didn't know him well. I feel bad about his death, but I have a business to run. Does that answer your question?"

Duke nodded. "I take it you're planning on staying around for a while?"

Traynor turned to the sheriff. "Until we're sure the computer and the security system are working."

"Well, let me know if I can help," said Hockney, sounding official and disingenuous at the same time. "Say, Thumps, why don't you walk me to the car."

Thumps looked around the computer room. Something didn't smell right. Not the fresh paint. Not the affluence. Beaumont stood at Chan's shoulder, following the lines of text as they flashed on the screen. And then again, maybe it was nothing. Just an ex-cop's imagination working overtime, trying to put round pieces into square holes.

Duke walked all the way to his truck before he said anything. "Just what the hell do you think you're doing?"

"What do you mean?"

"Claire put you up to this?"

Thumps started to shake his head, but Hockney stopped him.

"Let's get a couple of things straight. First, you're a photographer, right?"

"That's right."

"So, why are you playing cop?"

"I'm not playing cop."

"And you just happened to be in the neighbourhood." Duke stopped and looked at his fingernails. "You thought you'd just get in a couple of landscape shots before dinner?"

"Claire's worried about Stick, that's all."

"She should be. He's at the top of my list."

"Stick didn't kill anybody."

"Claire tell you where he is?"

"Fishing."

"Yeah, that's what she told me, too." Duke smiled and nodded. "Stay out of my way, Thumps, and stay away from my case. You mess this up because you want to impress Claire, and I'll eat you for lunch."

"You find the van?"

Hockney tried to keep the annoyance from showing. "No."

"So, Cooley was telling the truth."

"Maybe." Duke patted the top of Thumps' car and opened the door. "Why don't you show me some of those big city moves?"

"You asking me as a photographer?"

"Don't fuck with me, Thumps."

Thumps looked back toward the gate. "Maybe everyone's right. Maybe Takashi drove up here and worked on the computer. And maybe he left, just like Cooley says."

"You been talking to Cooley, too?" Duke took off his hat and ran a beefy hand through his hair. "You know, you're beginning to piss me off."

"Okay, I was curious."

The sheriff fixed his hat. "Then how'd Takashi wind up dead in the condo?"

"Maybe that happened later."

"'Course it happened later. He was killed in the computer complex."

"Forensics?"

"Blood on the floor by the monitor." Duke held up a plastic bag. Inside were two cigarette butts, skinny ones done up in dark brown paper with gold foil wrapper around the filters. "Not your ordinary cigarettes."

"Where'd you find them?"

"On the floor behind the monitor, along with an ashtray. As if they had been knocked over by a struggle."

"They belong to Takashi?"

"Good guess," said the sheriff. "Chan identified them. They're some fancy brand that Takashi got out of New York City. Odd thing was, we didn't find any cigarettes on his body."

"Maybe the killer was low on smokes."

"You call that help?" Hockney pulled out a pack of gum and unwrapped two pieces. "If Cooley's telling the truth, Takashi pulled in here around ten-thirty and left a little after noon."

"You think Cooley's lying?"

"Beth figures that Takashi was killed between nine and one."

"Beth sure about the time?"

"I'll tell her you said that."

Thumps smiled. If Beth said the murder took place between nine and one, then it did. And by the time she finished a complete autopsy, she'd have the time down to the hour.

"You think Cooley and Stick are in this together?" he asked.

"I'm not thinking anything. I'd just as soon hang the killing on that blond jerk." Duke gestured for Thumps to get in the car. "Smug asshole could slice meat with that attitude."

"They learn it in corporate school," said Thumps. "It's not his fault."

"Get in your car and get out of here. Before I arrest your ass. And I don't want to see you stopping and talking to anyone on the way out."

Thumps wanted to talk with Cooley about Takashi and Saturday morning, but the conversation would have to wait for now. No sense getting the sheriff any more annoyed with him than need be.

The good news was that Hockney looked as though he was going to be tied up at the complex for a while. With any luck, Thumps could beat him to Shadow Mountain and be in and out of Takashi's room before Duke arrived and turned the place into a crime scene.

But first, he needed to make a quick stop.

Six

Ora Mae Foreman was trying to think of another euphemism besides "handyman's special" for a bungalow on the south side that had been partially gutted by fire when Thumps walked into the offices of Sterling Realty. He was cute, Ora Mae thought to herself, as he swayed up to her desk. In a western sort of way.

"We're closed." Ora Mae wrote "good location" on a slip of paper and looked at it for a moment.

"Thought real estate offices never closed." Thumps fished a pen out of a holder on the edge of Ora Mae's desk. Sterling Real Estate was written in gold cursive lettering on the side. "These free?"

Ora Mae took the pen away. "You see anyone else in the office besides me?"

"No."

"That's because it's Sunday. The Lord's day. The day of rest."

"I was just out at the band office." Thumps tried to make it sound casual. "Claire said to say hello."

Ora Mae put the pen back in the holder. "Oh, really."

"That's what she said."

"Don't imagine a dead body made her day."

No, Thumps had to admit, it hadn't.

Ora Mae went back to her listing. "Fixer-upper" wasn't going to do the trick and neither was "a diamond in the rough."

"Claire hire you or something?"

"Not exactly."

Ora Mae leaned back in her chair and watched Thumps fidget. " 'Cause

I can only think of one reason why Claire Merchant would hire you."

Thumps shrugged.

"This about Stanley?"

"Not exactly."

"You know, it feels like you're messing with me." Ora Mae had a voice that carried like an explosion under water. "Why does it feel like you're messing with me?"

"Claire's just concerned."

Ora Mae pushed the listing to one side. "So, what exactly do you want?"

Thumps shifted around in the chair. "Does the name Genesis Data Systems mean anything to you?"

"Is this a lunch favour or a dinner favour?"

"How about a free photograph?"

"You owe me six already."

"Okay, lunch."

Ora Mae nodded and turned to her computer. "Genesis Data is the name of the company that got the contract for designing and installing the computer system at Buffalo Mountain."

"You didn't even have to look that up."

"So what?"

"For lunch you should at least have to look it up."

"Okay." Ora Mae fiddled with her keyboard, waited a moment, and then turned the screen so Thumps could see it.

"What is it?"

She shook her head. "It's a Web site. You ever hear of a Web site?"

"Sure."

"Watch closely, I'm only going to do this once. What do you want to know?"

"Do they have pictures?"

"Of what?"

"I don't know."

Ora Mae went back to the keyboard. "We've got pictures of the main office in New Jersey. We've got pictures of the board of directors. We've got pictures of the research labs."

Thumps leaned closer to the screen. The main building was a bright, glass square, sleek and modern. The picture of the board of directors told him little more, except for the fact that most of the individuals were young, younger than Thumps would have imagined.

"They're all kids."

"That's computers."

"What about the labs?"

There were six pictures of the research labs, each photograph exactly what you would expect—happy workers holding up pieces of what Thumps supposed was a computer. Except for the last picture, which showed a young Asian man flanked by two young women. The man was holding up what looked to be a tiny square of plastic, while the women looked on in happy amazement.

Ora Mae swung the screen back so she could see the man clearly. "Well, I'll be damned."

"Daniel Takashi."

Ora Mae fooled around with her mouse, and the picture scrolled up. "Thanks for sharing."

"I just found out."

Ora Mae hit a button on the computer, and real estate listings took over the screen. "Anything else, or can I get back to selling houses?"

"One more question," said Thumps, leaning on the chair. "How often are the units at Buffalo Mountain checked?"

"Once a day."

"Every day?"

Ora Mae looked at Thumps as if he had surprised her. "That's what's supposed to happen."

"But?"

"Some days I check them. Some days Clarence checks them."

"Clarence Fellows?" Thumps snorted. "Sterling's nephew?"

"Didn't your mother teach you manners?" Ora Mae shook her head. "Yes, Sterling's nephew. He was supposed to check them out Saturday night."

"Saturday night."

"Cheaper than a motel room, if you know what I mean."

Thumps was enjoying this more than he would have imagined. "Clarence still fooling around with Celia Brothers?"

Ora Mae batted her eyes at Thumps. "Goodness, but that's supposed to be a secret."

"Clarence and Celia were at the condos Saturday night?"

"No such luck. They were at a motel in Kalispell."

"Maybe I should talk to Clarence anyway."

"Sure," said Ora Mae. "If you want to drive over to Kalispell."

"He's still there?"

"Not coming home any time soon."

Thumps looked at Ora Mae. The woman wasn't just a little evil. She was pure evil.

"Seems Clarence's little secret wasn't as secret as he would have liked," she said.

"Barbara?"

Ora Mae nodded and began to chuckle. "Barbara and Celia had a little chat."

"Barbara knows?"

"Evidently Celia called her." Ora Mae was having difficulties keeping a straight face. "From the motel."

Thumps found he wasn't quite as amused as he had been. "Did they ... hurt him?"

Ora Mae shook her head. "Now you should know that violence is no way to settle your problems."

"He's alive?"

"Oh, yes," she said. " 'Course, he looks a little strange."

Thumps leaned back in the chair and waited. Ora Mae looked at the ceiling, and then she looked out the window.

"You going to make me ask?"

"They painted him."

"Clarence?"

"Bright red," said Ora Mae, her eyes dancing. "Right after they shaved his head."

Ora Mae was having too much fun. Thumps could see it was time to turn the conversation back to the matter at hand.

"So, who has keys to the condos?"

"Aren't any keys," said Ora Mae. "But you knew that already, didn't you?"

"Computer keypad, right?"

"That's right. You need a key card or a code."

"All the buildings the same?"

"Hardly," she said. "Every building is different. We have cards just for the condominums."

"How many?"

"Two cards here at the office. One for the agents and one that Sterling keeps."

"Who else has a card?"

"Probably Claire."

"Takashi?"

"More than likely."

Thumps glanced around the office. "I guess that means Sterling killed Takashi."

Ora Mae wasn't quick enough to catch all of the laugh before it jumped out of her mouth. "DreadfulWater, if you weren't such a lazy horse, I might just take you for a ride."

"Thought you were ..." Thumps let the rest of the sentence die and drift off the edge of the desk.

"Go ahead," she said. "You can say it."

"What I meant was ..."

"Don't worry. Your dick won't fall off."

Thumps could feel Ora Mae herding him over a cliff. "I'm not afraid to say ... lesbian."

"Praise the Lord! Another sensitive man."

"And I'm not lazy."

"Honey," said Ora Mae, leaning in, "you're the laziest man I've ever known, white, black, yellow, or red. But I hope you find the son of a bitch who did this before Claire comes to harm."

"Thought you said I was lazy."

"Being lazy and being good at what you do are two different things."

The half-hour drive to Shadow Ranch gave Thumps time to try to imagine Clarence bald and painted red, and to go over everything he knew so far.

Which wasn't much.

Item number one: The dead man was Daniel Takashi, a computer programmer working for Genesis Data Systems, the company that was installing the computer and security system at Buffalo Mountain Resort.

Item number two: Stanley Merchant, a.k.a. Stick, the son of the band manager and leader of the protest against the resort complex, had gone missing at almost the same time as the murder.

Item number three: The only way into the condominiums was with a computer key card. Or a code.

Item number four: According to George Chan, someone had introduced a worm into the computer system. Try as he might, Thumps could think of only one person who might have the skill to construct a worm and a reason to do so—Claire's son.

The body was particularly puzzling. It had been moved. That much was clear. But it hadn't been moved in order to hide it. Takashi had been killed in the computer complex. Why would someone lug the body over to the condos and drop it off in a wingback chair? If you wanted to move the body somewhere else, why not drag it into the woods? Carrying a dead body from the computer complex to the condos meant crossing at least four hundred yards of open ground. Too much of a risk. Unless you were desperate.

No, something was wrong. Thumps couldn't find it at the moment, but something was very wrong.

Shadow Ranch was a sprawling, upscale country club cleverly disguised as a western movie set. The Bunk House was a four-star hotel. The Watering Hole was a Las Vegas-style nightclub. The South Forty was a world-class eighteen-hole golf course. The property included a water slide/pool complex, tennis courts, riding stables, skeet-shooting range, and a modest, family theme park.

Buffalo Mountain Resort was impressive, but for size and range of activities, Shadow Ranch had it beat hands down. Except for the gambling. That was the difference, and if there was room enough in town for only one fast gun, Buffalo Mountain might just have the edge.

Shadow Ranch belonged to Vernon Rockland, and it was no secret that Rockland was unhappy about the new resort and the competition.

Actually, furious was the better word. Even before construction on Buffalo Mountain began, Rockland had lobbied the powers that be long and hard, complaining that the "playing field" should be level.

The joke was that the "playing field," as Rockland liked to call it, had never been level. The ability of the tribe to offer gambling had tipped the angle slightly in favour of the tribe, and, for the first time, people such as Vernon Rockland, who had always enjoyed business on a favourable slant, were irate to find themselves suddenly labouring across relatively flat ground.

Claire had tried to calm the waters by pointing out that Buffalo Mountain was set up for long-term residency, that most of its clientele would be older people who wanted a retirement property or families who were in the market for recreation opportunities. Shadow Ranch, she pointed out, catered to a more transient group, wealthy tourists who popped in to see the Rockies and what was left of the wilderness. In the end, there would be enough business for both resorts, she argued. It was a rationale that Thumps found both self-serving and reasonable.

Not that he believed it. And he was certain Rockland didn't.

Thumps parked his car in front of the hotel and walked quickly into the lobby, where the resort's air conditioning welcomed him with open arms. The girl at the front desk was very young and very attractive, very blond and very slim. In the age of international travel, where the staffs at major resorts were chosen for their racial and cultural diversity, Vernon Rockland was a dinosaur, a fossil from the old school of friendly colonialism, which continued to insist that things European and white be the standard against which everything else was measured.

"Hi." The woman had a gold badge pinned to her blazer that said Kimberly, and a mouthful of perfect, white teeth. Thumps ran his tongue across his own teeth in an effort to give them a last-minute polish.

"Hi," he said, trying to smile back without opening his mouth. "Where can I get information on your limousine service?"

"Right here," said Kimberly, her teeth flashing in the soft light of the lobby.

Thumps fingered the brochure. "A friend of mine is staying here. A Mr. Daniel Takashi."

Kimberly turned to the computer. "Yes, he is staying with us."

"He said the driver he had was excellent. A Native man."

"Native?" Kimberly's smile faded a bit.

"Indian."

"Oh, Indian." The smile was back. Kimberly reached under the counter and pulled out a map. "The Ironstone River Reservation is just to the west of us. We have a tour that goes through the reservation and then over to Glacier National Park."

"That's not what I want."

"It's one of our most popular tours."

Out of the corner of his eye, Thumps saw one of the resort's limousines pull up to the front door.

"Could I leave a message for Mr. Takashi?"

"You can call his room and leave a message on his voice mail."

"I'd rather write it down."

"Certainly," said Kimberly, and she handed him a pad of paper.

Thumps scribbled a message on the paper and handed it back. "I need to be sure he gets this."

"Absolutely," said Kimberly. She glanced at the computer and wrote a number on the back of Thumps' note. "If you like, I'll have someone take it to his room right away."

Thumps smiled, looked at the brochure for a moment, and then tapped his forehead as if he had forgotten something. "On second thought," he said, with all the charm he could muster, "forget the note. I think I'll surprise him."

"I'm sure he'd like that," said Kimberly. "I always like surprises."

"And I'll probably sign up for that tour," said Thumps. "It looks interesting."

The limousine was already heading down the lane by the time he got outside. It was too hot to run, and he slowed to a walk, following the dark sedan as it wove its way around to the back of the complex.

The garages were behind the hotel. When Thumps walked out of the shadows and back into the sun, Floyd Small Elk, Cooley's older brother, was washing one of the cars. Cooley was the bigger of the two, but Floyd was faster, stronger, and meaner. Thumps and Floyd had always been on good terms, but Thumps knew enough about the other man and his temper to know that that could change in a moment.

"Hey, Floyd."

Floyd froze, the hose in his hand.

"It's me, Thumps."

"Hey, Thumps," said Floyd. "You startled me."

"Sorry."

"What the hell you doing here."

"Won the lottery."

Floyd began laughing softly and turned the hose on the car. The spray hit the soap suds and cut them in half.

"I need some information."

"Information centre is back in town."

"Actually it's not for me. It's for Claire."

Floyd owed Claire big time, and if her name didn't flush out the information he wanted, Thumps knew he might as well head home and have a nap.

"Claire, huh?"

"Right."

Floyd put the sponge and the hose down and leaned against the side of the car. "What do you want to know?"

"Japanese guy named Takashi."

"What about him?"

"You were his driver."

"He complain about me?"

Thumps watched Floyd's eyes. "He's dead."

"Dead?" Floyd folded his arms across his chest so Thumps could see the muscles in his neck and shoulders. "You're kidding."

"Nope."

"Shit." Floyd looked at the garages. "You playing cop for Claire?"

Thumps shook his head.

" 'Cause you're beginning to sound like one."

"Old habits."

"What happened?"

"Someone shot him." Thumps waited to see whether Floyd was really hearing this for the first time. "At Buffalo Mountain."

Floyd leaned against the car. "I owe Claire."

"She's a generous woman."

"And I pay my debts." Floyd uncrossed his arms. "Yeah, I was his regular driver. Take him out to the resort around nine, pick him up around five."

"What about Saturday?"

"Just weekdays."

"He drove up to the complex around ten on Saturday and left a little after noon."

Floyd frowned. "Doesn't make any sense."

"Why not?"

"Every weekend, he rented a camper van and went sightseeing. Tourist stuff. He used to ask me where he should go."

"Every weekend?"

"Yeah," said Floyd. "You sure you're not playing cop?"

"Not anymore."

"And this is going to help Claire?"

"I hope so." Thumps turned and looked west. Shadow Ranch wasn't Buffalo Mountain Resort, but the view across the prairies all the way to the mountains was spectacular, and he could imagine himself sitting in a lawn chair by the side of the pool, eating his way from one meal to the next.

"A couple more showed up."

Thumps tried to pretend he didn't know what Floyd was talking about.

"Came in by helicopter."

"Short guy, slightly bald?"

Floyd picked up the hose again and let the water play over the car. "You don't do dumb cop worth shit. Blond guy and a woman. Good-looking. Corporate types. The kind that don't worry about money, either." He stopped the water for a second and looked at Thumps. "That it?"

Thumps shrugged. "You haven't seen Stick, have you?"

"Be sure to let Claire know I helped you."

As Thumps walked back down the hill, he tried to imagine what it would be like to be rich enough not to worry about money. Travel first class. Stay at the best resorts. Eat at the best restaurants. Own a car with air conditioning. It must be nice to be that rich. The rich certainly seemed to manage well enough.

Thumps stopped in the shade of the hotel. Kimberly had written "24" on the back of the note. Shadow Ranch had only two types of accommodations. Rooms and townhouses. Expensive and prohibitive. Comfortable and luxurious. Thumps didn't know Takashi's tastes, but he guessed that a top programmer in charge of a major project, staying in a strange town for more than a week would opt for luxury.

Twenty-four was a townhouse. Thumps quickly let himself in and hung the Do Not Disturb sign on the knob. It wasn't the Cascade at Buffalo Mountain, but it was very nice. He especially liked the gas fireplace with its carved oak mantle. The only inexpensive touch had been the lock on the front door.

Thumps walked through the rooms. The cleaning people hadn't been by yet. The bed was unmade and there were towels on the bathroom floor. Thumps checked the wastebaskets. Newspapers, a crushed cigarette pack, and a candy bar wrapper. There were clothes in the drawers—socks, underpants, and several T-shirts with sports logos on them—and a dark suit and a pair of dress shoes in the closet. Everything was where it was supposed to be.

On the desk was a laptop computer and a portable printer, along with several computer magazines. Thumps debated with himself for a moment and then turned the laptop on. He watched as it ran through its little dance of letters and numbers that made absolutely no sense. He was hoping the stupid machine would settle on a green screen loaded with icons, but instead he wound up with a black screen with a little rectangle that asked him to type in a password. Thumps didn't like computers in the first place, and this kind of nonsense wasn't going to help.

Okay, he had read somewhere that people pick passwords that mean something to them. Thumps tried "Takashi" in case the man had had a strong ego. Access denied. Next he tried "Geek" in case Takashi had had a sense of humour. Access denied.

This was fun. In quick succession, Thumps tried "Genesis," "Data," "Systems," "Genesis Data Systems," and "Buffalo" because he had run out of guesses. All access denied.

He left the computer to rot and checked under the bed and between the mattress and the box springs. It would be nice if Takashi had left a clue taped behind a picture hanging on the wall or tucked under the vanity in the bathroom. Thumps understood that he was probably looking for something that didn't exist, but once he got started, he was loath to give the search up. More disturbing, he found that he was enjoying himself.

Nothing.

Thumps sat down at the computer and wiggled it. There was a slot at the front that he vaguely remembered was for floppy disks, although the disks that he had seen Stick playing with hadn't looked particularly floppy. The slot was empty.

Thumps sighed and pressed the ESC button. Nothing. Then he pressed the F1 key. Nothing. He knew there was no point in getting angry with a machine, especially a computer, but part of him wanted to annoy the laptop as much as it was annoying him, and he toyed with the idea of pushing every button on the keypad until something happened.

Instead, he settled back in the chair and tried to breathe his frustration away. Which is when he saw two buttons at the front of the computer, next to the floppy slot. He pressed the first one and out popped what looked to be a battery.

"Wonderful."

The second button was no more help than the first. As he pressed it, a little drawer slid open. For a moment, Thumps thought he had found something, but the drawer was empty.

He pushed the drawer shut and checked the room one more time. Enough was enough, he told himself as he closed the door behind him. He'd find Stick if he could. Claire and the sheriff could take it from there.

Seven

Beth Mooney's office was a two-storey brick building that had once been the land titles office. Beth lived on the second floor and practised being a doctor on the first. She rented the basement out to the county as a morgue. Thumps had never been below the first floor, and he was more than happy to keep it that way.

He stepped into the foyer and pressed the button for the intercom.

"Yes?"

"Beth? It's me."

"Thumps?"

"Can I come up?"

"I'm down."

"First floor?"

"No, in the basement."

Thumps tried to remember whether he had any errands he could run first. "You coming up soon?"

"If you want to see me, you'll have to come down."

Thumps began counting the tiles on the floor. When he got to thirty-four, he reluctantly pressed the intercom again.

"Okay," he said, but he didn't really mean it.

The stairway down to the basement was dark and musty. Actually, it was more than musty, but musty would do just fine. Thumps didn't want to know what all the smells were or where they came from, and by the time he got to the bottom of the stairs, he was breathing through his mouth.

Beth was standing by the side of a steel table, dressed in a grey apron that had other colours on it as well. In her hand was a nasty-looking scalpel. Daniel Takashi lay on the table.

"What brings you to my kitchen?"

Thumps' stomach turned over.

"You okay?"

"Fine."

"Hey, come here," said Beth. "You'll be interested in this."

"No, I won't."

"Don't be a baby. It's a dead body, not a snake."

Thumps wasn't sure what a dead body and a snake had to do with each other, but all things considered, he was more inclined toward the snake.

"I've just finished up with the stomach. You want to see how it works?"

"No."

"It won't bite you."

"The Navajo don't like dead bodies."

"You're not Navajo."

"I have Navajo sensibilities."

"You're Cherokee," said Beth. "As I recall, the Cherokee like to create alphabets and take sovereignty cases to the Supreme Court."

"It was a syllabary, not an alphabet."

"Here," said Beth, and she handed Thumps a metal clipboard. "If you're going to stand around and take up space, you might as well help."

The form on the clipboard was a worksheet for a death certificate. The place for a name was blank.

"Daniel Takashi," said Thumps, almost to himself.

"Takashi? That his name?" Beth dropped her scalpel into a pan.

"He was a computer programmer." Thumps took his handkerchief out of his pocket and pretended to wipe his nose.

Beth picked up an electrical appliance that resembled a miniature skill saw. "No kidding." She pressed a button and the saw came to life.

Thumps didn't much like the look of the saw, and the high-pitched whine it made reminded him of the scream of an injured animal. "What's that thing for?"

Beth waved the little saw around in a circle. "I'm going to take a look at Mr. Takashi's brain."

Thumps could feel his body go numb.

"You all right?" Beth put the saw down and stripped off her rubber gloves.

Thumps found a stool just before he passed out. "Just fine," he said, but the words came out sounding like a moan.

"You guys are such a bunch of babies, you know that?"

"I'll be okay in a minute."

Beth smiled. "You had dinner?"

Thumps glanced at the corpse. "You're hungry?" he said, making sure to keep his teeth clenched.

"Starving," said Beth. "You can really work up an appetite down here."

The Golden Harvest was one of those combination restaurants that specialized in mediocrity at good prices, where you could serve yourself off the long steam table in the centre of the room or order from a menu and be assured of getting the same food.

Beth was a good sport. "I left a corpse for this?"

"The salad bar is terrific."

Thumps helped himself to the spaghetti on the supposition that the only way to harm pasta was to overcook it. Beth poked at the fried chicken.

"You really know how to turn a girl's head."

Thumps was trying to decide between the red Jell-o and the green Jell-o, when he saw Archie slide out of a booth and head his way, all smiles and good cheer.

"Hey, big shot," said Archie as he crossed the room, sweeping everyone out of his way. "Where have you been?"

Archimedes Kousoulas was one of those people everyone should have in their life. Whether they wanted one or not. Archimedes, or Archie as everybody called him, ran Chinook's only used book store. A Greek, originally from the island of Evia, he was a patchwork of distinct and disparate passions that ran from rare books to buried treasure.

Books were Archie's life, and he was happiest when he was searching attics, rummaging through estate sales, or surfing the Net, looking for first editions and hard-to-find volumes. A couple of months back, Archie had called Thumps on the phone to announce that he had found a rare first edition of Tony Hillerman's *The Blessing Way*, as well as a first edition of Evan Connell's *Son of the Morning Star* with the original soft paper jacket—for no other reason than that both books were about Indians.

"You're eating just the pasta?" Archie slipped in behind Thumps and followed him down the steam table.

"It's safe."

"They overcook it."

Treasure hunting, on the other hand, was Archie's passion. Not the Treasure Island variety or the "sunken galleon on a coral reef loaded with gold" kind. What Archie loved was western treasure. The army payroll. The strongbox from a stagecoach robbery. The fortune of some recluse who had hidden his money under the floor boards of his shack. Every minute that Archie wasn't on the prowl for another book, he was poring over letters and maps, researching western lore, confident that if he looked long enough he would locate that lost gold mine and become famous and rich, all at the same time.

"Hi, Archie." Beth's tray was bowing under the weight of the food she had heaped on the plates. "How go the books?"

Thumps liked Archie, but being in the man's energy slipstream was exhausting. He had gone on one of Archie's "treasure expeditions," partly out of friendship and partly out of curiosity, and one trip tromping through the wilderness had been enough.

"I have to get back to the shop," said Archie. "But for you, I can be late." He herded everybody to a booth. "So," he said to Thumps, "how come you don't come by and see me? I got some new postcards in."

"I've been busy."

"Busy? Taking pictures isn't busy," said Archie. "I'm the only one who buys them." He looked at Beth and smiled. "Do you know what this man does for a living?"

"I wouldn't call it a living," said Beth. "How you doing, Archie?"

"Fine. Always fine." Archie put his arm around Thumps' shoulder. "Do you know what this woman does for a living?"

"Don't remind me."

"That anatomy volume you wanted," Archie said to Beth as she began excavating a mound of mashed potatoes. "I think I know where to find one."

"Expensive?"

Archie shrugged. "We'll see. But first you eat. Then we talk." He got up from the booth. "I'll be right back. It's a surprise, so don't ask."

Thumps watched Archie head out the door, thankful that he wasn't going to have to spend dinner listening to the man's latest treasure story.

Beth leaned her head over the coffee cup and took a deep breath. "So, you didn't come by just to tell me the victim's name."

"Why were you going to ..." Thumps paused, appalled at what he was about to ask.

Beth waited to see if he was going to get to the end of the sentence. "Why was I going to cut open his head?"

Thumps could feel the waves of nausea rising up out of the depths of his stomach and heading for shore. "Yeah," he managed.

"Murder cases generally involve full autopsies."

"But he was shot. In the chest."

"Looks that way, all right. But I won't know for sure until I ..." Beth waved her finger around in a circle. "You know."

Thumps wondered about the smells that Beth worked with. Did they dissipate quickly or did they hang around like cigarette smoke, lurking in your hair or sticking to your fingers like an oil slick.

"Does the sheriff know you're nosing around?"

"I'm not nosing around."

"Could have fooled me." Beth raised the cup to her face and rolled it against her cheek. "So, why are you here?"

"Just curious if you found anything unusual."

"You want to tell me the difference?"

"Between what?"

"Curious and nosy."

The window behind Beth was bright, and the light tangled in her hair in a way that made Thumps think of cotton candy. The late afternoon sun also made him remember that he had missed his nap. He could feel his eyes begin to droop.

"I'm not that boring."

"I was up early."

Beth shifted and rested her head against the wall. "Okay, here's what I know. The man was Asian in his early thirties, and he was killed Saturday morning around eleven, give or take half an hour."

"That's it?"

"The last thing he had to eat was a doughnut and a cup of coffee."

"Hockney is going to be thrilled."

"How's the Jell-O?"

Thumps checked his fork. One of the tines was bent. How people could stand to eat with a bent fork was beyond him. He put the fork down and picked up a spoon.

"He's back," said Beth.

Thumps looked up just in time to see Archie come in the front door.

"Guess what?" said Archie as he slid in next to Beth.

Beth looked at Thumps.

"Don't look at him," said Archie. "He doesn't know anything."

Whenever Archie asked "guess what?" it was generally about treasure. When he wasn't in his shop, he was up in the hills, looking for caves, secret trails, and suspicious landmarks. Archie knew the mountains as well as most of the people on the reservation, but in all the years of looking, he hadn't found anything.

This didn't stop him, of course. Archie's philosophy was that if he hadn't found the treasure, then it was still out there. Thumps had to admit that this reasoning made sense. So far as it went.

"I know where the Aztec treasure is."

The Aztec treasure was the big cheese in this part of the world. After Cortes destroyed the Aztec empire, a small group of enterprising Spaniards under the leadership of one Antonio Garcia de la Vega supposedly slipped out of Mexico with a fortune in stolen gold. According to the legend, they got as far as the mountains around Chinook before they ran into the Blackfoot and had to take cover in a cave. Along with their gold.

In Thumps' opinion, all stories about lost treasure had slightly fantastic elements to them. This one was no exception, and what happened next in the story depended on who told it. Version one: the Spaniards were killed and the Blackfoot took the gold. Version two: some of the Spaniards escaped but had to leave their gold behind. Version three: the Spaniards hid the gold somewhere in the cave before they were killed to a man.

Archie liked them all. "You know where the Ironstone comes over Blackfoot Falls?"

"Didn't you look around there last year?"

"Maybe you could tell your boyfriend to shut up."

"My pleasure," said Beth, and she turned to Thumps. "Shut up."

"So, I'm looking around Blackfoot Falls, and guess who I see?"

"Okay, what did you see."

"Not what. Who."

Sometimes these conversation were short, but Thumps could sense that Archie was just warming to the story.

"An Aztec?"

"Tell your boyfriend to shut up again."

"He's not my boyfriend," said Beth.

"That's because you're a smart woman."

"Okay, Archie," said Thumps. "Who did you see?"

"Stick Merchant."

Thumps sat up.

"Ah," said Archie. "Now Mr. Smart Remarks is interested."

"You saw Stick at the falls."

"At the pools below the falls. And you know what that means, don't you?"

Thumps stopped listening and began putting pieces together. From the trailhead on the northwest side of the reserve, Blackfoot Falls was about a three-hour hike. If you were going to fish the pools below the falls, that was the way you would go in.

"When?"

"What?"

"When did you see Stick?"

"Saturday." Archie looked at Thumps and winked. "He was on his way to visit the Aztec treasure."

The trail to Blackfoot Falls ran in behind Buffalo Mountain Resort. But if you knew where to drop off the trail and had a reasonable sense of direction, you could make it to the resort in an hour.

"What time did you see him?"

"Who cares," said Archie, who wanted to get on with his story. "You know who killed the Spaniards, don't you?"

"The Blackfoot," said Thumps, trying to head Archie off. "When exactly did you see Stick?"

Archie shrugged. "Late afternoon. What difference does it make? The important thing is that I know how to find the Aztec treasure."

Beth leaned forward. "How?"

"All I have to do is follow Stick the next time he goes into the mountains."

"What was he doing?" Thumps nudged Beth's leg with his foot. "Was he fishing?"

"Fishing?" said Archie, looking at Beth for help. "Your boyfriend doesn't listen, does he?"

Beth gave Thumps a reproachful look and moved her leg. "So, did you follow him?"

"I was too far away." Archie made a disgusted noise. "By the time I got to the pools, he was gone."

Thumps took his money clip out of his pocket. "We should be going."

"Going?" Archie frowned. "You eat. You run. You going to get cramps."

"I have to get back to the office," said Beth. "I've got a guy waiting for me."

"A man?" Archie raised his eyebrows and forgot about Thumps for a moment. "You got a man?"

"Don't ask." Thumps shuddered as his brain fired a reflex glimpse of Daniel Takashi stretched out on the metal table in Beth's basement. "Look, did he see you?"

"Who?" said Archie.

"Stick."

"Of course not." Archie helped himself to some of Thumps' Jell-O. "What do you plan to do with your share of the Aztec gold?"

"Thumps gets a share?" asked Beth.

"Sure," said Archie. "He's my partner."

"Partner?" Thumps was beginning to feel uneasy. "You don't need a partner."

"You don't want to be my partner?"

"It's not that," said Thumps, but as soon as he said it, he wasn't sure that this was the right answer.

"Good," said Archie. "So, the first thing you need to do is talk to Stanley about the treasure."

"Me?"

"I think that's what 'partner' means," said Beth.

"You're Indian," said Archie, "and Stick's Indian. What's the problem?"

"Archie ..."

"We'll split it three ways even though you probably don't deserve a full share."

"I don't want a share."

"Fine. We'll split it two ways." Archie pushed away from the table. "I got to go back to work. Don't let me down."

"That was fun." Beth folded her napkin and tucked it at the side of her plate. "But I better not keep 'my man' waiting."

"He's dead."

"You know," she said, "for a photographer, you're quite perceptive."

Thumps stayed at the table and watched Beth through the window. Outside, the light was beginning to drop and flatten out against the sides of the buildings. Too late to do anything more. Time to call it a day and go home. Maybe Stick would show up with a string of fish and a good alibi. Maybe Duke would catch the killer. Maybe some rich guy from Los Angeles would fly in and buy a bunch of Thumps' photographs.

Maybe there was something good on television.

Eight

Freeway was waiting for Thumps when he got home, and she wasn't happy. Not that she was ever truly happy, unless you counted the eight to ten hours each day that she spent lying on her back in the sunlight.

"You hungry?"

Freeway closed both eyes and pretended to ignore him. Thumps walked to the refrigerator. Freeway opened both eyes, yawned, stretched, and stood up.

The can of wet cat food sat on the top shelf, away from everything else. And even though it was sealed in two plastic zip-lock bags, the smell of it seemed to work its way into everything—the tomatoes, the sliced ham, the cottage cheese, and especially the fruit, which was all the way at the bottom of the refrigerator in its own drawer.

Freeway began sliding across Thumps' feet the way water flows over rocks. "So, now we're pals again?" Cat food, Thumps grimaced, smelled like vomit. He tried to breathe through his mouth as he spooned the chunky brown lumps into a bowl. "Don't be a pig."

Freeway was not a dainty eater. She enjoyed shoving her nose into the bowl and sucking up the food like a vacuum cleaner. Thumps didn't particularly care that the cat was a slob, but he knew if she ate too fast, she would throw it all up on the carpet.

"Cute cat."

Thumps spun around and reached for his gun before he remembered that he no longer carried one.

"She's a little standoffish." Floyd Small Elk was sitting on the sofa in the shadows. "Hope I didn't startle you."

"Wasn't expecting company."

Floyd nodded. "Yeah, I can see that."

Thumps reached for the light switch.

"Leave it off."

Unlike Kimberly at Shadow Ranch, Thumps was not particularly fond of surprises. And finding Floyd Small Elk camped in his living room was a surprise. "How'd you get in?"

"Door was open. You weren't here." Floyd shifted his weight on the sofa. "I figured you wouldn't mind if I waited."

"You want tea or something?"

Floyd shook his head. "I can't stay. Friend of mine asked me to stop by."

Thumps put a pot of water on the stove. "And here you are."

Floyd smiled and nodded. "My friend was wondering if there was a … reward."

"Reward?"

"You know. For the dead guy."

"Takashi?"

"Yeah."

"You know who killed Takashi?"

"My friend might."

Floyd didn't have any friends. At least none that Thumps knew about. He was one of those men that other men left alone, a man who carried the stench of danger and pain with him wherever he went.

"Tribe has a shitload of money," said Floyd. "What do you think information like that would be worth to them?"

"Floyd …"

"Five thousand?"

There was only one person Floyd knew who might know something about Takashi's death.

"Ten?" Floyd waited to see if he would get a reaction. "Publicity like that couldn't be good for business."

Thumps decided to do a little fishing. "Floyd, if Cooley knows anything about the murder …"

"Good guess." Floyd cocked his head and smiled. "But Cooley don't know squat."

"But your friend does?"

"Maybe." Floyd leaned forward and stood up. "I hear Hockney is looking to hang this one on Stick."

"Stick didn't do it."

"You're guessing again, cousin." Floyd opened the door and let the warm night air float in. "Talk to Claire. Tell her I'll give her first option. But tell her not to wait too long."

The kettle on the stove began to whistle. Thumps slid it off the burner and turned back to tell Floyd that he was playing a dangerous game.

"Look, Floyd ..."

The doorway was empty. Thumps waited, half expecting the man to return, to pop his head in to tell Thumps something he had forgotten, the way that detective on television with the rumpled trench coat used to do. But Floyd was gone.

Thumps poured the water over the tea bag. Just what the hell was that about? When he had talked to Floyd earlier in the day, the man didn't have a clue about Takashi. Thumps was sure of that. Now he was acting as though he had everything solved. Thumps wouldn't put it past Floyd to try to run a con. But this didn't feel like a scam. Floyd had been sure of himself, almost pleased.

Whether or not Floyd knew who had killed Takashi, he was right about one thing. Claire would want the matter cleared up as soon as possible. Whatever else Claire was, she was an astute business woman, and having the resort splashed all over the newspapers as a dangerous place to vacation or to live would be very bad for business. Maybe Claire would pay Floyd for the privilege of not seeing the resort highlighted on the national news and dragged through the tabloids. Then again, maybe she wouldn't.

Thumps looked at the tea bag floating in the cup. He was tired, and it was late.

"Come on," he said to the cat, even though he knew that Freeway would only come when she was good and ready. Enough for one day. Tomorrow would be soon enough to begin again.

When the phone rang the next morning, Thumps opened his left eye just enough to see the clock on the nightstand. The first number was a six.

Thumps closed his eye, rolled over, and tried not to count the rings. Somebody wanted him awake. Telemarketers didn't call at this hour, so it had to be someone who thought they were his friend. Thumps didn't have many, and at this moment, he didn't want to talk to any of them. Including Claire.

On the thirteenth ring, Thumps snatched the phone off its cradle. "This better be good."

"You still asleep?" Duke sounded much too cheery for the news to be encouraging. "I catch you at a bad time?"

"I'm asleep."

"No, you're not."

Thumps sighed and buried his head in the pillow. "Goodbye, sheriff."

"Figured I'd check to see whether you've heard from Stick."

"And you thought six in the morning was a good time to call."

"You were the first item on my list of things to do."

"Terrific." Thumps was wrong about Duke's voice being cheery. It was exhilarated. Almost passionate.

"That's what I figured," said Duke. "Always best to take care of these things before they get out of hand."

"What things?"

"We need to talk to Stick." The sheriff paused and waited as though he were trying to find the right words. "We need to talk to Stick right away."

"Did we find something?" Thumps tried to keep the sarcasm under control.

"Sorry I woke you," said Duke in a happy singsong fashion that was particularly annoying. "You have a nice day."

Even before Thumps put the phone down, he knew the case had taken a turn, that the sheriff had indeed found something, and whatever it was, it wasn't going to do Stick any good. The call was Duke's way of letting Thumps know that the situation was now serious, that the alert going out for Stick's arrest would probably describe the boy as armed and dangerous.

The hot-water heater in the basement had slipped into an extended depression, and for the last six months, it would produce only lukewarm water that ran to cold whenever Thumps began shampooing his hair. It was an irritating and startling routine, but by the time he stepped out of the shower, he was wide awake. And hungry. There was nothing much in the refrigerator and no time to stop in at Al's for a leisurely breakfast. Instead, Thumps settled for a cold cheese sandwich with sliced banana. Protein, fat, carbohydrates, and fruit—all in the same package.

All the way out of town, Thumps watched his rear-view mirror, in case the sheriff was more devious than he imagined. Nothing. Just to be safe, he took the long way, even pulled off the road at the top of Benson's Coulee so he could see the road below him. Nothing. By the time he turned off the main road, he was reasonably sure he hadn't been followed.

The parking lot for the trailhead to Blackfoot Falls had six cars in it. Three were rentals—tourists probably, who had come west to visit the wilderness. One was a pickup truck with British Columbia plates. The sixth car was Stick's Mustang. Thumps felt the hood. Dead cold. So, Archie had been right. He had seen Stick.

From here, if you knew what you were doing, you could climb to the saddle at Dark Horse Pass and then go cross country for an hour and come in behind the resort. Or you could keep climbing and catch the Ironstone as it emptied out of a sheer canyon over Blackfoot Falls into a series of deep pools where the fishing was as good as it gets.

The car in the parking lot was good news. It offered the possibility that Stick had been telling the truth, that he had gone fishing. The Mustang was locked, but Thumps had it opened in a minute. There were tapes on the front seat, and a shirt and a pair of pants on the back. The trunk took a little longer to open. Inside, Thumps found a pair of dark green waders and a fly rod.

He sat down in the shade and put on his hiking boots. If Stick had come to the trailhead to go fishing, why did he leave his fly rod in the trunk? And if he had parked here and walked into the resort to kill Takashi, why not take the fishing pole with him to help establish his alibi?

Thumps stood up and looked around. It was mostly open country to begin with, and from where he stood in the parking lot, he could see all the way to where the trail rose into the foothills and dropped into the narrow valley behind the first range of hills. The hike looked a lot longer than he had remembered, and he debated throwing his sleeping bag on the ground, taking a nap in the shade, and waiting for Stick to come out on his own.

Thumps was still thinking it was a good idea as he left the parking lot and began the climb to the near ridge.

In his heart, he believed that he was in far better shape than he looked, and by the time he got to the top of the ridge and looked down into the valley, he knew he was wrong. His legs hurt. His back hurt. His head hurt. His arms ached, and the skin on the heels of his feet was beginning to separate. Resting didn't help. Every time he stopped, he could feel his muscles begin to tighten, and he could hear the insects behind him gaining ground.

You could fish the Ironstone at any of a dozen spots, but if you were serious about your fishing—and Stick was—you'd fish the pools below the falls. It was a hard spot to get to and difficult to fish, but the browns that lay in the shadows could bring down an elk. If Stick had gone fishing, that was where he would be.

Thumps checked the sky ahead of him for any sign of smoke, but that would have been too easy. There was the chance that he might stumble across Stick's trail, but only if Stick had marked it out with reflective tape. The cliché of an Indian gliding through a forest, alive to the vagaries of turned stones, broken branches, and scents on the wind, only happened in movies and on television. A fire trail he could follow. He might even be able to negotiate a well-used game trail. The more Thumps thought about what he was doing, the more he realized how crazy this expedition was. It would be desperately comic if, in trying to find Stick, he got lost or even injured. Wilderness might not be as wild as it once was, but it could still kill you if you took it for granted.

Thumps started down the trail into the valley. With any luck, he would get to the pools while he still had feeling in his feet. With a small miracle, Stick would be there waiting for him.

Thumps hadn't counted on a miracle and he didn't get one. The pools below the falls were deserted. He searched the rocks for any sign of Stick, but the only things moving were the big trout rising in the pools to take insects off the surface of the water. Thumps headed for the shade of the big boulders. It would be cool there, a good place to rest and think about what to do. Next to one of the larger rocks, someone had constructed a crude circle of stones. Inside the circle he saw the remains of a fire that had "tourist" written all over it. From the look and smell of the firepit, some idiot had lugged in a bag of self-starting charcoal briquettes. Thumps was sure if he poked through the ashes, he'd probably find pieces of melted marshmallow stuck to the stones and the charred remains of a cork or two. This wasn't Stick's work.

So, where was Stick going when Archie saw him? The good news was that there weren't many choices. South was the resort. North was more mountains. If you went far enough west, you'd wind up in one of the many small resort towns with hot springs and golf courses and motel beds that vibrated. Going east took you back to Chinook.

Thumps closed his eyes. A quick nap sounded appealing, but he knew that if he went to sleep, there was no telling when he would wake up. The great outdoors was nice, but he didn't fancy spending a night in the wild watching the stars and listening to wolves. Just as well, for Freeway wasn't the kind of cat who enjoyed having the house to herself. The last time Thumps had stayed out overnight, Freeway had unrolled the toilet paper, then pulled the cereal box off the counter and dragged it around the house.

Thumps was watching the water pour over the falls and arguing with his body about the nap when he suddenly remembered. Sikayopa. Stick had told him about it once when they had come to fish the pools, when Thumps and Claire had been serious contenders for each other's affections. Sikayopa. An ancient site, on the eastern face of the moun-tain, where you could see the sun rise. Where people had gone for gener-ations to seek visions. A ledge of black stone, darker than the rest of the mountain. In the shape of a crouching bear.

That must have been where Stick was going. Nothing else out here made any sense. What had Stick told him? An hour's climb, at most, from the pools. Directly above a large scree field.

Thumps got to his feet and dragged a boot through the firepit scatter-ing the stones and the ashes. Charcoal briquettes and marshmallows. It was a wonder they hadn't packed in steaks and a portable barbecue. But then again, maybe they had.

The climb out of the pools and over the first ridge was reasonably easy. But as Thumps stood in the narrow valley and looked up at the eastern face of the mountains, he could see that finding Sikayopa was going to be more difficult than he had hoped. There were at least four scree fields, and in the deep shadows, all of the rock was dark.

It took him the better part of an hour to find it. Set on the side of the mountain. A long, thick slab of black granite. And just below it, the bear in the rock. Thumps walked the base of the scree field, looking for a trail, a way up. But there was no easy way to get to the ledge. If he made a mistake, he would come sliding down the mountain as part of a small avalanche. A wrong step and he could break a leg.

Thumps sat down and gave plan B a try.

"Stick!"

He listened to his voice as it ran down the mountain and echoed in the thin air. It was loud enough.

"Stick! You up there?"

Somewhere off to the right, Thumps heard the distant clatter of rocks.

"Stick, it's me, Thumps!"

Thumps waited for his voice to disappear into the silence. It would be nice, he mused, if hard things could be done the easy way once in a while.

The climb was difficult, and as he dragged himself over the loose rocks and boulders, as his breathing turned to desperate gasps, Thumps began to imagine that Stick was waiting for him with a cold glass of lemonade and a bowl of fruit salad with cottage cheese. It was the thin air. Thumps understood that. But when he finally pulled himself onto the ledge, his shirt wet with sweat, his legs aching, his ankles bruised, his hands and arms cut and scraped, he was mildly disappointed to find it deserted.

The ledge itself was a narrow affair that ran back to a shallow cave. Someone had built a small fire at the back of the cave and had stayed long enough to have lunch. Or supper. Or both. Two apple cores and a banana skin lay near the firepit.

Thumps smiled and wondered if they were the fugitives from Ora Mae's fruit plate.

Not that any of this meant that Stick had been here. The fruit could have come from anywhere. The fire could have been started by someone who just needed to get away from everything for a while. Thumps didn't know much about vision quests but he knew they generally lasted more than one day. As far as he could tell, only one fire had been started. An overnight stay, maybe, or a day visitor.

Thumps walked the length of the ledge looking for clues. If the fire was Stick's, why would he have come here? If he had killed Takashi, he might have gone to the pools to establish an alibi, but why would he have come to this place? Thumps walked the ledge again, slowly this time. Nothing.

The cave was little more than a shallow bowl cut into the rock, deep enough to get you out of the weather. But the roof sloped quickly, and if you wanted to sit at the back, you had to crawl.

Enough was enough. Enough hiking. Enough stumbling. Enough crawling. Stick was damn well old enough to take care of himself. Thumps did not need to dash up hills to impress Claire. As he recalled, little he had ever done had impressed Claire. The light was starting to go, and if he hoped to get back to the parking lot before it was too dark to see, he would have to start back down now. He glanced at the cave one more time.

"Hell!"

Thumps got down on his hands and knees and made his way inside. From the entrance, the roof of the cave looked as though it sloped down until it met the floor, but as he got to the back, the roof suddenly and unexpectedly opened up into a small dome, a rock bubble, where he could sit up.

Thumps dragged himself into a comfortable position against the rock and rested. It was pleasant, he had to admit, for a cave. He picked up one of the apple cores. It was fresh. So was the banana peel. He was reaching for the second apple core when he saw the buffalo. At least, that's what it looked like. A crude drawing of a buffalo scratched into the roof of the cave. And then a second drawing, this one of a man with a spear. As Thumps' eyes adjusted, he could see that the roof was covered with drawings of animals and people. And symbols. Rain, clouds, a river, lightning. Some of the drawings looked bright and fresh. Others looked older. A few appeared to be as old as the rock itself. Off to one side, someone had scratched "Dalton loves Celeste" into the wall. High on the roof, another artist had drawn a reasonable facsimile of Mickey Mouse.

Thumps ran a hand through the fire, rubbed the soft ashes between his fingers, and smelled them. There was no mistaking the scent. Sage. He had smelled it often enough at powwows and ceremonies. Someone had come to pray. To leave an offering.

It was so close, he almost didn't see it. A piece of string. Above his head, hanging off a rock shelf. But as Thumps moved to one side and reached up to grab it, he realized that it might also be a tail. It would be just his luck to stick his hand into an animal's nest. Something small and bitey that did not like fingers. Or worse. Thumps tried to shut those thoughts away by humming a round-dance song. His hand found the shelf, and he cautiously dragged a finger across the rock in time with the music. He found it on the second pass and was relieved that it didn't feel like a tail at all. Slowly, he began to pull on the string until it stopped.

Okay.

Thumps pulled a littler harder, increasing the pressure until something popped out of the rocks and hit him in the chest.

"Shit!"

The object lay in his lap, and for that brief moment, it looked very much like a small rodent. Thumps rolled to one side and knocked it away before it got any bad ideas.

"Damn!"

Now it didn't look so much like a small rodent. It looked more like a bag. A leather bag with a rawhide tie. Moose hide, from the look of it, and not commercial moose hide, either. Thumps held the bag to his nose. This leather had been smoke cured and hand worked and he was reasonably sure he knew what it was. A medicine bag. Something you didn't fool around with. Whoever had left it here had left it for a reason.

Thumps turned the bag over in his hands. It hadn't been in the cave long. He saw no sign of weathering or any hint that animals had been at it. Mice loved hide like this, and given the opportunity, would have chewed the bag to shreds. So, should he open it? Thumps hated philosophical questions like this. A traditional Indian would not open someone else's medicine bag. Thumps did not think of himself as a traditional Indian, but neither did he like to think of himself as an assimilated

Indian. What would a photographer do? No help there. How about a police officer? That was easy. A police officer would open the bag. No question. To hell with culture. To hell with tradition. Get the facts. Catch the crook.

Thumps sat in the cave and squeezed the bag, feeling for what was inside. He wasn't sure squeezing medicine bags was allowed. Not that it helped. Whatever was in the bag was shapeless and spongy. Except for four small soft lumps.

He sighed. No point in sitting here all night trying to figure out a way to open the bag that would not offend his sensibilities. Which left only two options. Leave the bag where he had found it and assume it had nothing to do with Stick or Takashi. Or take the bag with him and figure out what to do later. Thumps shook his head at the logic he was about to embrace. It wasn't okay to open the bag, but it was okay to take it. Brilliant. Truly impressive. Very modern.

He shoved the bag into his pocket. He'd get back to the pools before dark. From there, with any luck, he'd be able to follow the trail down to the parking lot. Maybe the moon would be up.

Thumps stopped for a moment, suddenly pleased with the prospect of a walk in the woods. Living in cities had changed his life in ways he had hardly noticed, even a city the size of Chinook. And as he made his way down the side of the mountain, he realized that he couldn't remember the last time he had seen the stars. Or watched the moon rise into a night sky.

Nine

The notion of a romantic stroll through the woods in moonlight under an ocean of stars proved to be extravagant. Almost as soon as Thumps left the pools, heavy cloud cover moved in, turning the trail down the mountain into a slow fall down a deep well. He crashed against rocks, ran into tree branches, tripped over roots, and by the time he stumbled into the parking lot, he was bruised and cranky.

He had heard that medicine bags could provide protection against all manner of mischief. Evidently, questionable decisions such as walking around in the mountains in the dark were not covered.

The parking lot was empty, except for the Volvo. The rentals were gone. The truck with the British Columbia plates was gone. Stick's Mustang was gone. Thumps brushed the dirt off his clothes and thought about screaming. If he had just waited in the parking lot, he would have found Stick and saved himself the hike. Instead, all he had to show for his troubles were lacerations, torn pants, and somebody's medicine bag.

Thumps tried not to think about the bag. Now that he had it, and he was off the mountain, he was not at all sure he had done the right thing. Maybe he should have left it alone. Or maybe he should have opened it on the ledge. If he hadn't discovered anything of interest inside, he could have closed the bag, put it back where he had found it, and pretended that nothing had happened. Now he was stuck doing things the hard way.

Thumps had been to Moses Blood's place two or three times, but those visits had been during the day when he could see his way around. At night, distances lengthened out and directions shifted, and Thumps drove by the turnoff twice before he finally found it. Moses called the track that led to his house a "driveway," but that's because Moses had a warped sense of humour. No stretch of the imagination could turn the deep ruts carved in the prairies into something as genteel as a driveway. In the glare of the headlights, they looked like canyons, and Thumps had to make his way down to the river as much by feel as by sight.

Moses lived on about fifty acres of bottom land overlooking the river. There was a chicken coop, a barn, and about forty trailers in various stages of decay. Over the years, for reasons Thumps could only guess at, people from the reserve had brought their poor and tired trailers to Moses for safekeeping. And over the years, he had arranged the trailers in intricate patterns so they resembled a giant maze or an enormous patchwork quilt. Even Ora Mae would have been hard pressed to describe it.

The lights were on. Thumps parked, stood by the car, and waited. Unlike the sky in the mountains, the prairie sky was clear, and the moon was rising, bright yellow and full. Go ahead, thought Thumps as he watched the stars sparkle overhead, have a good laugh.

It took a while for Moses to come out, but when he did, he had two cups in his hands. "Been expecting you," he said.

Ten or twelve years back, an ethnographer from a big university in California spent several weeks with Moses collecting old stories. Each day, when the ethnographer showed up, Moses would say, "Been expecting you." Each day, no matter when the man arrived, Moses would say, "Been expecting you." Towards the end of the visits, the ethnographer told Moses about the role of visions in primitive cultures and how some people believed they could see the future.

"Look at you, " said the ethnographer. "You know I'm coming before I get here."

"That's right," said Moses.

"So, maybe you can see the future."

"See it all the time."

The ethnographer was delighted and went back to California dragging behind him stories of Indian mysticism, psychic ability, and spirituality.

"For a white guy," Moses told his great-niece after the man had left, "he wasn't too bright."

"You told him you could see the future?"

"You bet. Look out the window. What do you see?"

"The main road."

"The minute the future turns off the main road, I can see it."

Thumps took the tea and let the twists of steam run over his face. "How you doing, Moses?"

"Been expecting you."

Thumps smiled and sipped at the tea. It was hot and sweet. "Thought I'd stop by and say hello."

Moses looked out into the night. "Is it a big problem or a little one?" In the distance, Thumps could hear a coyote working its way across the coulees.

"It's not exactly a problem."

Moses nodded. "Then you better bring it inside," he said. "You never know when an owl might be listening."

In contrast to the complications and angles of the trailer park behind Moses' house, the inside of his place was surprisingly simple. It was basically one large room. The kitchen sat at one end and a large-screen satellite television sat at the other. In between was a Formica kitchen table and chairs, a purple Hide-A-Bed, and a white Naugahyde recliner. As far as Thumps knew, Moses slept in the kitchen, for the house had no other room except for the bathroom.

Moses took the tea kettle from the stove and set it on the table. "It's a new recipe I'm trying."

"Traditional?"

"Don't think so, but who knows these days. I saw it in *News From Indian Country*. There's this good-looking Native doctor, Dr. Marie Micak, and she said this tea will help you get slim."

"Diet tea?"

"Who knows." Moses scooped two spoons of sugar into his cup. "It's got one-half cup of dried watercress, one-half cup of dried kelp, and one-quarter cup of chamomile flowers in it."

"Tastes pretty good."

"It's better with sugar," said Moses.

Thumps took the bag out of his pocket and laid it on the table. He knew Moses wasn't going to look at it right away because there was other business to take care of first.

"You haven't been out for a while."

"Saw Claire today."

"Lots of things been happening," said Moses, and he helped himself to another spoonful of sugar. "Some of them are regular, and some of them are pretty strange."

Thumps wasn't sure whether Moses knew about the body at the condos. Since the old man didn't have a phone, he might not know. Thumps had always found that odd. A big-screen satellite television and no phone.

"They cancelled North of Sixty. That was a regular thing."

"That got cancelled a while back."

"It was okay." Moses shifted in his chair. "But those people up there at Lynx River didn't have much of a sense of humour."

"It was a serious show."

"Laughing and crying are good for you," said Moses. "But being grim all the time will only make you sad."

"So what do you watch now?"

"Magnum P.I. reruns. That's one tricky fellow. One time he was accused of murder. It looked pretty bad for him." Moses stopped as if he was trying to remember the plot. "And sometimes I watch Northern Exposure."

"That had Indians in it."

"You bet," said Moses. "Sidekicks."

Thumps had had these kinds of conversations with Moses before, conversations that started off well enough but then took a turn when Thumps wasn't looking and left him standing by himself in a field.

"Sidekicks?"

"That's right," said Moses. "Indians make the best sidekicks. You ever hear of a guy named Tonto?" He poured Thumps another cup of tea and put his hand on the bag.

Thumps leaned back in the chair. "It's not mine."

"Someone lost it?"

"Not exactly."

"'Cause if you stole it, I don't know that I can help."

"I borrowed it."

"Ah," said Moses. "Okay. Borrowing is okay."

Thumps leaned forward and looked at his tea. There were little yellow specks floating in the brown liquid. He hoped these were the remains of the chamomile flowers.

"I found it at that ledge. Where people used to go for visions."

Moses poured himself another cup and let the sugar slowly fall off the spoon like sand in an hourglass. Thumps picked up his own cup and waited. He could have lied and told Moses that he had found the bag at the trailhead or in the parking lot, but he knew the old man could see through a lie as easily as most people can see through a window.

"You want to watch a movie?" Moses got to his feet and came back with the remote control.

"What's on?"

"Everything. You ever see *Die Hard*?"

"Sure."

"They kill a lot of people in that movie."

"That's Hollywood."

"That's what white people do best." Moses pressed the on button and the television sprang to life. "They make good movies." On the television, a bunch of good-looking men and women in spacesuits were fighting with a bunch of giant bugs. "Ho," he said, "I've seen this one before. The bugs almost win." Moses turned down the sound. "Just like Indians." Moses rubbed the bag with his thumb. "You want me to open it."

"Yes."

"But you were worried it might be sacred or something."

"I wasn't sure."

"Always pays to ask." Moses switched channels. Jodie Foster was talking to Anthony Hopkins, who was sitting in a jail cell. "That guy there is a cannibal," he said and quickly switched to another channel. "The stuff they show on television."

"Can you open it?"

Moses put the remote on the table and picked up the bag. "Don't need me for this." He untied the strings and emptied the bag on the table. "It's not a medicine pouch."

Thumps looked at the clump of tobacco on the table. Wonderful. Someone had left an offering, and Thumps had made off with it.

"Is this what you were looking for?"

"No."

"How about this?"

Moses shook the bag again and four gold tubes fell out. At first, Thumps didn't recognize them. It was only when he picked one up and turned it over that he realized what it was.

"Looks like a filter tip," said Moses. "Always good to leave tobacco when you go to the mountains." He ran a finger through the tobacco. "But you don't have to leave the filters, too."

There was no mistaking it. The filters on the table were the same as the ones the sheriff had shown him at Buffalo Mountain.

"Is it a secret?" said Moses.

"Maybe," said Thumps.

"It's okay. I won't tell anyone," said Moses. "I'll be your sidekick." And the old man began laughing softly to himself. "You want to watch a movie?"

"It's getting late."

"That's the good thing about television."

"What's that?"

"It's there twenty-four hours a day."

Moses walked Thumps out to his car. The moon was gone, but the stars were brilliant. "Now, that's a big screen," said Moses.

"Maybe I should stop by sometime and pick you up," said Thumps. "We could catch dinner in town and go to a movie."

Moses looked up at the night sky. "They got stars like this at the movies?"

"No."

"Then I guess I'll stay home." Moses turned and started back to the house. And then he stopped. "He didn't do it, you know."

"Stick?"

"No. Magnum. The killer turned out to be a hit man from Chicago."

Thumps looked at the filter tips in his hand.

"Same as Stanley," said Moses.

"What?"

"He didn't kill anyone, either."

"How did you hear about that?"

"Saw it on television." Moses pointed the remote at the sky and clicked it several times. "Good news," he said. "It doesn't work out here."

"You wouldn't happen to know who did kill the man at the resort?"

"If this was television, it would be a hit man from Chicago."

The way back along Moses' driveway wasn't as easy as the way in. Thumps' mind was on other matters besides his driving, and his oil pan paid the price. The filter tips sat on the seat beside him. In the starlight, the gold foil seemed to glow.

He should have said no. When Claire had asked him to find Stick, he should have just said no. It was the sheriff's job to solve crimes, not his. But now that he had started, he knew he was in too far to turn around and walk out.

Ten

The hardest decision Thumps had to make each morning was when to get out of bed. Nine was too early. Ten was okay. Eleven was even better because, by then, he could forget about breakfast and go straight to lunch. Some people might see this as a sign of laziness, but for Thumps sleeping in was a way of reminding himself that he was his own boss. When he was a cop on the California coast, late mornings had not been an option. Now that he was an artist, a fine-art photographer, and not tied to someone else's schedule, most days were his to do with as he pleased.

Today was not one of those days. All the dashing about in the last while had screwed up his rhythm, and by the time the sun had begun its climb up the eastern slope of the mountains, Thumps was awake. Three early days in a row was obscene, and as he stood under the shower, he reminded himself that self-employed people should at least have the luxury of arranging their business day. Not that Thumps was exactly self-employed. To be sure, he had a small pension from the State of California, but if he added up the number of photographs he had sold in the last four months, self-unemployed might be a better description.

As soon as Thumps stepped out of the tub, Freeway jumped in and began lapping at the pool of water that never seemed to drain away completely. Thumps had considered pouring a bottle of something nasty down the pipe to unclog it, but he worried that Freeway might wind up stiff and cold on the porcelain. Of course, there were times when he wanted to strangle the cat. And he wasn't sure he would really miss her. But after Eureka, he knew he didn't have the stamina to manage many more losses in his life. Even minor ones.

As he stood in front of the bathroom mirror and tried to decide whether or not he needed to shave, Thumps began sorting through his options for the day. He had already been up to Buffalo Mountain twice. He had talked to Cooley. He'd been in the mountains looking for Stick and did not plan to do that again. He'd been out to Shadow Ranch to visit with Floyd, and Floyd had stopped by to visit with him. He'd even broken into Takashi's room and searched it. The sheriff would love that one. And he had been to see Claire. As far as he could tell, he hadn't missed anything. Yet, with the exception of the cigarettes, he hadn't found anything either. Takashi was still dead. Stick was still missing. And aside from some vague notions about the possibilities of political protest gone wrong, he didn't have a clue as to why the crime had taken place.

Thumps folded his jeans and put on a pair of cotton slacks instead. Most of his good shirts were in the laundry. The rest hadn't been ironed yet. In the end, all he could find that was reasonably appropriate was a dark green golf shirt with "Paradise Canyon Golf and Country Club" tastefully stitched on the front. Thumps set his runners on the shoe stand in the closet and went looking for his old Rockports. He found them sitting on top of a shoebox.

Shit.

Thumps did not remember putting the box there. Couldn't remember where he had put it, though he imagined he would have tried to put it somewhere he wouldn't find it. Now it was too late to put it back or try to hide it again.

The box was empty except for a police-evidence bag and a handful of photographs. All that was left of his career as a cop. All that was left of Anna and Callie. Thumps sat down on the floor and took the photographs out of the box. It was a mistake, one he had made any number of times. It was a mistake and he knew it, knew where it would lead, knew how it would leave him feeling, knew how close to the edge it had taken him in the past. But he also knew that once the memories were loose, there was no putting them back in the box.

Not until they had done their damage.

·   ·   ·

It was late morning before Thumps backed his car out of the driveway and started the long run across the flat back of the prairies to Shadow Ranch. He rolled the windows down all the way to keep the heat and depression at bay, and he put a tape in the cassette player and sang along with the twangy, nasal voice of some Hank Snow wannabe. But nothing helped. Instead, he found himself sliding toward the edge as the interminable whining verses about unfaithful women, hard-headed men, and lost dogs, rolled into a chorus that celebrated being drunk, broke, and on the road again. Thumps liked country-and-western music well enough and probably would have liked it a great deal more if none of the songs had words.

Floyd was the wild card in the game. He had been Takashi's driver. Maybe the two of them had gotten chummy. Maybe Takashi had told Floyd something.

Maybe, maybe, maybe. That's what Thumps liked about crime and about life in general. There was always an endless string of maybes to play with. Maybe after he talked to Floyd again, he'd stop in and see Vernon Rockland. Maybe Rockland would invite Thumps to bring his photographs out to Shadow Ranch for a one-man show.

Maybe, maybe, maybe.

After all, Shadow Ranch did have an art gallery, and in addition to the usual suspects—landscape painters, woodcarvers, and stoneware potters—Rockland had already featured several photographers.

The first photographer that Rockland had brought to Shadow Ranch was a woman from San Francisco who did black-and-white ocean scenes with craggy rocks and backlit waves. Thumps liked the ocean and he was impressed with the photographs, each one a technical marvel of exposure, masking, and toning, but the overall effect of all the photographs in one room was more romance than he could stomach.

The second photographic show consisted of large colour prints of clowns.

Hockney's cruiser was parked in front of the main lodge. Thumps pulled in behind him. So, the sheriff had finally gotten around to searching Takashi's room. It had taken him long enough. But now that Duke was on the prowl, Thumps knew that he should stay away. Stay away from the townhouse. Stay away from Floyd. A smart man would retreat into the hotel, where it was air-conditioned and cool. A smart man would find Rockland, have a leisurely cup of coffee, and talk about photography. But Duke's phone call was chewing at him, and curiosity is a powerful mistress. And, in the end, she dragged him up the red-gravel path to the townhouses.

Sure enough, Takashi's apartment was taped off and Duke was standing in the doorway.

"Hi, sheriff."

"This one of those coincidences?"

"Saw your car."

" 'Cause I don't believe in them," said the sheriff. "What about you?"

"Came up to talk to Rockland about photography." Thumps could see past the sheriff and into the room. It looked the same. "So, what's all this?"

"What's it look like?"

Thumps shrugged. "A crime scene?"

Andy Hopper came out of the room carrying a large box. "It's not there, Duke."

"You look everywhere?" The sheriff did not sound happy.

"Not many places you can hide a laptop." Andy stood there holding the box, waiting for the sheriff to make up his mind. "You want me to keep looking?"

"No. Lock it down."

Thumps tried not to appear too anxious. "You lost a laptop?"

"It's the dead guy's room," said the sheriff. "But I'm guessing you already figured that out."

"Takashi?" Thumps hoped that he sounded surprised.

Andy was back. "I put the box in your trunk. You sure the Jap had a computer?"

"Japanese," said Hockney.

"Right," said Andy.

Oh, he had a computer all right, thought Thumps. It was on the desk yesterday.

"You know what a laptop looks like, don't you, Andy?"

"Sure thing, Duke. My nephew has one." Andy grinned at Thumps.

"What do you think?" he said, his mouth a short, mean line, thin as a razor. "This the way city cops do it?"

Duke stopped Andy with a glance. "Talk to the maid again."

Thumps watched the deputy lumber down the lawn. "Your tax dollars in action."

"He's a good cop," said Hockney.

"No, he's not," said Thumps.

Duke smiled, but not in a particularly friendly way. "So, I suppose you want to know why I phoned you yesterday."

"You mean it wasn't a courtesy wake-up call?"

"We found a print." The sheriff hitched his pants and waited.

"At the computer complex?"

Hockney nodded.

"Good work."

"Don't you want to know whose print we found?"

"We know that already, don't we?"

"Indeed we do." Duke fluffed his feathers. "Stanley Merchant."

Thumps let the sheriff get the strutting out of his system. "So, where did you find the print?"

"On the mouse by the main monitor. Thumbprint on the left side. Good one, too." Duke nodded and walked into the townhouse. "Come on. Maybe you can give us a hand."

Thumps followed the sheriff inside. The townhouse seemed even more vacant than it had the day before.

"The townhouses get maid service once every two days." Hockney stood in the living room with his hands on his hips. "Today's the day."

"Wonder how much one of these places costs."

"Every morning, the resort leaves a newspaper on the porch."

"Bet they're more than we can afford."

"Woman at the gift shop said Takashi bought a golf magazine and a couple of those computer magazines."

Thumps looked around the room. He already knew where Duke was going.

"The maid who cleaned the room two days back said there was a laptop on the desk along with a printer." Hockney sat down on the sofa and closed his eyes.

"And you're wondering where it is."

The sheriff kept his eyes closed, but he began to smile as if he was thinking of a good joke. "Hell, I wonder where everything is." He pushed off the sofa. "Where are the newspapers? Where are the magazines? Where's the laptop and the printer?"

"Anything in the trash?"

"Nothing."

"The maid clean the place early?"

"Nope."

"You figure someone has been through here?"

"That's pretty good for a photographer."

"Don't think Stick did it."

"Don't much care if he did or didn't. But I do want to talk to him. You know what I mean?"

"If I knew where he was, I'd tell you."

Duke was chuckling as he left the townhouse. "Sure you would."

Coming from the dark of the building back into the light was painful. The sun was blinding, and Thumps had to close his eyes and turn away. A small crowd of tourists had gathered around the pool to watch the performance. Several people had video cameras and were filming the entire boring drama of police officers walking into a townhouse and then walking out again. By now, all of them would know that there had been a killing, and even though the murder itself had happened miles away, being this close to a dead man's room was probably more excitement than they had ever had on a vacation.

Thumps shielded his eyes from the sun. "One of these days you're going to have to do something about Andy."

"By tomorrow, a lot of people are going to be looking for Stanley." Hockney pulled his hat over his eyes and glanced at the clutch of police cars. "Things could go south real quick. You know what I mean?"

Thumps didn't say anything, but the warning was clear enough. He had been involved in manhunts before, and he knew about the kinds of enthusiasms that could overtake men turned loose to hunt other men. It didn't matter whether you were a cop or some local with a gun along for the ride. Running with a pack was exhilarating.

• • •

The lobby of the Shadow Ranch Hotel was airy, decked out in light woods and bevelled glass. Thumps started there.

"Mr. Rockland is in the coffee shop." The man at the front desk hung up the phone and pointed Thumps down the hallway. "He'd like you to join him."

"Thanks."

"Is DreadfulWater really your name?"

"Yes, it is."

"Two words or one?"

"One, with a capital W."

"What is it?"

"It's Cherokee."

"No kidding."

Rockland was having coffee with Elliot Beaumont and George Chan. And Virginia Traynor.

"Thumps." Rockland was all smiles. "Sit down. Join us. This is—"

"We've met," interrupted Beaumont. "At the computer complex."

Rockland cocked his head to one side and looked at Thumps questioningly.

"I was taking pictures for the sheriff," said Thumps.

"Ah," said Rockland. "That's right. But Thumps is also a fine-art photographer. As a matter of fact, I've been meaning to call you about a show."

"I assume you take pictures of things other than dead bodies?" Beaumont meant it as a joke, but his timing and intonation were off.

"I do landscapes and portraiture."

"Mr. Chan dabbles in photography," said Traynor.

"Digital." Chan poured cream into his coffee until it turned beige.

"And are you a good photographer, Mr. DreadfulWater?" Traynor's voice was smooth and controlled.

"Yeah," said Thumps. "I'm good."

"Elliot tells me you're helping the sheriff with the murder of Daniel Takashi."

"Nope. I just take pictures."

"Somehow, you don't look like someone who just takes pictures."

"Thumps used to be a cop," said Rockland. "Didn't you?"

"In California," said Traynor. "If I'm not mistaken."

It was Thumps' turn to be impressed.

"Weren't you involved in the ... Lava Murders?" Traynor picked up her coffee cup and looked at Thumps across the rim. "Isn't that what the newspapers called them?"

"Obsidian." Thumps didn't like the direction the conversation had taken. "The press called them the Obsidian Murders."

"Did the police ever solve them?" Traynor settled back in her seat.

Whoever was in charge of Genesis Data Systems' security was good. Traynor already knew the answers to the questions she was asking, and she was letting Thumps know that she knew.

"No."

"As I recall," said Rockland, who could probably feel the tension in the air, "you have a tee time coming up."

"Maybe Mr. DreadfulWater would like to play with us," said Traynor, and this time there was warmth at the edge of her voice.

"I don't think Thumps plays golf," said Rockland.

"Paradise Canyon Golf and Country Club," said Traynor. "Or did you just buy the shirt?"

A business woman with a sense of humour. Thumps liked that. "I'd love to play," he said.

"But?"

"No clubs." Thumps shrugged. "No shoes."

"Not a problem." Traynor didn't even turn to Beaumont. "Tell the people at the pro shop that Mr. DreadfulWater is going to play with us." She glanced at her watch. "We'll meet at the first tee in half an hour."

Thumps watched her leave the room, Beaumont and Chan close on her heels like leashed dogs.

"Now there is one cold bitch," said Rockland softly, almost to himself.

Thumps slid out of the chair. "I better get ready."

"What about it?"

"What about what?"

"A show of your photographs."

"Sure. Tell me when." Thumps tried to make his voice sound as casual as possible.

"Just don't make them too expensive," said Rockland. "Tourists like to think they're getting a bargain."

Thumps left Rockland to his coffee and went straight back to the front desk.

"Mr. DreadfulWater," said the man, smiling. "With a capital W."

"That's me."

"How can I help you?"

Thumps wasn't sure whether he liked the man or not. Not that it mattered. "A friend of mine is staying here. I was supposed to meet her, but I've forgotten her room number."

"Is that Ms. Traynor?"

Thumps should have been surprised, but he wasn't. "Yes."

"She said you'd probably forget, and that if you asked, it was okay to give it you." The man wrote the number on a piece of paper. "Have a nice day."

Thumps slipped the piece of paper into his pocket and headed for the pro shop. He wasn't sure how nice the day was going to be, but it had certainly turned out to be worth the trouble of getting out of bed.

Eleven

The pro shop at Shadow Ranch was one long room with golf clubs set up in display boxes along the walls and golf clothing dangling from chrome display racks. The selection of golf goodies wasn't as large as you would find at one of the big-box golfing stores, but everything that Shadow Ranch offered was expensive.

The young man at the desk was bright-faced and cheery. "Hi. You must be Mr. Dreadful."

"DreadfulWater."

"Ms. Traynor asked us to take care of you." He paused and looked at Thumps as if he were sizing him up for a suit of clothes. "She said she thought you were about a seven handicap."

Traynor was guessing, but she was a good guesser. "Last time I looked, I was an eight."

"Do you have any preference in clubs?"

"Whatever you have in rentals will do."

"Rentals?" Jimmy looked pained.

What Traynor had meant by "take care of him," Thumps discovered, was the purchase of a complete golf outfit.

"Where do you want to start?"

The sun was pouring in through the windows of the pro shop. All around him the racks of golf clubs gleamed in their polished wood stands, the shafts flashing in the light like drawn swords.

"Rentals will do just fine."

"Have you seen the new Calloways?"

They were right—money does corrupt. And in spite of his best efforts,

Thumps left the pro shop with a new pair of two-tone FootJoy shoes, a floral Tommy Bahama golf shirt that he was unable to resist, a stone-washed Titleist cap, and several sleeves of expensive balls that were guaranteed to fly farther and straighter. As he walked down to the first tee, he tried to imagine that he was a successful investment banker just up from the city for an afternoon on the links, not an unsuccessful photographer who had been rented for the day.

Virginia Traynor, Elliot Beaumont, and George Chan were waiting for him. Traynor looked at the clubs and nodded.

"A man of principles."

Thumps strapped the bag to the back of the cart. "I don't play much anymore."

"Let's play teams. Elliot is a ten handicap. George is a twelve." Traynor turned to the two men. "Cowboys and Indians. I get the Indian. Is that all right?"

It wasn't really a question, and everyone understood that it wasn't.

"A hundred dollars a hole?"

The game was getting unpleasant and they hadn't even teed off. Thumps glanced at the other men to see whether they were going to object. He had no reason to think that they would. And they didn't.

"Too steep for me," said Thumps.

"Then we'd better not lose," said Traynor, and she took her driver out and walked to the tee box. "I'll play from the blues," she said, "just to even things out."

For some reason, Thumps had thought that Traynor was simply an astute business woman with an attitude. But by the time they had reached the first green, he could see that he had been mistaken. Quite a few of the men he had played with in the past saw golf as a form of recreation. Others had approached the game as a competition. Traynor understood it as a blood sport.

Her drive was two hundred and thirty yards straight down the fairway. Her second shot, a three wood, was a laser to the hundred yard marker. Her third rolled to within four feet of the cup. Beaumont was much longer off the tee but in the sand with his second. Chan had a slice that sent him into the woods and a tendency to jump at the ball that made his shots erratic.

Thumps wasn't exactly burning up the course. The clubs felt strange in his hands after all these years, the swing awkward and rushed.

Traynor birdied the hole. Beaumont put in a solid par, and Chan scrambled for a bogey. Thumps got lucky and parred the hole with a fifteen-foot putt.

"See?" said Traynor as they climbed into the cart. "That wasn't hard."

The game quickly settled into a pattern. Beaumont and Chan won the holes where distance counted, and Traynor and Thumps won the holes where accuracy was rewarded. Thumps had expected Traynor to be talkative, but by the time they got to the turn, the only conversation had been small talk and silence.

The tenth tee was backed up.

"You want something to eat?"

Traynor sent Beaumont and Chan up to the clubhouse with the order and settled back in the seat. "I didn't ask you along just for the golf. I suppose you knew that."

Thumps nodded.

"And I hope you didn't mind my running a background check on you."

"Not much to check."

"On the contrary," said Traynor. "I was impressed. So much so, I'd like to hire you."

"As a photographer?" Thumps knew the answer to the question before he asked it.

"Genesis Data Systems is a small company." Traynor slipped into her corporate voice. "We specialize in security and computer systems for casinos."

"Good business?"

"Good enough," she said. "But there's a lot of competition. And it's hard to break into the big time."

"Vegas and Atlantic City?"

"Sure, but the real growth market is Internet gambling and Indian gaming. Do you know how many tribes in the States and Canada are planning casinos?"

"Lots?" said Thumps.

"In five years the number of Indian casinos will triple."

"The Mashantucket Pequot casino?"

"That's just one of them."

Thumps had an idea where this conversation was headed. "Buffalo Mountain isn't exactly going to be a gold mine."

"Buffalo Mountain is our in. We've got a casino computer system that is light-years ahead of anyone else's. Which means we have about a nine-month headstart before the rest of the industry catches up with us. A year at the most. If we can get the system running at Buffalo Mountain, and if it works as well as we project, we'll be able sell our system to every new casino that comes on-line."

"It's that good?"

"It's better. But if this project falls through because of Daniel's murder ..."

"No more golf?"

Traynor's eyes brightened, but Thumps could see she wasn't happy. "Someone may be trying to sabotage the company. I don't know why. And I don't know who."

"I'm not a cop anymore."

"The sheriff tells me that he's looking for a young man, an Indian."

"Stanley Merchant."

Traynor nodded. "If Daniel was killed by someone out to destroy my company, then I have to know who and I have to know right away. But if Daniel was killed as some sort of political protest over Indian gambling ..."

"Then it's not so serious."

Traynor could see the trap. "It won't kill the project."

"Takashi's still dead."

"I can't do anything about that."

Thumps could see Beaumont and Chan as they came out of the clubhouse with the food. Beaumont had his cellphone out, and was walking and listening at the same time. Thumps wondered whether they taught those kinds of skills at corporate school.

"I'm a photographer."

"You used to be a good cop."

"I used to be a good golfer, too."

Thumps liked women who knew what they wanted, but over the years, he had come to the slow realization that, like most men, he liked them better in theory than in practice.

"I don't care who killed Daniel. But I do need to know why." Traynor leaned forward and looked down the tenth fairway. "Do you know why I play golf?"

Thumps appreciated questions that might have a right answer. "Because you like the game?"

"I hate the game. It's expensive. It's boring. Country clubs are testosterone waste dumps." She paused. "That must sound cranky and petulant."

"Nope."

"So, how can I see some of your photographs?"

"Stop by next time you're in town."

"I will."

Beaumont held up his cellphone.

Traynor unwrapped a sandwich, sniffed at it, and passed it to Thumps. "Can it wait until we finish?"

Beaumont nodded. "It can wait."

The rest of the game was quiet and relatively pleasant. Traynor held up her end of the small talk, and by the time they got back to the clubhouse, Thumps knew where she had gone to school, how she had gotten into the casino computer business, and why she didn't like nuts in baked goods.

"I really would like to see some of your photographs."

"Any time."

Traynor turned to Beaumont and Chan. "I'll drive Mr. DreadfulWater back to his car. Get us a tee time for tomorrow."

Beaumont nodded. "Morning or afternoon?"

"Afternoon," said Traynor. "I want to go to Buffalo Mountain in the morning."

The golf course parking lot was filled with expensive cars. Thumps hadn't noticed it before, and as Traynor drove the cart down the rows of bright and twinkling Mercedes and Porsches and Lincolns, he found himself hoping that his Volvo looked a little better than he remembered.

"Thanks for the shirt and the shoes."

Traynor shook her head. "Think of them as payment."

Thumps wasn't sure what he wanted to say.

"For your time today."

He unlocked the Volvo and opened the doors. "Good chance the sheriff will find who killed Takashi."

Traynor flashed a smile. Thumps wasn't sure whether it was fire or ice. "I don't like chance," she said. And she turned the cart around and headed back to the clubhouse.

No, thought Thumps as he stood by the car, waiting for the heat to pour out, I'll bet you don't.

Thumps took the back way to the hotel and buried his car between an elephant of an RV and a GMC Kingcab with chrome running boards and spoke wheels. He wasn't trying to hide the Volvo, exactly, but neither did he want to announce the fact that he was hanging around. If he was right, whoever had killed Takashi was still in the vicinity. Takashi's room had been searched and sanitized, which meant the man's death wasn't a simple thing. If Stick and the Red Hawks had killed Takashi, the killing should have been the end of it. Why kill a man to stop the casino project and then take the time to search his room? Why kill a man to make a political point and then steal his computer? No, something else was going on, and as improbable as it seemed, Floyd might have tumbled to it. But murder was a dangerous game. Did Floyd know what he was getting into? More to the point, did he care?

The limousine garage was deserted. Thumps had never ridden in a limousine and it wasn't on his list of things to do. The idea had little appeal. Now a Porsche or a Jaguar, that was a different story. A sports car you drove yourself. Something you could push into the corners and open up on the straightaways. Something low and sleek with a manual transmission. That was driving.

Riding in the back of a rich man's bus was not.

Thumps wondered whether Traynor had a limousine as well as a helicopter. She looked more like the sports car type, but you couldn't tell with women. If they chose their cars the same way they chose their men, anything was possible. And nothing had to make sense.

"Can I help you?"

Thumps hadn't seen the man and was forced to think faster than he wanted to. "Hi."

The man was young and thick and in good shape. There was no handy name tag on the lapel of his blue blazer, but Thumps guessed he was hotel staff.

"Are you looking for something?"

The truth was Thumps was snooping, but he knew he would have to come up with a better answer than that. Luckily, he knew a number of ways to gain time in order to construct a more plausible story. Asking questions was one of the best.

"Is this the limousine garage?"

"Is there a problem?"

The man came forward, his weight evenly distributed, his hands out of his pockets, stopping short of the distance an assailant would need in order to attack him before he could react.

Security.

Thumps was glad he had allowed himself the golf shirt. He hoped the man knew his name brands.

"I was looking for one of the drivers." He pitched his voice in a way to suggest that he owned the place.

"Are you a guest at the hotel?"

Thumps had hoped the man would not ask that question. "I believe I left my glasses in the car."

The man reached into his jacket the way you would reach for a gun. "Eagle One to base." He man held the walkie-talkie sideways against his mouth the way they did it in crime dramas. "I have a guest at the garage. Says he left his glasses in one of the limos."

"I *think* I left them there," said Thumps.

There was a pause, and then an indistinct voice crackled back. Thumps couldn't quite hear what base had to say about guests wandering around the garage looking for lost glasses, but he supposed that base had an official procedures book and was even now leafing through it to see what to do.

"Okay," said Eagle One, and he slipped the walkie-talkie back into his jacket.

At this point, Thumps mused, one of three things could happen. One, Eagle One could ask for identification, take Thumps' name and phone number and promise to pass it on to hotel security, who would notify him if the glasses were found. Two, Eagle One could invite Thumps to come to security with him so they could search though the lost-and-found bag for non-existent glasses. Or three, Eagle One could check with the front desk and discover that Thumps was not a guest, just a local photographer cleverly disguised as a successful golfer.

"I asked at the front desk," said Thumps, trying to sound impatient and annoyed, the way rich people do when they don't get what they want. "And they suggested I come out here and talk to the driver."

Eagle One blinked.

Good, thought Thumps. He understands arrogance.

"What was the driver's name?"

"Floyd. I believe it was Floyd something. Really, I would have expected a resort such as this to have a better system in place for dealing with misplaced articles."

"We have a lost and found."

"Excellent," said Thumps, working on his enunciation. "Could you give them a call on your radio?"

"They don't have your glasses."

"Well, perhaps the driver has them."

"He's not in today."

Normally Thumps would have quit while he was ahead, but the golf had left him feeling important. "Really? I'm sure I saw him earlier."

"He called in sick."

"Ah," said Thumps, jamming his hands in his pockets and pouting, "then there's little else to do but lunch." He turned away and then turned back. "What's your name?" It was an excellent ploy, and he congratulated himself for thinking of it.

"Ah ... Steve. Steve Webster."

"Well, Steve. Thank you for the assistance." With that, Thumps strolled out of the limousine garage as if he had no place in particular to go and all the time in the world to get there. And he didn't look back. Not even after he got to the front doors of the hotel.

The coffee shop was almost deserted. Thumps slid into a booth at the back and looked at the menu. Coffee was two dollars and fifty cents a cup. Pie was six. A cheeseburger without fries was twelve. No wonder the place was empty.

"Hi, did you have a chance to look at the specials?"

The waitress was a young woman with a gold tag on her blouse that said Ruth. Just out of high school. All enthusiasm and energy. A happy bubble. Thumps wondered whether this was a summer job before university or the beginning of a fulfilling career carrying plates of food to tourists.

"How's the Cowboy Chili?"

"Terrific."

"How about the cheeseburger?"

"It's terrific, too."

"And the soup."

"All our food's terrific."

"Terrific," said Thumps. "What do you eat?"

The girl kept smiling, but he could see a hint of distress or embarrassment at the corners of her mouth. "They don't let us eat here."

"Food can't be that good."

Ruth glanced at the cash register. The bubble burst, and her smile slid into a conspiratorial grin. "It's not."

"The chili?"

"Bland."

"Soup?"

"Dry mix."

"Burger fresh?"

"Shipped in frozen." Ruth was having a good time. "And twenty-five percent fat."

While Thumps was reasonably sure that Ruth had no idea who had killed Takashi, he knew one thing for certain. Working at the Shadow Ranch coffee shop was not a career move.

"What do you suggest?"

"Al's in town."

University. Ruth was definitely going to university.

"I'll have some coffee and a piece of cherry pie."

Thumps settled into the booth and took out a pen. On his napkin, he made two columns. At the top of one, he wrote Stick. At the top of the other, he put an "X."

Under "Stick" he wrote "opportunity" and "motive." Thumps sighed and crossed them off. The opportunity was circumstantial. No one had seen Stick at the complex. No one had seen Stick with the dead man. So far as Thumps knew, Stick hadn't threatened Takashi or Genesis Data Systems. And even if he had the opportunity, the motive was weak. No matter how Thumps imagined the crime, it made no sense to kill Takashi. Not if your goal was to stop the complex. So why had Takashi been killed? Traynor's problem seemed to have more to do with the death than the protest. If she was right about someone trying to sabotage her company, then killing Takashi might make sense. He was a key player at Genesis. His death might slow the project and allow a rival company to step in. Industrial espionage was big business. Maybe dog-eat-dog was no longer just a figure of speech. Maybe today's dogs were armed.

By the time Ruth returned with the coffee and the pie, Thumps' deductions had deteriorated into circles, squiggles, and wavy lines, and the neat columns were buried under cartoon tornadoes and funny faces.

The pie was of no better quality than his deductions. Canned cherries set adrift in a sea of bright red Silly Putty, sugared to taste. The crust was cosmetic, with the consistency and taste of damp cardboard.

"How's the pie?"

"Terrific."

"You want anything else?"

Thumps had a quick flash. "How much are your doughnuts?"

Ruth shook her head. "Sorry," she said. "We don't serve doughnuts."

"Okay. Just the bill."

"Are you charging it to your room?"

Now there was a delicious thought. Dishonest, to be sure. No, not dishonest, exactly. Clever. Maybe even satiric. A joke among friends.

"Room 243," said Thumps. "Can I charge the tip to my room, too?"

"Absolutely."

Thumps felt expansive as he walked out of the Shadow Ranch coffee shop and stepped into the bright afternoon light. The day had not started off well, but it had picked up speed and was moving along nicely. New golf shoes. A new golf shirt. Eighteen holes on a course he couldn't afford to play. And a dreadful lunch. All on corporate America. To be sure, there was still a dead body to deal with, Claire's prodigal son to locate and clear of any suspicion, and a chat to have with Floyd to find out what he knew. But right now, Thumps was warm and sleepy. A nap would be nice. That's probably what Freeway was doing at this very minute. Stretched out in a square of sunlight on the bed, rolled up on her side, her head twisted over at an impossible angle to catch as much warmth on her chin as she could manage. Lazy damn cat.

Yes, Thumps grumbled to himself, a nap would be very nice indeed.

Twelve

Thumps wasn't sure how it had happened, but as he drove back into town, he realized that he was now looking for two men. And if he assumed that neither Stick nor Floyd had anything to do with Takashi's death, then technically—and ignoring the sexist assumptions—he was looking for three men.

As he examined the dilemma logically, it was clear that he should concentrate on finding Floyd and talking to him. The killer certainly did not want to be found, and evidently neither did Stick. In Thumps' experience, people who were determined not to be found could stay hidden for a long time. Sometimes they could disappear altogether. Without a trace.

Stick would show up eventually. Native people seldom ran too far from home, and even those who went away always seemed to return. But if Thumps were right, Takashi's killer probably had no such ties, and each day that went by made it less likely that he would ever be found.

Thumps was already in Chinook before he remembered that he didn't know where Floyd lived. Cooley still lived with his mother on the reserve, but Thumps couldn't imagine Floyd bunking there.

The gas gauge was below the empty mark, a meaningless caution since the gauge had stopped working two years ago. But just to be safe, Thumps pulled into the Shell station, filled up, and checked the phone book. No luck. He could ask around, but that would take time, and Floyd would hear that Thumps was looking for him. Floyd had found Thumps, but it didn't mean that Floyd wanted Thumps to find him. As Thumps had discovered in his other life as a cop, people were funny about things like that. And Floyd, did not seem to have a well-developed sense of humour.

Ora Mae was at her desk looking over the new listings when Thumps walked through the front door. She glanced up and shook her head. "Well, aren't you the looker."

"I was playing golf."

"Well, la-di-da. I thought golf was a rich white boy's game."

"It is."

"You ain't no rich white boy, honey. And unless I've lost touch with the better labels of this world, you can't afford those rich white boy's clothes, either."

"It was business."

Ora Mae shook her head and went back to the listings.

"I need some information."

"Do I look like an information centre?"

"It's for Claire," said Thumps. "I need to know where Floyd Small Elk is living."

"Floyd? That mean sonofabitch?"

"He's not in the phone book."

"'Course not. Most folks in town wouldn't rent him a bench."

Thumps tried charm. "But you know where he lives, don't you?"

"You sure this is for Claire?"

Thumps crossed his heart.

"Okay, this one is free." Ora Mae wrote an address on a piece of paper and held it out. "So, what you going to do? Arrest him or just take his picture?" On the wall was a large poster advertising Buffalo Mountain Resort. Ora Mae caught him looking. "Just because you found some fancy clothes doesn't mean you can even afford the dreaming."

"Why do you suppose Takashi wound up in the condos?"

"Don't you mean how?"

"No. The man's a computer programmer. Every day of the week he goes from Shadow Ranch to the computer complex at Buffalo Mountain. Every evening he goes from Buffalo Mountain back to Shadow Ranch."

"It's called a routine."

Thumps walked up to the poster and put a finger on top of the computer complex. "If he's at Buffalo Mountain, then he should be here." He moved his finger across the poster to the condos. "But he winds up dead here. Why?" He waited to see whether Ora Mae wanted to help out.

"Is this a philosophical question or are you asking me about the security system?"

"There's a security system?"

Ora Mae looked back at Sterling's office. The door was closed. "DreadfulWater, does this line of bull work on any women you know?"

Thumps blinked and sat down in the chair by Ora Mae's desk.

"Now, if you want to ask me about the security system at Buffalo Mountain, just do it. Don't waltz me around with how Mr. Dead Guy got from point A to point B."

"What's the security system like?"

"That's better."

Ora Mae began sorting through the listings on her desk.

"You going to tell me?"

"Honey, they call it security because how it works is a secret."

Thumps hadn't wanted this job in the first place. And between being a rent-a-golfer for Genesis Data Systems and a punching bag for Ora Mae, he was beginning to get pissed off.

"It's a computer-controlled security system." Ora Mae leaned forward on the desk. "All the outside doors to the condos are on key cards."

"What about the computer complex?"

"Key cards."

"Same card?"

"Are you kidding? Each building has a separate card."

"Could someone break in?"

"Sure, if he had the right equipment and enough time."

"Cameras?"

"At the entrance to each building, and in the hallways and stairwells. There are sweep cameras for the parking lot and the immediate grounds."

"And?"

"They're not operational yet." Ora Mae picked up a pen and wrote a note on one of the listings. "Any more questions?"

Thumps looked at the poster. The tribe had done well. All he had to do was help keep the resort from going down the toilet. "Only one. How would you carry a body from the computer building to the condos without being seen?"

"I thought you wanted to know why, not how."

"Humour me."

Ora Mae looked at the poster. "Probably through the maintenance tunnels."

Thumps could hear the hesitation in her voice. "But?"

"But you'd have to have a master key card."

So, that's how it was done, Thumps thought to himself. From the guard station, Cooley had a clear view of the entrance to the condos. The killer might have risked moving the body, hoping Cooley wouldn't see him, but why take the risk if you had a better way?

"Would Takashi have had a master key card?"

"I don't see why not. He would have needed one to check out all the systems." Ora Mae lowered her eyes and her voice. "Hear you've been hitting on my woman."

"I just bought her dinner."

"Platonic, right?"

Thumps hitched his pants. "Absolutely."

Ora Mae fished a pen out of her drawer and slid it across the desk. "Keep it that way."

Bridge Street started off as a two-lane road that ran behind the industrial section of Chinook. Once it crossed Lincoln, it turned into a narrow, weedy laneway that dead-ended in the Songbird Trailer Park. According to Ora Mae's note, this was where Floyd was living.

Number fifty-seven was a beat-up single-wide with a blue-and-white awning and a high porch that sagged to one side. What was it about trailers that Indians liked? Probably the price. Or maybe after being pushed from one end of the country to the other, Native people had gotten attached to having wheels on their homes.

Thumps parked the car across from the trailer.

"You got business here?"

Thumps turned to find a large man in a T-shirt and shorts. Cradled in the crook of his arm was a pump shotgun.

"Or you just a tourist?"

"I'm visiting Floyd Small Elk. Number fifty-seven, right?"

"Cop?"

"No."

"You got a name?"

"DreadfulWater. Thumps DreadfulWater."

"Bert," said the man. "You're parked in my driveway."

Thumps couldn't see anything that resembled a driveway. In fact, there was no room for a driveway, unless Bert moved the trailer off the lot.

"Do you know if he's home?"

"Ask him yourself." Bert and his gun headed back inside the trailer. "You got three minutes to move your car."

Number fifty-seven looked quiet. The screen door was closed, but the inside door was open. It didn't mean that Floyd was there. Chinook was one of those towns where people actually felt safe leaving their doors open.

Thumps knocked. If Floyd was home, Thumps didn't want to surprise him.

"Hey, Floyd. It's me, Thumps."

The air wafting through the screen door was cool. Floyd had air conditioning. Thumps knocked again and peered in through the screen.

"Hey, Floyd!"

If Floyd wasn't at Shadow Ranch and he wasn't at home, half a dozen explanations were possible. Maybe he really was sick and in bed. Or maybe he had gone to the doctor's. Maybe he was grocery shopping. Maybe he was seeing someone. Or maybe Thumps wasn't the only person to whom Floyd had talked.

There were those maybes again.

Thumps was running through the range of possibilities when he heard the first sound, the irritating creak of a door opening somewhere inside the trailer. And then silence.

"Floyd?" He tried the screen door. "We need to talk."

The second sound was hard, quick, and metallic, and Thumps was just able to duck away from the door as the first two shots tore through the aluminum siding where his head had been. He didn't wait to see where the next one went. He rolled off the porch in one motion, in time to see Bert come charging out his front door.

"Get down!" shouted Thumps as he slid across the hood of his car to the safety of the far side. Two more shots. Thumps heard the first one hit the Volvo. The second zipped across the road and rattled off Bert's cast-iron barbecue.

"What the hell!" For a large man, Bert was amazingly fast. As Thumps crouched behind his car, Bert pumped and lowered the shotgun in a single motion and blew four large holes in the side of Floyd's trailer. "Floyd, you stupid sonofabitch!"

If it was possible to be in the wrong place at the wrong time, Thumps was there. In the middle of a crossfire with no place to go. If the shooter in the trailer didn't get him, Bert probably would. All Thumps could do was huddle against the rear tire as Bert and whoever was in the trailer lobbed bullets at each other.

And then, as quickly as it started, the shooting stopped. No yelling. No gunfire. No birds singing. Just the smoke from Bert's shotgun and the nasty smell of cordite. Thumps eased his head over the hood of his car, making sure he wasn't in Bert's direct line of fire.

"That was a new barbecue, you stupid sonofabitch!" And Bert put two more shots into the trailer, sending Thumps diving back to the safety of his tire. "Thirty percent off at Kmart!"

"Stop shooting!" shouted Thumps.

The trailer looked completely peaceful now. Behind him, Thumps could hear Bert shoving more shells into the shotgun.

"You got a gun?"

"No."

"I got a pistol in the house you can use."

Thumps had carried all sorts of guns and rifles when he had been a cop, and he hadn't cared much for any of them. The National Rifle Association's assertion that guns didn't kill people, that people killed people, was disingenuous at best. Actually it was bullshit. Guns were dangerous. All by themselves, they were dangerous. People just made them more dangerous. When you had one in your hand, you felt invulnerable. You felt protected. You felt empowered. Most of all, having a gun made you feel you had a God-given right to use it, that once you had gone to all the trouble of loading it and cocking it, you should use it.

"Bert." Thumps slowed himself down, so Bert could understand each word individually. "Call the police."

"Hell," said Bert. "No way they could miss that little celebration."

"Call them anyway."

Bert stood there for a moment, looking petulant and hurt. "Yeah, well, just remember, I saved your life."

The inside of Floyd's trailer was dark and cool and didn't look much the worse for wear—if you didn't count the bright sunshine streaming in through the bullet holes in the walls. One of Bert's blasts had hit the stove and shattered the glass front. Another had blown a hole in one of the cupboards, and thick brown liquid was dripping onto the counter. It looked like syrup, but Thumps wasn't all that interested in knowing whether he was right or not.

"Floyd."

The living room and kitchen were empty.

"Floyd, it's Thumps. I don't have a gun." Thumps eased the bathroom door open. "That was Bert."

If Thumps had been in the trailer when Bert opened up, he would have headed for the bathtub. But this idea wouldn't have been as good it sounded. Instead of cast iron and porcelain, the tub was one of those thin plastic affairs that could barely hold water.

He worked his way down the narrow hall. Floyd was in the master bedroom. On the floor. Thumps didn't have check the man's pulse to see whether he was dead or alive.

"Jesus, did I do that?"

Bert was standing in the doorway, his shotgun at the ready.

"No, you didn't do that."

"Yeah, but I might have."

"Did you call the cops?"

"Not yet. What do you want me to tell them?"

"Tell them there's been a shooting."

"You sure I didn't do that?"

Thumps sighed and took the shotgun from Bert with a little more enthusiasm than was needed. He worked the pump until he was sure the gun was unloaded. "You see any pellet holes in the walls?"

Bert looked around the room. "No."

Thumps gestured to Floyd's body. "That look like a shotgun wound to you?"

Bert cocked his head to one side. "No way. Small calibre."

"Exactly." Thumps handed the shotgun back to Bert. "Now call the police."

"So, I didn't kill him."

Thumps could feel himself getting cranky. "Better luck next time."

"Right," said Bert, and he lumbered back down the hall and out the front door.

Thumps followed him as far as the kitchen. The back door by the side of the refrigerator was open.

The backyard was nothing but hard dirt and sunburnt weeds. The shooter must have left this way. Thumps stood on the steps and looked around. Beyond the yard, the slope ran down to the river. The willows were thick there, and a man could disappear quickly.

Thumps thought about trying to track the shooter. There was no easy way to get through the willows without leaving some sort of sign, a sign that even Thumps could follow. Then again, the man was armed, and tracking him through heavy cover could be deadly.

Maybe Thumps should put Bert on the scent. Men with guns. The idea had a certain poetic tension. Not that the contest would be fair. If the killer was waiting in the willows, Bert would be a large and easy target. Besides Bert wasn't the killer type. For all his noise, he was probably little more than an irresponsible gun enthusiast.

When Thumps came out of Floyd's trailer, Bert was relaxing on his porch. The shotgun was nowhere in sight.

"You want a beer?" He held up a six-pack.

"No, thanks."

"You want to know who killed Floyd?" Bert belched once, a controlled and almost delicate burp.

"You know who killed Floyd?"

Bert nodded. "Some people think that because I'm fat, I'm stupid. Bet you get that all the time."

Thumps sucked his stomach in.

"Being Indian," said Bert. "People see you're Indian, and right away they figure you're going to steal something they have."

Touché, thought Thumps, more than a little embarrassed that Bert had caught him out.

"I had a couple of Indian friends who used to say they were Italian. But

Indian fat or Italian fat or poor-white fat is still fat. You know what I mean?"

Thumps knew exactly what Bert meant.

"So, it pains me to tell you that your friend Floyd was killed by an Indian."

"An Indian?"

"Sure as hell wasn't an Italian."

Thumps didn't want to ask the next question. "What did he look like?"

Bert opened a can and took a long drink. "Good-looking kid. Skinny. No ass. Maybe twenty. Long hair. Wore it in a ponytail."

A couple of dozen young men from the reserve probably fit that general description, but Stanley Merchant fit it perfectly.

"You talk to him?"

"He asked me where Floyd lived."

"What was he driving?"

"Green Mustang." Bert looked over at Floyd's trailer. "He didn't park in front of my driveway."

So, Stick had been to visit Floyd. That was not good news. When Bert repeated his story to Sheriff Hockney, as he certainly would, Duke would see Floyd's murder as an attempt to cover up Takashi's murder. And that would settle any questions of Stick's guilt.

"You hear anything?"

"Heard them yelling at each other."

"You hear a gunshot?"

"*The Simpsons* were on."

"When did he leave?"

"Don't know," said Bert. "Before you got here. He a friend of yours, too?"

Thumps looked back down Lincoln Street, out past the Songbird Trailer Park gates. In a little while, the sheriff's white Ford would be tearing along the road, and Thumps would have to explain what he was doing at Floyd's place and how the trailer had gotten shot up. No matter how Thumps tried to slice his story, it was going to come out thin.

"No point your waiting around," said Bert. "Sheriff's going to have a lot of questions."

"What are you going to tell him?"

"Not going to lie," said Bert. "He'll ask me about Floyd, and I'll tell him what I know. Then he'll ask me about the holes in Floyd's trailer, and I'll have to tell him about getting shot at." Bert looked at his barbecue with mournful eyes. "Just got it two days ago."

"He'll ask you if anyone came by to see Floyd."

"Maybe. And if he does, I'll have to tell him about the kid with the Mustang."

"He may ask you if there was anyone else."

Bert smiled, and Thumps could see that he had been wrong. The man did have a sense of humour. "Maybe he will, and maybe he won't. Not my place to do his job." Bert waved his hand toward the entrance to the trailer park. "Of course if he finds you here, I won't have to tell him anything."

"Thanks."

"Hell," said Bert, "you didn't shoot my barbecue."

Thumps was out of town before his breathing returned to normal and his heart stopped banging around in his chest. Things were definitely getting out of hand. Takashi was dead. Floyd was dead. The sheriff was not a happy man to begin with. Two killings in his town in a week were going to make him downright unpleasant.

Thirteen

Thumps did not drive to the townsite and the band offices. Claire would probably still be stuck in meetings, and the last thing Thumps wanted to do was to exchange artillery rounds with Roxanne. At the top of Old Man Coulee, he turned off and headed west. While no one on the reserve owned land outright, different families had occupied particular pieces for so long, no one questioned their right to be there. The high, hard ridge at the foot of the mountains, and the circle of bottom land that had been created as the Ironstone looped its way south, had always been Merchant land. It had been Claire's great-great-grandfather's summer place. Her great-grandfather had built a cabin there. Her grandfather had added a barn.

Her father had left the land, moved his family into the townsite, and gone to Los Angeles to find work. While he was away, the barn burned down, and the cabin collapsed under the weight of wind and weather. But when he returned, years later, the land was still there. He didn't build anything but he did what his great-grandfather had done and moved his family onto the land each summer. When her father died, Claire did what her great-grandfather had done and built a house.

Claire's house sat on high ground overlooking the river. It was a prefab house, a remnant of one of the many economic ventures that the tribe had been encouraged to try. The majority of these had been the bright ideas of some eager bureaucrat in Washington, ideas that were generally ill-conceived, always under-funded, and never supported any longer than the next election.

The house was a long rectangle wrapped in sky-blue-and-white aluminum siding, and it reminded Thumps of Floyd's trailer, except that it was larger and didn't have wheels. It was not a pretty house, nothing like the ones featured in the home-and-garden magazines, and Claire's only attempt at landscaping had been to drop a pad of four large concrete slabs in front of the porch. The rest of the yard was dirt and long grass. Thumps had always thought that houses on the prairies looked tentative, as though they didn't quite belong, as though they had paused on the land to rest a while before moving on.

He pulled his car to the west side of the house where no one could see it from the road. Normally, he would have left it out in plain sight so Claire wouldn't be surprised when she came home, but there was the off-chance that Stick might show up, and if he saw the Volvo parked in front of the house, he might run.

As Thumps sat in his car and waited, his stomach began growling, and he suddenly realized that he had missed lunch. The cherry pie and coffee were long gone, and the shootout at Floyd's trailer had delayed dinner. Now he was stuck in the middle of nowhere, with nothing to eat. Maybe Claire would feed him when she came home.

Thumps got out of the car and walked to the edge of the ridge. Below him, the Ironstone snaked across the prairies, black and silver in the early evening light. The temperature was beginning to drop, but it would never fall anywhere near comfortable. Thumps settled in on the shady side of a basalt outcropping and watched the river.

Now there were two deaths. Takashi's was still a mystery, but Floyd's was simple enough to figure out. He had been killed because of what he knew or what he thought he knew. Had he tried to extort money from the killer? Why had Stick gone to see Floyd? A teenager with a passion for justice and an ex-con with a taste for larceny shouldn't have much in common. Yet Bert's description left no doubt that Stick had been to the trailer.

In the end, everything came back to Stick.

Claire didn't get home until the sun was long gone behind the mountains. As soon as he saw her car coming up the road, Thumps stepped out from behind the house so she would have time to adjust to his being here.

"Hi."

Claire had a dress on and she looked good, but she didn't seem any happier than the day before, and as she stepped out of the car, Thumps realized that his appearance had probably raised her hopes. He tried to look as sombre as possible.

"Nice dress."

"You don't have to do that."

"What?"

"You don't have to look like bad news."

"It's not all bad news."

"You found Stanley?" Claire could see the answer on his face, and Thumps knew it.

The mountains had turned a deep blue in the evening air, and the dark clouds were ringed with light. Thumps didn't want to tell Claire about Floyd. Not right away. Not with this panorama to look at. Not until he got something to eat.

"You eat yet?"

"Why?" said Claire. "You asking me out?"

Dinner was hot dogs and baked beans out of a can. And a salad. All in all, it was good. The ketchup helped. Claire didn't say much. A little shop talk about the council and about Roxanne's showing up at the band office with a new boyfriend.

"Where's he from?"

"Why does he have to be from somewhere else?"

It was a rhetorical question. Roxanne had long ago worked her way through all the men, eligible and otherwise, in the immediate vicinity.

"They serious?"

"Roxanne thinks so."

"That why you're wearing a dress?"

Claire dumped her plate in the sink. "Had a meeting with the bank. And the FBI gave us a call."

"Takashi?"

"Dead body on reservation land is an FBI body." Claire stood by the sink and looked out the window. "You know that."

Which was all Claire needed—the FBI, the sheriff, and Genesis Data Systems, all scurrying around the reserve, turning over stones, kicking up dust, and making a nuisance of themselves.

"Good news is they're backed up with a couple of bank robberies right now and won't be able to get to us until next week."

Claire found some ice cream in the back of the freezer and crushed a few Oreo cookies over it. "All right," she said as Thumps was chasing the last bits of cookie around his bowl. "You've been fed."

Thumps put the bowl down and tried to think of an easy way to tell Claire how he and Bert had spent their afternoon. "Floyd Small Elk is dead."

"Floyd?" Claire was more puzzled than shocked. "How?"

"Shot."

"An accident?"

"No."

Claire nodded her head, but her mind was elsewhere. "You want coffee?"

"Sure."

He did not want to be the one to tell her that Bert had seen Stick with Floyd just before Floyd was killed. That was the sheriff's job. Thumps had seen enough messengers shot in his time.

Claire came back to the table with two cups. "Floyd was Takashi's driver."

Thumps sipped the coffee and tried to look relaxed. "Good coffee."

"You drove all the way out here to tell me that?"

"I wanted to see you."

"We talking about sex?"

There was no give in Claire. Sometimes Thumps liked that and sometimes he didn't. Claire's face was beginning to harden, like poured concrete.

"Sex is fine with me." Thumps smiled so Claire could see he was kidding. It didn't work.

"What's Floyd got to do with Stanley?"

"Probably nothing."

"Damn you, DreadfulWater."

Thumps had run out of room and he knew it. "Stick was seen at Floyd's trailer just before Floyd died."

"He didn't kill Floyd."

"Nobody says he did." Thumps reached for the coffee cup, but Claire's eyes stopped him.

"Does the sheriff know?"

"No," said Thumps quietly, "but he will."

Claire leaned forward on the table. Thumps could almost feel the air leaking out of her. He hoped she wasn't going to cry, because he had never figured out what to do with women who cried. Nothing ever seemed to work. It was as if you were supposed to let them cry, that, in the end, crying wouldn't hurt them. The problem was that whenever a woman Thumps was with cried, he felt guilty, as if he was somehow to blame. Which wasn't always fair. If Claire started crying now, Thumps was going to feel guilty about not finding Stick. Or he was going to feel guilty about letting Claire down. And then he'd start feeling guilty about how his life had gone, about what had happened in Eureka, about his real failures and what they had cost him.

Claire kept her head down, but the leaking had stopped. "Don't worry," she said. "I'm not going to cry."

"You want some coffee?"

"I have some coffee." She raised her head and looked at him. "What I would like is for you to ... hold me."

"Sure."

"I'm not talking about sex."

"Sure." Thumps looked around the room. "You want me to do it at the table, or someplace else?"

Claire pushed away from the table and walked stiffly to the sofa.

"Look, I don't think Stick killed anyone." Thumps came over and sat down beside her. "But he's going to have to give himself up."

Claire slowly leaned into Thumps' side, nestling up against him as if she planned on going to sleep. He wasn't quite sure what to do. He let his arm slide down the couch. It landed on Claire's shoulder with slightly more force than he had intended, but she didn't jump and she didn't pull away.

"I'll find him."

Claire put her hand on Thumps' chest. "What are you thinking about?"

Why did women always ask that particular question? Thumps suspected that there was a right answer, an answer he had never hit on, and that everything else was wrong. That was one of the great joys of sex. You didn't have to carry on an intelligent conversation. And you didn't run the risk of being accused of not listening. Sex had its own problems to be sure. What to do afterwards, for instance. Talk, cuddle, apologize, explain, compliment, support, sympathize, reassure. Go to sleep.

Thumps could feel his right leg begin to cramp. "I don't know," he said, pressing his toes against the floor. "I was just thinking how nice this is."

Claire snuggled in tighter. Her body seemed to melt around his, and her hand slid down his chest to his belt buckle.

"This is relaxing."

No, it's not, thought Thumps. This is definitely not relaxing. And he was sure that Claire could tell that he wasn't relaxed.

"Are you relaxed?" she asked.

That was the benefit of being with the same woman for a period of time. While Thumps and Claire had not been steady lovers, exactly, he had gotten used to a number of her signals.

"The lights aren't too relaxing."

"Then turn them off."

That was signal number two. Thumps slipped away from Claire, took two giant steps across the room, hit the light switch, and slid back into her arms without leaving a ripple.

Kissing Claire was one of Thumps' favourite things to do. There was no rush in her, which was fine with him. She liked long, lingering kisses that were gentle and brushing rather than hard and crushing. And she liked to be touched. Everything slow and patient. She especially liked to have the sides of her breasts rubbed, and as Thumps moved his hand under her arm, Claire buried her face against his neck, shifted her thighs, and ran a hand along his leg.

"You don't feel relaxed."

For the next little while, Thumps worked on undoing Claire's dress, which was one long line of buttons, and Claire worked on undoing Thumps' belt and unzipping his pants. Thumps had slightly more trouble with the buttons. One of them got hung up in a looping thread, and he couldn't figure out which way it went, and Claire had to give him a hand.

"Careful."

The bra was a bigger problem. As long as Claire had the dress on, all Thumps could do was bunch the damn thing up around her neck. It didn't look particularly erotic in that position, and each time he tried to nuzzle her nipples, it would fall down and he would have to push it back up with his nose.

"Is the bra a bother?"

"No."

Claire's nipples were another of Thumps' favourite things. They were large and very sensitive. Better yet, they were dark brown, almost black, and Thumps began to lose himself in soft skin and warm butter.

He was glad Claire had worn a dress. Dresses were much sexier than jeans. With jeans, you had to peel them off—the way you shuck an ear of corn. With a dress you could slowly push it up the thighs, pausing as you went to touch and caress.

"Take my panties off."

Thumps buried his face in Claire's chest. "You want to go to the bedroom?"

"No," said Claire, and she pulled Thumps' underpants down and gently pushed him off the sofa.

Claire's bed was comfortable and cozy. The floor was another matter. It was hard, and the shag carpet was scratchy. But Claire was on top now, and that soft butter feeling was back, and even if he got a few rug burns on his tailbone, it wouldn't be the end of the world. Thumps ran his hands across Claire's bottom, arched his back, and shifted his hips.

"No," she said, leaning forward and letting her breasts fall against his chest. "I want to do it."

Thumps closed his eyes and sighed as Claire reached down and moved him into position.

"We should use a condom," she said.

"A condom?"

"Yes."

Thumps tried to think whether he had a condom, and if he did, where it was. "I don't think I have one."

"Neither do I."

He could feel Claire's warm wetness against him and it was affecting his thinking. "What about something else?" he said between breaths.

"Like what?"

"Saran wrap?" Thumps didn't know why he said this, but it was the only thing he could think of.

"You just want to screw me."

"Yes."

Claire lowered herself onto his thighs. "All right."

Thumps wasn't sure he would have noticed that someone had come into the room, if the person hadn't turned on the lights.

"Mom!"

Claire was off Thumps in a flash, leaving him in what he supposed was a rather silly-looking position, especially to someone who was standing above him and looking down the way Stanley Merchant was at that moment.

"What the hell are you doing?"

Since Claire had never taken off her dress, she was able to get decent in a flash. Thumps wasn't quite so agile. Pulling his underpants on was a quick enough task, but getting his jeans up from around his ankles was difficult and time consuming.

"Jesus, you two were screwing."

"We were making love." Claire turned on her son. "And where the hell have you been."

Stick was outmatched. Thumps had been there, and he knew the kid didn't have a chance.

"Don't change the subject," Stick whined. "You were naked."

"You've seen me naked before."

"Yeah, but not with him."

Thumps thought about leaving and letting Claire and Stick work this out, but there were other matters to sort through that were more pressing and serious than being caught with his pants down.

"This is disgusting, Mom."

Thumps got off the floor so that he wouldn't have to continue looking up at Stick.

"Where have you been?" said Claire.

"I'm hungry," said Stick, and he headed for the kitchen and the refrigerator. "What's to eat?"

"The sheriff's looking for you." Thumps could see no value in playing around.

Claire put herself between Thumps and her son. "He only wants to ask you a few questions."

"He thinks you killed Daniel Takashi," said Thumps.

Thumps believed that you could tell a lot about people not by how they answered questions but by how they reacted to them. Stick kept his head buried in the refrigerator.

"Did you?"

"We out of ham?" asked Stick.

Thumps glanced at Claire. He could see she was caught in the middle—not sure whether to protect her son or light into him for his bad manners. She decided on the latter and slammed the refrigerator shut, barely giving Stick time to get his arms and head out of the way.

"Hey!"

Claire was on him like a hawk on a prairie dog. "Sit down!"

Stick looked at Thumps, and then at his mother. He didn't like it, but he sat.

"First, where the hell have you been?" Claire's voice was low and hard.

"Fishing." Stick lowered his eyes and tried being surly. "And don't swear."

Even Thumps could see it was a lie. But Claire didn't change her tone or pace. "Did you kill Daniel Takashi?"

"No."

"Do you know who did?"

"No."

She waited for a moment and then turned to Thumps. "Satisfied?"

"What?"

"You heard him," said Claire. "He said he didn't kill Takashi."

Thumps could see that he had better move slowly. "Yeah. And I believe him."

"Who asked you," said Stick, who obviously thought he could take out some of his grievance on Thumps.

"But the sheriff isn't going to be so easy."

"So, screw him," said Stick.

Enough was enough. Stick had already cost him three days' work.

Thumps had spent most of an afternoon and an evening stomping around in the mountains. He had endured Roxanne, dodged the sheriff, and negotiated his way around Claire's emotions.

"Let me lay it out for you." He moved in close so Stick could see his pores. "The sheriff thinks you killed Daniel Takashi, and before morning, he's going to think that you killed Floyd Small Elk as well."

"What?"

That was genuine. Stick hadn't known that Floyd was dead.

"He was shot."

"You think I killed Floyd?"

"You went to Floyd's trailer today."

"Says who?"

"You were seen." The sneer on Stick's face vanished. "So here's what we're going to do. You're going to go with me and your mother to town and talk to the sheriff."

"You've got to be kidding."

"Au contraire." Thumps paused to let the sarcasm sink in. "By now, you're the most popular man in the state, and there is nothing the sheriff would like better than to find you, shoot you, tie you to the hood of his truck, and drag your sorry ass back to town."

"Thumps ..."

Thumps didn't have to turn to see the concern on Claire's face. He could hear it in her voice.

"No sense lying to the boy."

"I'm not a boy."

"Then stop acting like one, and tell us what you know."

"I don't know anything."

Another lie. Stick did know something. Thumps had never doubted that for a moment. The coincidences that linked Claire's son with Takashi and Floyd were too neat to be random.

"Please, Stanley." Claire sounded tired now. "Listen to Thumps."

Thumps could see Stick running through his options. "Forget it," he said. "You don't have any options."

Stick leaned against the sofa and looked at the ceiling. "Okay, but I need a shower, and I need something to eat."

"That's fair enough," said Claire.

Stick clumped down the hall to the bathroom. "We got any Kraft dinner?"

As soon as Stick had closed the bathroom door and Thumps heard the shower, he turned to Claire. "I should probably call the sheriff and let him know we're coming in."

Claire put a pot of water on to boil. She didn't look at Thumps. "What's going to happen to him?"

"If he tells the truth, he'll be okay."

"He is telling the truth."

Thumps took Claire in his arms. "No, he's not."

Claire pushed away, more out of distress than anger. She rummaged through the cupboard. When she looked back at Thumps, she had tears in her eyes. "This is all he wants to eat these days," she said, tearing the top off the box.

"I'll help him as much as I can."

The tears were streaming down Claire's face. She stood by the stove, her body shaking.

"You want some more coffee?" she said, trying to seal off the tears and smile at the same time.

"Sure."

Thumps sat at the table and tried to come up with a plan. Stick was going to need an attorney. So far, all the evidence against him was circumstantial. He had led the protest against the casino project, but there was nothing to indicate that he knew Takashi or bore him any ill will. The fact that he was at Floyd's place just before Floyd was killed was also circumstantial. More important, he had no motive. The sheriff couldn't even come close to proving that Stick had anything to do with Takashi's death. And if Stick hadn't killed Takashi, then he had no reason to kill Floyd.

Of course, if Stick had killed Takashi and Floyd had found out, then Stick would have a motive for killing him. But Thumps suspected that there were other people more interested in Takashi's death, people who had managed to stay in the shadows, so far.

The water on the stove began to boil before Thumps noticed that Stick was taking a long time in the shower. He went to the door and knocked on it.

"Stick, food's on."

He turned the handle. The door was locked.

"What's wrong?" Claire was at his side. She had stopped crying.

Thumps tried the door again. "Stick!"

Claire took the handle and turned it hard. "Stanley!"

Thumps put his shoulder into the door and forced it open.

"Shit!"

Stick's clothes and his runners were in a pile on the floor. The shower was running, but there was no Stick in the tub.

"Damn it, Stick!"

Thumps rushed to the front door and out onto the porch. The air was warm and sweet with the smell of wild sage and willow. The moon was just above the horizon, and the stars were full and bright in the black sky. But Thumps wasn't looking at the stars and he wasn't looking at the moon. He was looking at the taillights of Stick's Mustang as it raced off across the prairies and into the night.

Fourteen

Thumps stayed at Claire's house that night. They didn't have sex. They didn't even sleep in the same bed. Thumps spent the night on the sofa, wrestling with a short blanket and a lumpy pillow. Turning the two deaths over and over in his mind.

He had just gotten comfortable when the sun, which evidently didn't give a damn about either killing, decided to get the day started. The first strong blast of prairie light caught Thumps full in the face. At first, he thought someone was fooling around with a floodlight. He tried turning away and burrowing under the cushions, but the sun was relentless, and he was forced to find himself a shady spot on the floor. Or get up.

In the end, he got up and put on a pot of coffee. Claire's kitchen was a war zone. The counter was littered with crumbs and bits of lettuce. The bean cans hadn't been rinsed. And the mustard and ketchup were standing around with nothing to do.

Most of Claire's dishes and flatware were floating in the sink, in a cold, greasy swamp that gave off a hazy hint of decay. It wasn't that Claire was lazy when it came to housework. She just believed that the longer you allowed things to soak, the easier it was to get them clean.

Thumps drained the sink, ran fresh water, washed the dishes, and set them to dry in organized lines in the rack. He found a box of Coco Puffs in the cupboard. But there was no milk in the refrigerator, just a carton of something called "Hawaiian Punch." Thumps listened for any movement from Claire's room. She was either asleep or pretending to be asleep. Not that it mattered. Given the events of the last few days, she needed all the rest she could get.

The Coco Puffs floating in the Hawaiian Punch looked particularly unappetizing, but Thumps was hungry and had a second bowl. Claire, he remembered as he rummaged through the cupboards, didn't care much for multi-grain bread, bread with bits and pieces of grains and seeds that bothered your tongue and got stuck between your teeth. Thumps had no particular problem with white bread. Aside from the fact that it had no taste and no texture.

At least Claire believed in butter.

Thumps took his coffee to the bathroom and shut the door. Mornings were never a pretty time for him, but today he was feeling particularly dishevelled. And lost. Coffee would help. So would a shower. But hot water and soap weren't going to wash away the feeling that he had screwed up.

By the time Thumps stepped out of the shower, the bathroom was foggy and warm. There was a tube of menthol toothpaste on the edge of the sink, the bright white kind with a glowing blue gel swirl running through it. He squeezed a gob on his finger and reluctantly pushed it around the inside of his mouth. Jesus! What was wrong with regular toothpaste?

Thumps was wiping a hole on the mirror and considering using Claire's razor to tidy up his face when he noticed Stick's clothes on the floor. Finding a clue in Stick's jeans would be too much to ask, and Thumps was not sure how Claire would feel about his looking. Though, with a murderer on the loose, Claire's feelings weren't really the issue.

The jean pockets were empty. The shirt pockets were no help either. Thumps kicked at Stick's runners. They were wet and covered with tiny grey spots that looked for all the world like mould blooms. The laces were shreds. The black rubber bottoms had begun to separate from the black nylon tops. And the inside lining had deteriorated into a soft, soggy pulp with an odour that reminded Thumps of Claire's sink.

He saw it by accident. The thin edge of something white and much too clean to be part of the shoe. Something just under the insole. Thumps was not keen to put his finger anywhere near the inside of Stick's shoe. Fortunately, there was a toothbrush on the side of the sink. He hoped it was Stick's, but at this point, he wasn't particular. It wasn't his. He slipped the butt end of the toothbrush under the insole, pried it up, and shook whatever it was into the sink.

What it was was a card. A white card. A white plastic card with a magnetic strip. No name on it. No markings.

Thumps let the rest of the clothes lie where they were. Stick was Claire's son. She could figure out what to do with them.

It took a little rummaging around in the kitchen before Thumps found what he needed. A pair of rubber gloves and a utility knife. And a flashlight. The gloves were a light rose colour. He would have preferred green or yellow, but these would have to do.

The morning air was dead calm and had an unexpected but welcome chill to it. As Thumps stepped off the porch and walked to his car, he played back his conversation with Stick. His instincts told him that Stick had been telling the truth about not killing Takashi or Floyd. But he had lied about going fishing, and he had lied about not knowing anything about Takashi's death.

More troubling was Stick's attitude. He hadn't been frightened. And even though he had taken off, he wasn't running. Thumps didn't like what he was thinking. Surely Stick wasn't trying to solve the case himself. The damn idiot! That would explain why he had gone to see Floyd, and why he had come home. He hadn't come home to hide. He had come home to change his clothes. And eat.

Thumps turned out of the driveway and pointed the nose of the car due west. Back to Buffalo Mountain Resort. Things were beginning to go in circles. Big circles. Little circles. In most Native cultures, circles were good. But for police work, circles were maddening. Culture notwithstanding, Thumps was more than ready to stumble onto a straight line.

Cooley was waiting for him when he drove through the gate. Cooley and Floyd had not always got along, but they were brothers, and Cooley wasn't going to be happy about Floyd's murder. That is, if he knew about it yet. Thumps couldn't imagine that Duke hadn't notified the family by now. There was no reason to keep Floyd's death a secret. But as Thumps pulled up to the guard shack, Cooley was smiling as he always smiled.

"You're up early."

"Figured I get some photography in."

Cooley sucked on his lips and nodded. "I hear early morning light is the best."

"Okay if I park up by the condos? I'd like to do some shots of the river."

"Place is still a crime scene. Not supposed to let anyone in." Cooley leaned on the car. "Except members of the crime team."

"That would probably include me," said Thumps, holding onto the steering wheel as the car dipped to one side.

"Think so?"

"I took the pictures of the dead guy."

"How about my brother?" Cooley's smile evaporated, and Thumps felt the man's fingers tighten on the car. "Did you take pictures of my brother?"

So, Cooley knew. Thumps could see it in his face now. And he could hear it in his voice.

"No," said Thumps, hoping Cooley wouldn't detect the lie. "I didn't find out about it until this morning."

"Sheriff's looking for Stick pretty hard."

"Stick didn't do it."

"Sheriff thinks he did."

"Hockney's blowing smoke," said Thumps. "I'm really sorry about your brother."

"Floyd lived his life." Cooley shrugged. "He was a screw-up. Everyone knew that."

Thumps wondered whether Cooley or the sheriff knew that he had been at the trailer, had discovered the body, and had skipped out. It had been a dumb thing to do. He didn't think Cooley would hold it against him, but Thumps knew that if the sheriff found out, he could expect to lose a body part. He should have called the murder in himself. But if he had, Hockney would have known for sure that Thumps was playing cop again, and more body parts would have gone missing.

Cooley stood back from the car and folded his arms across his chest. The man was massive, but anyone who thought that he was fat and happy and inoffensive would be making a fatal mistake.

"If you see Stick, you tell him I said hello." Cooley patted the roof of the car the way you might pat a dog or a favourite horse. "Tell him Floyd's brother said hello."

Thumps eased the car away from the guard shack. Great. Stick was beginning to resemble a pizza. The sheriff wanted a piece. The folks at Genesis Data Systems wanted a piece. Cooley wanted several pieces. By the time the FBI arrived, there'd be nothing left but the box.

He parked the car in the top parking lot so Cooley could see it from the guard shack. Then he hauled his camera backpack out of the trunk, along with the wooden tripod, and made a production of strapping everything on. Cooley stood by the side of the shack watching him.

Wave goodbye, Thumps reminded himself. Act casual.

The Ironstone was about a quarter of a mile from the condos, and the walk through the trees was a pleasant one. By the time he got to the river, Thumps had almost convinced himself to spend the rest of the morning taking photographs of the water, retiring to his darkroom, and leaving the detective work to the professionals. He even went so far as to set up the camera and take several light readings before conscience and obligation regained control.

But he left the camera set up at the water's edge. If anyone asked, he could say he was waiting for better light or for the right moment. If Cooley wandered down to the river, at least it would look as though Thumps were working. And if what he had in mind didn't pan out, he could always come back to the camera and take a few shots, so the trip out wouldn't have been a complete waste of time.

Thumps worked his way back to the condos, keeping high ground between himself and the guard shack. Going in through the front door was too public and too open, but if he was right, the side door would do as well.

By the time he got to the north side of the condos, he was out of breath. Thumps wasn't sure whether it was the altitude or the adrenalin. Or whether he was just getting too old for this kind of nonsense.

The locking mechanism on the door was a small steel box with a slot and two tiny lights. One red. One green. Thumps took the plastic card out of his pocket and slipped it into the slot. Red light.

He removed the card, checked the magnetic strip, and put it back in the slot. Red light.

Maybe the lock was like the ones in expensive hotels, where guests had to slide the card in and out with one motion.

Green light.

Thumps turned the handle and the door swung open. So far, so good.

The eighth floor was quiet. Duke had sealed the Cataract with a large paper patch that said Crime Scene, and had strung yellow Crime Scene police tape across the doorway. Breaking the seal was a crime, but Thumps had already lost count of how many laws he had broken in the last few days. Breaking into Takashi's room. Failing to report a murder. Leaving the scene of a crime. Impersonating a rich golfer. The list was impressive.

Thumps took the rubber gloves out of his pocket. They were too tight, and as soon as he put them on, he could feel his hands begin to sweat. It took less than a minute to cut the seal with the exacto knife and to pick the lock. Anybody looking closely would be able to see that the crime scene had been compromised, but Thumps hoped that by the time questions were raised, the case would be solved.

If Thumps had killed someone and wanted to leave the body in a condo, he would have chosen one of the larger units. A unit with more class. A unit closer to the elevator. Why drag the body all the way to the Cataract? He walked to the window and looked out. From here, he could see the parking lot and the computer complex. One thing was sure. Takashi hadn't been brought to the Cataract for the view.

It didn't make sense. It didn't make any sense at all. Thumps smoothed the cut edges of the seal and reset the tape. This was the place where the crime ended. Maybe this was the place to begin. Maybe if he could follow the events backwards, he could figure out what had happened to Takashi and why he had been brought here.

Keep it simple, Thumps reminded himself as he walked down the hall to the elevators. Do it by the numbers.

The basement of the condo complex was an underground parking garage, and it was pitch black. Thumps turned on the flashlight, but it didn't make much of a dent in the darkness.

Ora Mae had said that all the buildings were connected by service tunnels. If the sheriff was right about Takashi's being killed in the computer complex, the tunnels were the only safe way to move the body between the two buildings. Thumps played the light up and down the garage, and tried not to allow his imagination to get out of hand. It was not just dark in the garage. It was dark and damp, with the wet smell of fresh concrete and the oppressive weight of silence. The only sound was the echo of Thumps' footsteps, as they rolled off the cold walls and came back as low moans and growls. While Thumps knew better, he felt as though he were lost in the belly of some large beast. And that he was not going to get out.

It took him twenty minutes to find the door. The card opened it as easily as it had the first door. So, Thumps could go anywhere in the complex he wanted, and right now he wanted to go somewhere bright and airy that didn't remind him of Beth's workroom. There was no way to tell which way he was going or which building he would wind up in. But by the time Thumps got to the door at the other end of the service tunnel, he didn't care.

He wasn't sure what he would find when he opened the door, but he wasn't expecting another basement. Another basement with no lights. The flashlight began to stutter. Thumps shook it, but instead of coming back to life the way flashlights are supposed to do when you shake them, this one died all at once. Terrific. With the light, he had been stumbling around in the dark. Now he was reduced to groping. He put his hands on the wall and slowly followed it around the room until he found a set of stairs going up.

Up was good.

At the top of the stairs was another door with another card slot. Mercifully, Thumps could see a whisper of light under the door frame. Salvation was at hand. Better yet, as he stepped through the doorway, he found himself back in the computer complex. Just where he wanted to be. Almost as if he had planned it. And once his breathing returned to normal, he might even congratulate himself.

If Thumps had felt slightly out of his league sitting in front of Takashi's laptop at Shadow Ranch, standing in the Buffalo Mountain computer complex staring at a bank of large boxes with little lights made him feel like a Neanderthal just out of the cave. Everything considered, he had been better off in the garage with a dead flashlight.

If the answer to Takashi's death was on the computer, Thumps would never find it. If the answer was somewhere else in the computer room, he had half a chance. He circled the room and tried to imagine what might have happened.

There were any number of ways to reconstruct Takashi's murder, but Thumps preferred two. One, the killer was in the process of sabotaging the computer. Takashi arrived unexpectedly. They argued. They fought. Takashi was killed. Or two, the killer was waiting at the complex for Takashi. Takashi arrived and was killed.

Both possibilities were simple enough, but Thumps had learned to distrust coincidence long ago. During the weeks Takashi had spent working at Buffalo Mountain, he had never come out on a Saturday. Each and every weekend, he had rented a van and gone sightseeing. But this particular Saturday, he had shown up. Why? How did the killer know Takashi would be there? The idea that the killer and Takashi had just happened to appear at the complex at the same time was too pat. Even for a Neanderthal.

And coincidence aside, how had the killer gotten past Cooley? Cooley would have certainly noticed a second car. No car could mean that the killer had been on foot with a reasonable knowledge of the terrain. And that turned all the suspicion back on Stick and the Red Hawks.

Unless Cooley was lying. Unless Cooley had been involved in the killings.

Maybe the murder had nothing to do with the computer. Maybe Takashi had been fooling around with someone's wife. Maybe he had annoyed someone at a bar. Thumps stopped in mid-thought. He was getting desperate, beginning to sound like a television detective. Even if Takashi had gotten someone murderously pissed off, why would the killer go to the trouble of sneaking into Buffalo Mountain Resort on foot instead of driving over to Shadow Ranch and killing Takashi there?

Thumps sat down in the chair and spun it around. Something was missing. How did Takashi and Floyd fit together? The simplest answer was that Floyd had figured out who had killed Takashi, was trying to blackmail the murderer, and was killed for his troubles. Thumps liked that answer. Neat. Uncomplicated. Believable.

Spinning around did not help. It was making him dizzy and turning his mind away from the killings to more mundane concerns. The walls of the computer complex, for instance. As Thumps turned in the chair, he noticed that the walls were all painted grey. Not a particularly nice shade, either. Maybe the colour was supposed to be a soothing complement to the irritation of computers. Not that the painters had done a very good job. Now that he was looking at it, he could see that the paint job on the far wall was streaked and uneven.

All the money Claire and the tribe had thrown at the resort, and they couldn't even get a good paint job.

Thumps walked the length of the room. The bloodstains that Hockney had found suggested that Takashi had been killed while he was working on the computer. Takashi was shot from the front, so he probably saw his killer. Either he knew his killer, or he didn't see the danger until it was too late.

Thumps sat down in the chair again. Maybe Takashi was sitting at the monitor. He heard a noise behind him, turned around, and was shot before he had time to react. Thumps turned in the seat to face the wall with the bad paint job. Bang, bang, you're dead.

Damn! That wall was a real annoyance. Thumps rolled the chair across the floor and looked at it from a different angle. Now it looked fine. He rolled the chair back the other way. It looked fine from here, too. He rolled the chair slowly back toward the main keyboard.

There it was. The bad paint job. You could see it only when the wall caught the light in a particular way, from a particular angle. Maybe it was the murders. Maybe it was the shootout at the Songbird Trailer Park. Maybe it was exhaustion. Whatever the reason, Thumps had the strong urge to find a can of paint and a roller and do the job right.

He bent the gooseneck lamp on the monitor table and aimed it at the wall.

Sloppy bastards.

And then he saw it. So large and clear, he couldn't believe he hadn't seen it before, couldn't believe that no one else had seen it before. Thumps grabbed the lamp and began playing the light across the wall.

"Sonofabitch."

Beneath a thin layer of paint, he could see the shadows of letters. Letters that had been painted over. There was an R and an H and a W. Thumps worked the lamp and watched as the light pulled words off the wall.

Red Hawks.

Someone had scrawled "Red Hawks" across the wall in large letters. And someone had tried to cover it up.

Thumps took a coin from his pocket and began rubbing at the paint. It peeled away easily, revealing a layer of shiny black paint.

"Nice gloves."

Thumps froze.

"You need some help?"

Thumps turned slowly, letting the light trail off across the floor. Cooley was standing in the doorway, smiling the way he always smiled. But Thumps wasn't looking at Cooley's face. He was looking at the rifle Cooley had pointed at his chest.

Fifteen

On Thumps' list of the things he liked about guns, having one pointed at him was near the bottom. Especially when the person with the gun was the brother of a man who had just been murdered.

"Kinda hard to photograph the river from here." Cooley cocked his head at the wall.

Thumps kept his hands up where Cooley could see them. "There's a good explanation."

"I'll bet there is."

"I'm really sorry about lying to you."

"No big deal," said Cooley, and he lowered the nose of the rifle to the floor. "You get used to it. Floyd used to lie to me. So did my old man. Hell, politicians lie to me all the time."

Thumps let his hands drop by degrees. He was reasonably sure that Cooley wasn't going to shoot him. But Cooley was angry, and you couldn't always tell what angry people were going to do just by looking at them.

"Where'd you get the gloves?"

"I can explain that, too."

"Nice colour."

Thumps peeled the gloves off. His hands were wet and pasty-looking, as if he had left them underwater too long.

"Red Hawks," said Cooley, looking at the wall. "Old Duke is going to be pissed off he didn't spot this the first time out."

"It's not what it looks like."

"It is what it is."

"You really don't think Stick did this."

"They don't pay me enough to think."

Whoever had painted "Red Hawks" on the wall had wanted the world to see it. The letters were large and well formed, the kind of letters you used to see in books on penmanship.

"We're going to have to call it in."

"I don't know," said Cooley. "We could always lie to the sheriff. I'd like that."

"No point in looking for trouble."

"Seems to me, we've got trouble already," said Cooley. "If we call the sheriff and tell him the truth, he's going to be angry with you for snooping around and messing with his case."

Thumps sighed. Cooley didn't know how right he was.

"And he's going to scream at me for letting you in."

"We have to tell him about this."

"I suppose we do," said Cooley. "But maybe we could rearrange things a little first."

Thumps was impressed. For a guy who wasn't paid to think, Cooley was doing a pretty good job. "You want to tell the sheriff you found this?"

Cooley shrugged. "If I tell him that I found it, he won't need to yell at you."

Thumps nodded. "And if he doesn't know that you let me in …"

"Then he won't yell at me," said Cooley.

Thumps reminded himself for the hundredth time not to judge a person's intelligence by their size. "You'd do that?"

"Sure," said Cooley. "Who knows? By now, there may be a reward."

"You won't mention I was here?"

"Do the math," said Cooley. "If I tell Duke that you were here, he'll probably throw your ass in jail."

Thumps had to admit that was a real possibility.

"And if you're in jail," Cooley continued, "who's going to find Stick for me?"

So, it wasn't generosity.

"I can't do that, Cooley."

"You don't have to catch him."

"What if he didn't kill Takashi or Floyd?"

"Then he's got nothing to worry about."

Thumps searched Cooley's face for a sign that he could take the man at his word. "I'm going to need time to figure this thing out."

"Sure." Cooley's smile was back, but it was a painful smile. "Floyd's not going anywhere."

As Thumps rolled through the gates of the resort and turned onto the main road, he wondered whether Cooley had heard the second lie. The one about time. The last thing Thumps needed was more time. The more time he had, the less likely it was that anyone would find who had killed Takashi and Floyd. What Thumps needed was a clue. A big, straightforward clue. Something plain and easy to read. Like writing on a wall.

But like everything else about this case, the writing on the wall didn't make any sense. If Stick and the Red Hawks had killed Takashi, why would they have wanted to advertise it? And if they had wanted to advertise it, why cover it up? Unless they'd second thoughts—remorse, fear, maybe panic—and then had tried to paint over the evidence.

As Thumps thought about the case, he realized that the problem wasn't too few clues—it was too many. Someone had shot Takashi. Someone had moved his body. Someone had shot Floyd. Someone had painted "Red Hawks" on the wall of the computer complex. And someone had tried to paint over the words. In Thumps' experience, clues tended to work toward agreement, like pieces of a puzzle. The more you had in place, the clearer the picture. This case had more than enough clues, but they tended to contradict each other.

Just like the Obsidian Murders.

The memory was in his head before he could block it. Thumps tried to shove it back where it belonged, back into the darker places of his mind. But the similarities between what had happened on the California coast and what had happened at Buffalo Mountain nagged at him. Similarities not with the killings, but with the confusion around each murder. That case hadn't made any sense, either.

One summer, bodies began showing up on beaches along the northern California coast. Ten people in all. Five women, four men. One child.

There had been no similarity in their ages, their occupations, or their friends. Five were from the area. Five were on vacation or travelling through. Each body had been left just above the high-tide line, arranged in the sand as if part of a grotesque mosaic.

The Obsidian Murders. That's what the press had called them. Because in the mouth of each victim, the killer had placed a small piece of obsidian, something you wouldn't find on a beach, something the killer brought with him.

Then, as quickly as they started, the murders stopped, and all that remained to mark a summer of terror were the pieces of investigative flotsam—bags of physical evidence, photographs, forensic reports, psychological profiles. And a police force that was exhausted, humiliated, and defeated.

The sign welcoming travellers to Chinook took Thumps by surprise, and as he turned the corner by the Burger King, he realized, with some concern, that while he could remember going over every haunting detail of that summer on the California coast, he couldn't remember making the drive from Buffalo Mountain to town.

There were three places in town where Thumps was reasonably sure a person could get doughnuts. Not that he was a connoisseur of doughnuts. In fact, he hated the damn things. Doughnuts and cops might be more than just an occupational joke, but in Thumps' case, there was no truth to the rumour. Even as a kid, he couldn't stand the soft, bready texture or the way doughnuts folded up in his mouth like a wet wash rag. He especially hated the thick slick of sugar that snapped off in thin sheets like broken glass and filled his mouth with an unbearable sweetness.

Thumps stopped at Tim Hortons first, a chain that owed most of its success to its coffee. Thumps had to agree that the coffee was better than average, but what he liked about Hortons were the paper cups they used. Thumps was no fonder of Styrofoam than he was of doughnuts.

The girl at the counter looked to be twelve.

"Hi," she said. "Can I take your order?"

"I'll have a medium coffee."

"Anything in it?"

"Black."

"Would you like a doughnut?" asked the girl, each word bouncing out of her mouth like a ball.

"No."

"We have some really fresh apple-cinnamon muffins."

Maybe younger than twelve, Thumps thought. Only the very young could be this happy.

"Do you know who works the morning shift during the week?"

The girl smiled and handed him his coffee. "I've only been here a week. But I can ask Jill."

"I'd appreciate that."

"She's been here a month."

Jill, as it turned out, had worked the morning shift for the past three weeks. But she didn't remember Takashi stopping in for coffee and doughnuts on a regular basis.

"We try to remember our regulars," she said. "Have you seen our ads on television?"

"He was Asian. Late twenties."

"Sorry. Did Jackie tell you about our fresh apple-cinnamon muffins?"

Thumps' next stop was Sugar and Spice, an upscale boutique bakery that a couple from New York had opened a few years back. Gordon and Linda Packard were nice enough, but Chinook wasn't Manhattan, and some of the exotic breads and desserts that Linda served up were lost on the locals. Thumps suspected the Packards didn't like doughnuts any better than he did but had decided to make a few to try to fit in.

They hadn't seen Takashi, either.

"What time would he have come by?" asked Linda.

"Probably between seven and eight."

"No chance," said Gordon. "We don't open until nine."

Thumps wasn't even sure that doughnuts and coffee were a regular stop for Takashi. Just because Beth had found doughnuts and coffee in the man's stomach didn't mean he ate them every day. But what Thumps knew about human nature gave him hope that doughnuts were, in fact, a part of Takashi's routine

Dumbo's was Thumps' last good hope. Morris Dumbo was a skinny reed of a man who enjoyed complaining the way some people enjoy chocolate. He was an uncomplicated, unrepentant mix of bigotry, sexism, and general vulgarity, a social garbage can on legs. Morris believed that everyone had a God-given right to smoke, drink, and shoot at anything that moved or got in the way, and that all food consumed by civilized people should be deep-fried.

Thumps had eaten at Dumbo's a couple of times, and that had been enough. He had nothing in particular against fried food, but the oil Morris used to make his French fries, chicken parts, and fish sticks looked and tasted as though it had been squeezed out of the crankcase of a diesel. Why his doughnuts were considered the best in town was a mystery to Thumps. But they were. Among those in the know, Dumbo's doughnuts were regarded as the Cadillacs of cholesterol.

Dumbo's looked ordinary enough from the outside with its complement of pickups and semis hunkered down in the parking lot. The brown clapboard building was covered with crudely painted red-and-white signs that advertised everything from "good food" to "Indian souverneers." Some time in the not-too-distant past, Morris had strung Christmas tree lights along the eaves of the building. But instead of taking them down after the holidays the way most people did, Morris left them up so he'd have something to turn on for a special occasion. When George W. Bush beat Al Gore out for the presidency, Morris had left them on for a week.

Inside, the place was pretty much like any number of beat-to-shit western cafés. Tables with plastic tablecloths and mismatched chairs. Wood floors. Bathrooms marked Stags and Does. What made the place unusual was the large area behind the counter where Morris had set up a television set, a dirt-brown sofa, a pressboard coffee table, two end tables, and a Budweiser clock. As far as Thumps could tell, this was where Morris lived.

Morris was wiping down the counter when Thumps came through the door.

"Hey, chief. Long time, no see."

Dumbo's was dark, much like Al's, but the odours were sharper and uglier. If meanness had a scent, Thumps reasoned, it would probably smell like this.

"You see what our wop mayor is trying to do?"

"The swimming pool?"

"Fucking waste of money. Am I right?"

Thumps wanted to tell Morris that he wasn't right, that the community pool the city was finally going to build was a great idea, but he didn't want an argument. He wanted information.

"What'll ya have?"

"Friend of mine stopped by here Saturday." Thumps knew he was on thin ice. Morris had probably heard about the murder at Buffalo Mountain. But there was the chance that he hadn't paid any attention to it. Or didn't know that two plus two was four. "Takashi. Daniel Takashi."

Morris' face remained blank. "Never heard of him."

"Asian guy. Late twenties," said Thumps. "He really liked your doughnuts. Said yours were the best."

"You got that straight."

"We were supposed to drive over to Glacier last Saturday," said Thumps, making it up as he went along. "Kick around for a week or two."

"That so."

"But we missed each other." Thumps shook his head. "A real pain."

Morris' eyes closed down into slits. "I got food to serve."

Thumps glanced around. There were two truckers at a table by the window. Otherwise the place was empty. "Now, I got to catch up with him."

Morris had a thin, razor mouth and short brown hair that sat on his bony head like a scrub brush nailed to a brick. He was not a pretty man, nor was he particularly ugly. He was simply unpleasant.

"You want coffee or what?"

Thumps sighed and took a five-dollar bill out of his pocket. "Sure."

Morris brightened up a little. "Doughnut?"

For the next hour, Thumps sat at the counter and listened to Morris storm about everything from welfare to the price of liquor. In the lulls, he would float the conversation around to Takashi, doughnuts, and coffee, slowly dragging information out of Dumbo the way an auger drags dirt out of a hole.

"Came in every day," Morris told him. "Black coffee and a chocolate long john."

"Must have really liked your doughnuts," said Thumps, with all the enthusiasm he could muster.

"Who cares what they like. Long as they pay and keep their mouths shut."

Thumps ate the doughnut slowly and toyed with the idea of going to the bathroom and putting his finger down his throat before the fat and the sugar and the caffeine hit his bloodstream all at once.

"We were going to do some fishing."

"That so."

"But my alarm didn't go off." Thumps wasn't sure he could finish the doughnut, no matter how long he sat and talked. He had no idea how Takashi had managed to eat one of these things each day or why he would want to.

"Got nothing against your friend, but do you know what those people do?" Morris got the coffee pot and refilled Thumps' cup. "They come over here and take over. They buy up all the real estate. They steal our timber. And our government gives them a bunch of money so they can sell their televisions and their cars for less than we can make them." Morris paused and looked around the room. "That's what happened to that slant up at Buffalo Mountain, you know."

"What?"

"He tried to buy up the resort and the tribe killed him."

"No kidding."

"First smart thing those Indians have done in a long time."

That was the nice thing about hate, Thumps thought to himself as he prodded the doughnut with his fork to see whether it had any weaknesses. You didn't have to be right. You just had to be committed.

"What really heats my grease is that they get rich screwing us. You know what one of those leather jackets costs?"

Thumps pushed the doughnut to the edge of the plate. He was contemplating an unfortunate accident, the doughnut tripping and falling to its death, when he heard the echo of the question. "What?"

"Your buddy, chief. That fancy leather jacket he wears every day. Indian Motorcycle Company. My brother says those damn things start at five hundred."

Thumps forgot about the doughnut. "An Indian Motorcycle Company jacket?"

"Along with that cute little San Francisco 49er cap and those fag dark glasses so you couldn't see his eyes."

"Saturday?"

"Every day."

"And a 49ers cap?"

"A real pussy team. The Niners haven't been worth watching since Joe Montana left. Now there was a real American."

"He didn't wear a sports jacket?"

"Joe Montana?"

"No, Takashi. When he stopped by on Saturday."

Morris leaned on the counter. The man's breath was foul, and Thumps had to turn his head to one side to find calm air. "Why the hell would a man wear a sports jacket if he was going fishing?" Morris thought about this for a minute and started to smirk. "You know what happened, don't ya, chief? He stood you up."

"Stood me up?"

"For a broad."

"He came in here with a woman?"

"Don't have to see them to know they're around." Morris touched the side of his nose with his finger. "I can smell them."

Thumps tried to picture the man as a baby, and he wondered whether Morris' parents had bothered to read the instructions on the Q-Tip box.

"That morning, he picked up two cups of coffee. You drink yours black, am I right?"

"That's right."

"So did your friend," said Morris. "But the other cup had cream and sugar in it."

"But you didn't actually see a woman?"

"Who else drinks coffee with cream and sugar?" Morris picked up the remote control and turned on the television. "You can't trust them, ya know."

"Women?"

"Chinks," said Morris. "But you're right. Women aren't much better."

The first thought Thumps had, as he stepped out the front door into the late afternoon sunlight and walked to his car, was to take off all his clothes and burn them. But his next stop wasn't going to be much of an improvement over Dumbo's. In fact, if the other day was any indication, it could be worse. Best to wait, he told himself, and burn everything at once.

Sixteen

Thumps had no idea what kind of hours Dr. Beth Mooney kept, but as he pulled up to the old land titles building, he hoped that she was playing doctor in her family-practice office, checking runny noses, and not playing coroner in the basement, cutting up corpses.

"Beth. It's me, Thumps." He listened at the intercom to see if he could tell which floor she was on.

"Come on in."

"Up or down?" He crossed his fingers and hoped for the best.

"Up."

"Second floor?"

"All the way."

Thank you, Thumps whispered to himself. Thank you.

Beth and Ora Mae had organized the top two floors of the building into sleeping and living areas. There were three bedrooms and a bath on the third floor, spacious and well appointed. The kitchen and living areas were on the fourth floor, bright, open rooms with high ceilings, large warehouse windows, old wood floors, and exposed brick walls.

As Thumps climbed the stairs, he thought about his own place. Or, to be more precise, he tried not to think about it. Comparisons were only going to make him unhappy. Fortunately, by the time he had dragged himself up to the third floor, he had forgotten about comparing anything and was concentrating hard on breathing.

Ora Mae was waiting for him on the fourth-floor landing. "You'd think carrying that big camera of yours around would keep you in better shape."

"I am in good shape," said Thumps, but he had to catch his breath between the "in" and the "good."

"We could hear you puffing all the way up here."

"That was just controlled breathing."

"Your breathing gets any more controlled, and you're going to wind up in Beth's kitchen."

Thumps stood on the landing and looked into the stairwell. It was the high ceilings. The building was only four stories, but with fourteen-foot ceilings on each floor, the climb from the ground up was longer than normal. He considered pointing this out.

"And don't be telling me about high ceilings," said Ora Mae.

Now that Thumps had caught his breath and was able to focus on matters outside his body, he noticed that Ora Mae was dressed in a pair of paint-stained white bib overalls, a long-sleeved shirt, and a white painter's cap.

"You're not painting the place again?"

Ora Mae had a passion for painting. In the time that Thumps had known the two women, Ora Mae had painted the flat that she and Beth shared at least eight times. Beth was not as keen on paint as Ora Mae was. In fact, Thumps recalled, paint tended to make Beth surly.

"Don't start something you can't finish," said Ora Mae, pointing a paintbrush at his head.

Beth was sitting on the sofa in the sun, reading a book and drinking a cup of coffee. There were tarps over much of the floor and green tape around all the window casements. On one wall was a series of painted stripes in various shades of yellow.

"So, which one do you like?" Ora Mae gestured at the wall.

Thumps didn't like this kind of guessing game. He knew that if he guessed wrong, he was going to hurt someone's feelings.

"I don't have an eye for colour."

"Must be a real advantage in something like photography."

"I'm a black-and-white photographer."

"World's not black and white," said Ora Mae. "This a business call or you just looking for a free meal?"

"Business," said Thumps.

"Last time you came around doing business," said Ora Mae, "Floyd Small Elk wound up dead."

"I heard."

"I'll just bet you did."

Thumps ignored the implication and tried to look unconcerned.

Beth turned a page in her book. "Sheriff thinks that Takashi and Floyd might be related."

Thumps shrugged and looked at the wall with the stripes. He rather fancied the deep yellow one that had just a hint of brown to it. A solid colour that would give the room weight.

"But I haven't done Floyd yet," said Beth, without looking up from her book.

Thumps closed his eyes and concentrated on reassuring his stomach. "I'm not here about Floyd."

"Then what do you need?" Ora Mae put down the brush and picked up a roller on a long pole.

"I need to look at Takashi's stuff," said Thumps.

"Sorry," said Beth. "Beth is done working for today."

"Just a quick look."

"Beth is reading and is not to be disturbed."

Ora Mae rolled a long line of light yellow paint on the wall. "You could help me paint."

"I just need to check something." Thumps tried to make his voice sound casual, but Ora Mae heard it and stopped rolling.

Beth looked up from her book. "Don't tell me you know who killed Takashi."

"Not exactly," said Thumps.

"See this?" said Beth, and she held her book up. "It's a murder mystery. I'm on page one hundred and fifty-four, and I already know who did it."

"Come on." Ora Mae put down the roller and jiggled Beth out of her comfortable position. "I've always wanted to see someone solve a crime."

The second floor of the building was set aside for Beth's medical practice. When she wasn't rummaging through dead bodies, she ran a small clinic whose patients consisted mainly of single women and their

154

children. The first floor was the coroner's office proper, complete with a large desk, a computer, and a long row of grey filing cabinets. It wasn't as depressing as the basement, but it had some of the same musty smells as the morgue below.

"All right," said Beth as she turned on the light. "What's so important?"

"You still have Takashi's clothes?"

"His clothes?"

"Yeah."

"This better be good." Beth went to a tall metal cabinet, unlocked the door, took out a large plastic bag, and laid it on the desk. "Wear these," she said, handing rubber gloves to Thumps and Ora Mae.

Thumps opened the bag, slid the clothes out, and arranged each item on the desk.

"You looking for something special?" said Beth.

He stepped back. "What do you see?"

"I hope this isn't one of those Indian vision things," said Ora Mae.

Beth sat down in the chair behind the desk and leaned forward on her elbows. "Clothes," she said. "Now, could we get this ride started?"

Thumps ran a hand across the T-shirt. "How many entry wounds?"

"You took the pictures," said Beth.

"Three entry wounds, right?"

"Right."

"How many exit wounds?"

"Two. One bullet stayed in the body."

"So how come there are no bullet holes in the jacket?"

Ora Mae smiled. "He wasn't wearing the jacket."

"He was when the body was found," said Thumps.

Beth nodded. "And that proves ...?"

"And no Indian Motorcycle jacket," said Thumps, more to himself than to anyone in particular. "Was there a pair of sunglasses? Or a 49er cap?"

Beth pursed her lips and looked at Ora Mae. "You let him take me away from my nap for this?"

"You were reading a book." Ora Mae turned the lapel of the sports coat over and whistled. "My, my," she said.

"What?"

"This is a Brioni."

"Is that good?"

"Very expensive," said Ora Mae.

Thumps felt the material to see whether he could tell. "Like ... Armani?"

"Honey," said Ora Mae, "nobody wears Armani anymore."

"This is certainly fun," said Beth. "Are we done?"

"How expensive is this ... Bri ... Brio ..."

"Brioni."

"Right."

"Couple thousand," said Ora Mae. "At least." She picked up the socks and rolled the material between her thumb and forefinger. "And in this corner, we've got standard mall-issue jeans, T-shirt, and bikini underpants."

"What about it, Officer DreadfulWater?" said Beth. "You wear bikini underpants?"

"Thumps is the boxer type," said Ora Mae.

"Those big balloony things?" said Beth.

"White!" said both women at once and began grinning.

Thumps held up a hand in an effort to get the situation under control. "So, we've got a guy who runs down to the mall, picks up jeans, T-shirts, and underpants, along with a two-thousand-dollar sports coat."

"You won't find Brioni at a mall."

Beth yawned and started folding Takashi's clothes. "You had dinner?"

Thumps' stomach rumbled discreetly. "What are you having?"

"Liver and onions," said Ora Mae.

Thumps swallowed hard and smiled. "I should get back. I've got some printing to do."

Beth turned out the lights and locked the door. "For what it's worth, looks like Floyd was shot with the same calibre gun that killed Takashi."

"They were killed with the same gun?"

"I didn't say that. I said the calibre was the same." Beth started up the stairs and stopped. "So, which colour did you like?"

Thumps didn't hear the question. He was watching Ora Mae's shoes as she started up the stairs. "What?"

"Yellow," said Beth, "Which shade of yellow did you like?"

156

Ora Mae's shoes were covered with tiny paint spots. Like mould blooms. Thumps could see them clearly. And what he saw did not make him happy.

"The dark yellow," he said, turning and heading down the stairs. "I think I like the dark yellow best."

Archimedes Kousoulas' house was a two-storey white frame with green trim. The second floor was the Aegean Book Shop. Archie was folding plastic covers for dust jackets.

"So," he said, "you decided to stop by."

"I stop by all the time."

"Here," said Archie, "look at these." He opened a drawer and took out several old postcards.

Thumps' secret vice was collecting postcards with Native themes. Preferably, historical themes.

"What do you think?"

"I've got a Sherman Institute one already."

"Same as this?"

The postcard was a side view of Sherman Institute with its Spanish architecture and its broad boulevards. At the far end of the main boulevard was a regiment of white-and-black figures that Thumps could not make out. Probably Indian children on their way to some affair or other. Off to one side, to help the children on their way, was a marching band.

"No."

Archie shrugged. "So, now you have another."

The second card was a photograph of an Indian lacrosse team from Weleetka, Oklahoma. The postmark was 1907. The one-cent stamp on the card was green, with a portrait of Benjamin Franklin.

"This is nice."

The third card was a slightly romantic rendering of the United States Indian hospital at Claremore, Oklahoma, complete with an American flag hanging from a flagpole and a border of yellow and red flowers laid in at the edge of the property.

"How's the investigation coming?"

Thumps looked up from the cards. "You should ask the sheriff."

"You and Beth going out?"

Thumps frowned. Archie had a devious way of sneaking up on questions. "No. Why?"

"You took her out to dinner."

"I owe her."

"You owe me, too."

"I know."

"But you don't take me out to dinner." Archie shook his head. "Even after I go to all the trouble of finding you nice cards for your collection."

"I'm looking into things for Claire."

"I think Sterling did it."

Thumps smiled. "Why?"

"Because I don't like him." Archie nodded, agreeing with himself. "And the man doesn't read. How can you trust a man who doesn't read?"

"Sterling didn't do it."

"Too bad," said Archie. "So, what do you want?"

"I just came by to see you."

"You know the story of the Trojan Horse?"

"More or less," said Thumps.

"That stuff only works once."

Thumps chuckled. "I need to know anything you can find out about Daniel Takashi."

"The dead guy?"

"You know everybody in town."

"I already asked."

Thumps' face gave him away.

"Don't look surprised," said Archie. "You're not the only one who gets curious."

"Claire called you, too."

"We're friends. Like you and me."

"And?"

"And nothing. Takashi stayed to himself. Went out to Buffalo Mountain every day. Went back to Shadow Ranch every evening. Ate most of his meals in his room. Didn't hang out at the bars. Didn't go to movies. Every weekend he went sightseeing."

"Great."

"Bet he was a reader."

"Why?"

"People who live by themselves generally read."

"How much for the postcards?"

"Next time you come by," said Archie, slipping the cards into a plastic envelope, "bring me a nice photograph of a mountain."

It was evening by the time Thumps got home. Freeway was waiting for him at the door, and she was not amused.

"You hungry?"

Actually, Thumps was a little hungry himself. He took the cat food out of the refrigerator and spooned it into the bowl. The bread was on the counter, but the ham had vanished. He tried to remember whether he had eaten it or had forgotten to buy any.

"You eat my ham?"

Freeway had her face buried in her food and wasn't in the mood for small talk. There was half a tomato in a plastic bag and most of a stick of old cheddar cheese in the refrigerator door. Thumps settled for those. Along with the opened bottle of Pepsi that had gone flat.

Okay, he thought, as he settled on the sofa, turned on the television, and looked around the room, it's not Ora Mae and Beth's place, and it's not one of the condos at Buffalo Mountain, but it's home.

Behind him, he could hear Freeway choking on her food.

"Slow down."

As Thumps ate the sandwich, he began putting together all the pieces that seemed to fit. Daniel Takashi was a programmer for Genesis Data Systems. He came to Chinook to program the computer at Buffalo Mountain Resort. Five days a week, he would leave Shadow Ranch in a limousine driven by Floyd Small Elk, get a cup of coffee and a doughnut at Dumbo's, and then drive out to Buffalo Mountain. On weekends, he would rent a camper van and go sightseeing. The Saturday he was killed, he had rented the camper van. But he hadn't gone sightseeing. He had stopped at Dumbo's, but this time he had bought two cups of coffee.

First question. Who was the second cup of coffee for?

Takashi got to Buffalo Mountain around ten, was killed at eleven, and left a little after twelve.

Second question. How was that possible?

Takashi was killed in the computer complex, where someone had spray-painted one of the walls with the words "Red Hawks." But his body was moved to the condos, and the wall was painted over.

Third question. Why?

Floyd Small Elk was killed just after he had sounded Thumps out about selling the identity of Takashi's killer to Claire.

Fourth question. What did he know?

Thumps was finishing off the last of the sandwich and going over what Ora Mae had told him about Takashi's clothing when he remembered that he had definitely bought ham. He went back to the refrigerator and began moving things around. The bottle of Pepsi. Mustard. Ketchup. A bowl of macaroni. Photographic paper and film. Cat food. Half a can of baked beans.

No ham.

Thumps checked the trash can he kept by the side of the sink. The plastic container that the ham had come in was sitting on top of the pile, along with the wrapper for one of Thumps' precious dark-chocolate Häagen-Dazs bars. He touched the wrapper. It was still cold and wet.

"Sonofabitch."

Okay, that did it. As if spending four days running around chasing smoke and getting shot at wasn't enough. Now this. Enough was enough.

The basement should have been pitch black, but when Thumps got to the bottom of the stairs, he could see the faint amber glow of the safelight spilling out of the doorway to the darkroom. He leaned against the wall. The door should have been closed. The safelight should have been off.

And as he stood there in the dark, listening for any sounds, he was sorry he hadn't grabbed his gun from the lock box. If he had guessed wrong, Thumps suddenly realized, the mistake he was making could be fatal.

Seventeen

Stanley Merchant was relaxing up on a sleeping bag by the side of the long stainless-steel sink, a pair of headphones strapped to his ears. His eyes were closed and his head was bobbing in time to the music while he sucked on a short, flat stick. All that was left of Thumps' Häagen-Dazs bar.

Thumps stood in the doorway and went through his options. He could do this hard or he could do it easy. With everything that he had had to endure in the last little while, in large part because Stick wanted to play loose cannon, Thumps was inclined to do things the hard way.

"Hey!"

The effect was marvellous. Stick's head snapped up, the earphones went flying, and his body lifted off the concrete floor.

"Jesus! You scared the hell out of me."

"You're in my darkroom."

"You could have knocked or something."

"You're eating my food." God, thought Thumps, he was sounding like one of the three bears.

Stick found his headphones and turned the CD player off. "Where have you been?"

"Where have I been?" Thumps could feel his blood pressure climbing. "I've been looking for you."

"Well, I've been here waiting for you."

"And eating my food."

"I was hungry."

"That was a Häagen-Dazs bar."

Stick shrugged. "You've got another one."

Thumps turned on the lights, pulled the chair out from under the enlarger table, and sat down facing Stick. "This better be good," he said. "This better be real good."

"Hey, I'm being framed."

Thumps held up a hand. "Tell me something I don't know."

"That's it."

"I'm going to call Hockney."

"Hockney hates me."

"I'm not overly fond of you myself."

"Yeah," said Stick, with a smirk, "but you like my mom."

Stick was a good-looking kid, tall and skinny, with a crooked smile that made him seem endearing. And he was smart. Which only went to prove that good looks and brains weren't always a winning combination. To be blunt, Stick was a pain in the ass, had always been a pain in the ass. Thumps knew that young men Stick's age could be self-absorbed, and he knew that most of them grew out of it. In Stick's case, Thumps didn't have time to wait.

"You know, if I can figure things out, the sheriff won't have much trouble doing the same thing."

"I didn't kill Takashi or Floyd," said Stick.

"Then why'd you move Takashi's body?"

It was an old cop trick. Throw a hot question into the middle of the conversation and see what happened. What happened was that the smile on Stick's face vanished. Good, thought Thumps. I've got his attention.

"I didn't move Takashi's body."

"You used the maintenance tunnels and the garage to get him to the condos."

Stick tried to tough it out. "Was this after I shot him?"

"No," said Thumps, "this was after you painted the wall." He was enjoying this exchange more than he could have imagined. "Or maybe you moved the body first and then painted the wall."

"You're crazy," said Stick, but his voice had lost its cocky edge. "You can't prove that."

"Won't have to," said Thumps. "The sheriff will do it for me. And he won't even have to try."

Stick's body tensed up. Thumps settled into the chair, blocking the only way out of the darkroom.

"I'm going to make it easy for you," said Thumps. "The sheriff already knows that Takashi was killed in the computer complex. As soon as he finds Red Hawks painted on the wall, he's going to have all he needs to get a search warrant for your mother's house." He paused so Stick could hear every word. "And as soon as he finds your runners, he's going to come after you with everything he's got."

Stick frowned. "My runners?"

"The ones with the grey paint spots on them."

Stick looked at his feet before he could stop himself.

"Not those," said Thumps. "The ones you left at your mother's house. When you painted over the wall, you got paint on your shoes. Duke will find them. He'll test the paint. And it'll match the paint on the wall. He sure as hell is going to find out that you went to see Floyd just before he was killed."

Stick's entire body was rigged for flight. His eyes were measuring the distance to the door, calculating his odds of getting past Thumps.

Thumps shook his head. "Forget it. Besides your mother, I'm the only friend you have."

"So, what are you going to do?"

"I'm going to keep you from getting killed." Thumps moved out of the way to give Stick a straight run at the door. "But if you want to be stupid, be my guest."

Stick looked at Thumps, and he looked at the door. Then he leaned back against the sink.

"All right," said Thumps. "Let's start at the beginning."

For the most part, he had guessed right. While the Red Hawks had opposed the resort as a whole, arguing that it pandered to rich whites, their main complaint was with the casino and the potential problems that recreational gambling seemed to drag along in its wake. Drugs, alcohol, violence. When public protest didn't work, Stick came up with the idea of sabotaging the main computer.

"All the slots are controlled by the main computer," said Stick. "You know what that means?"

The plan was to create a virus, a computer time bomb that would go off

163

periodically, changing the odds on the machines and scrambling the security systems. It would be, the Red Hawks reckoned, a public-relations nightmare. Slot machines paying off on every pull. Slot machines not paying off when they were supposed to. Key cards not working. Smoke alarms blaring. Surveillance cameras going wonky. Guerrilla warfare. Civil disobedience.

The more Stick talked, the more Thumps could see that the young man fancied himself a latter-day Thoreau with a computer.

"Not a worm?"

"A worm? No, it was a virus."

"You're sure?"

"I know the difference," said Stick. "But when I got there, I found Takashi."

"Why not call the police? Why move the body?"

Stick looked at the ceiling. "Do the math. Someone kills Takashi. Someone paints 'Red Hawks' on the wall. Who do you think the sheriff is going to figure that someone is? If I move the body and paint the wall, I buy time to figure out what's happening."

"Why move him to that particular condo?"

"Did you really used to be a cop?"

"I'm tired and I'm hungry," said Thumps. "Just answer the damn question."

"So I could see the computer building. In case the guy who killed Takashi came back."

"And then you went to see Floyd."

"Floyd drove Takashi around. Maybe Takashi said something to him."

"And?"

"Nothing," said Stick. "Floyd told me to get lost."

"So, you saw Floyd."

"Yeah, I saw him. But he was kind of weird."

"Weird?"

"He wouldn't let me in his trailer." Stick smiled his crooked smile. "Talked to me through the screen door. Like he had a woman in the bedroom or something."

Thumps stood up and pushed the chair back under the easel. "Let me be the first to congratulate you on screwing up magnificently."

"What the hell do you know?" Stick got to his feet defiantly.

"Well, let's see," said Thumps, and he held up one hand and spread his fingers. "One, I know about the cigarettes you took off Takashi."

"What cigarettes?"

Thumps gestured at Stick's shirt pocket. "Those ones."

Stick's reaction was predictable. He looked.

"Two, I know about the bag you left in the mountains."

"How ...?"

"Three, I know about Takashi's key card that you hid under the insole of your sneakers. That's how you got access to the tunnels and the condo." Thumps paused for everything to sink in. "How am I doing?"

"You found the key card?"

"I used to be a cop," said Thumps. "What I don't know is how you got into the computer complex in the first place."

"That was the easy part." Stick waited. "Want to guess?"

"Floyd?"

"Sure. There are two ways to get in."

Thumps nodded. "Key card or you can punch in a code."

"Right."

"And Floyd saw Takashi punch in the code?"

"Beats pulling out a card every time."

"But why would Floyd give you the code?"

"He didn't," said Stick. "I bought it off him."

That made sense, Thumps thought. Floyd wasn't in the business of giving anything away for free.

"So," said Stick. "What are we going to do?"

Thumps leaned against the wall. "There is no 'we.'"

Stick looked stunned. "You going to turn me in?"

"No, you're going to turn yourself in."

"The hell I am."

Arguing with Stick was like arguing with a horseshoe. "Okay," said Thumps, "suit yourself."

It took Stick a moment to react. "You're not going to turn me in?"

"Nope."

"And you're not going to tell the sheriff you saw me?"

"Nope."

He didn't make any move to get past Thumps. "Why not?"

"The sheriff will find you soon enough."

"No, he won't."

"Sure he will. Maybe not today. Maybe not next week. But he'll find you." Thumps looked at the empty plate. "And when he does, he's not going to treat you to a ham sandwich and an ice cream bar."

Stick shoved his hands in his pockets. "I could stay here for a while."

Thumps turned to go back upstairs. Maybe he was wrong about Stick. Maybe the kid was just plain bone-stupid.

"What if I have some evidence?"

"Evidence?"

"Yeah," said Stick. "Maybe I know why Takashi was killed."

"Well, that would be peachy." Thumps hoped Stick could hear the sarcasm.

"I mean, I don't know exactly why he was killed. But I have an idea."

Thumps didn't like where this was heading. "And where is this evidence?"

"In my car."

The alarm bells should have gone off as soon as Thumps found Stick in his darkroom. But for some reason, they hadn't.

"Your car?"

"Yeah."

"Where?"

"Where what?"

"Where did you leave your car?"

"In the alley."

"Behind my house?"

"Yeah," said Stick. "What's the problem?"

"Shit! How long have you been here?"

"I don't know. Couple of hours."

As soon as Thumps got upstairs, he turned off all the lights, stepped to the front window, and looked out. There were several cars on the street. Thumps recognized them all.

"What the hell's wrong?"

Thumps kept his voice low as he watched the street. "Did I mention that the sheriff is looking for you?"

"So."

"So, he's also looking for your car." Thumps glanced at Stick's face to see whether anyone was home.

"He's not going to check every alley in town."

"He doesn't have to," said Thumps. "He knows where I live."

The backyard was tiny, with hardly enough room for grass, but the people who had owned the house before had had ambitions for the area. And a subscription to one or more of those do-it-yourself magazines. They had put in a flagstone patio that started off well enough, with all the stones levelled and interlocked, the joints packed tightly with sand. But as it ran away from the house and out to the plywood gazebo, the pattern began slowly to fall apart, until the stones had simply been dropped and left to rot. From the gazebo, which had inexplicably been stained a deep chocolate brown, the previous owners had begun excavation for what Thumps could only guess was supposed to be a pool. By the time they had dug down three feet, they had evidently run out of patience with the project and with each other.

Thumps had bought the house partly because it had been cheap, the product of a less-than-amicable divorce, and partly because it had a high-ceilinged basement where he could put a darkroom. When he first moved in, he thought about finishing the yard, but by the time he had unpacked the boxes and painted the rooms, the weeds had already taken over the patio and the pool—if that's what the excavation was supposed to be— and had turned the hole into a seasonal pond complete with mosquitoes and toads. Most of the time, Thumps pretended that his lot ended at the back door, and on the rare occasions that he did venture into the back-yard, he ventured out only to knock down the weeds, so his neighbours wouldn't report him to the city.

Thumps kept the flashlight pointed low as he and Stick made their way through the yard.

"Watch your step."

"You ever going to fix this place up?"

"I like it natural."

Stick's car was leaning against the side of the wood-slat fence that marked the end of the backyard. Thumps didn't need the light to see that the fence, like the yard, was in need of attention. Maybe when Ora Mae ran out of rooms at the old land titles office, she'd come over and bring her brushes.

Thumps lifted the gate and swung it open. In the distance, a dog was complaining about something.

"Why didn't you just park the car out front and call Hockney?"

"So, why are you helping me?"

"I'm not helping you."

"You just want to have sex with my mom."

Yes, Thumps said to himself, that would certainly be preferable to babysitting her son. "Just show me what you've got."

Stick went around to the back of the car. "It's in the trunk."

Thumps looked down the alley. The dog had stopped barking, and the night was suddenly very quiet. The trunk opened with a long, agonizing creak.

"What the hell ...?"

Thumps moved to the trunk quickly. "What's wrong?"

"Cool." Stick pulled something dark and heavy out of the trunk and threw it over his shoulders. "What do you think?"

It was a jacket. A leather jacket.

"Pretty nice, eh?" Stick turned around so Thumps could see the Indian Motorcycle Company crest on the back of the jacket. And the two small bullet holes in the leather.

Thumps grabbed Stick's arm. "Where the hell did you get that?"

"Hey, easy," said Stick, pulling his arm back. "It was in my trunk."

"Shit." Thumps stepped from behind the car and swung the light into the yard.

"What's wrong?"

Thumps saw the muzzle flash at the same moment he heard the first shot hit the car. The second shot hit Stick and spun him around.

"Get your hands up!"

Thumps was on the ground before the third shot shattered the side window. Stick was draped on the trunk. Thumps found his belt and dragged him in behind the wheels of the car, just as a fourth shot tore through the rear panel. Someone was running through the garden now, crashing through the weeds. Thumps glanced under the car just in time to see a set of legs fly across the flagstones and hit the edge of the pool.

"Sonofabitch!"

Whoever had tumbled into the pool had tumbled in hard. Thumps rolled Stick over and tore the jacket open. The boy's shirt was soaked with blood, but it was too dark to see the wound. Wherever the bullet had hit him, it wasn't good.

"Shit!"

Suddenly there were lights everywhere as police cars roared in from both ends of the alley. Thumps pulled Stick's shirt up and began feeling for the wound.

"Drop your weapon and show us your hands."

"I've got a man down."

"Drop your weapon!"

"It's a flashlight, you asshole!"

"Drop the weapon!"

Thumps held the flashlight out and let it roll off his fingers. Then he raised his hands above his head, making sure that every movement was slow and deliberate.

Eighteen

Stick was still unconscious when the ambulance arrived. Thumps had found the wound and stopped the bleeding, but he wasn't sure that was going to help. Stick had been pale and still, and the pulse that Thumps had been able to find was weak.

"Going to have to arrest you." Sheriff Hockney watched as they loaded Stick into the ambulance.

"For what?"

"Harbouring a fugitive, for starters."

"Stick wasn't under arrest."

"And resisting arrest."

"We didn't resist anything. We got shot at."

The sheriff looked over at Thumps' backyard. "Andy says he identified himself and that you shot at him."

So the cowboy with the gun had been Andy. Thumps should have guessed as much.

"Would it hurt your feelings if I told you Andy is a liar?"

"He hurt his ankle real bad falling into that trap of yours."

"It's not a trap, it's a sunken garden. And I'm sorry he didn't break his neck."

Hockney put his beefy hand on Thumps' shoulder. "You know as well as me what happens when cops get shot at."

"And just what the hell did we shoot at him with?"

Duke picked the flashlight up and looked at it. "Hard to tell what a man has in his hand in the dark."

"Bullshit. No cop is going to mistake a flashlight for a gun."

The sheriff nodded. "We could argue about this all night, and it would go down to Andy's word against yours. How do you suppose that's going to play?"

"The way it's going to play is that you let a trigger-happy racist off his leash and he shot a kid."

"That kid was wanted for two murders."

Duke had evidently asked Bert the right questions. "I thought you wanted to question him about Takashi."

"Not anymore," said the sheriff. "Here's what we're going to do. I'm going to ask you some questions, and if I like the answers, I'm going to let you go. But if you try to screw with me, I'm going to handcuff you and drag your sorry ass to jail."

"I don't know any more than you do."

"That's not a good start. Why were you hiding the Merchant kid?"

"I wasn't hiding anybody."

"Found a sleeping bag in your darkroom. Plate with crumbs on it and a Popsicle stick."

"It was a Häagen-Dazs bar, not a Popsicle. And he broke into my house and raided my refrigerator."

"You want to press charges?"

"I found him when I got home."

"But you didn't call me."

"I was trying to talk him into giving himself up."

"Out here? By the car? In the dark?"

Thumps didn't like this one-way flow of information. Did Hockney know about the wall at the computer complex yet? Did he know that Thumps had been at Floyd's? Thumps was on thin ice, and he knew it. And he knew that the sheriff was waiting for him to break through.

"Stick said he had some evidence that might point to the killer."

"And where would this evidence be?"

"He said it was in his trunk."

"And was it convincing?"

"I don't know. Andy shot him before he could show me what it was."

"Good news," said the sheriff. "I can show you." Hockney opened the door of his squad car and took out the leather jacket. "You ever see this?"

Thumps shook his head. "No."

"Me neither," said the sheriff. "But I know a few things about this particular jacket. First, it's expensive. This one goes for about five hundred dollars." The sheriff turned the jacket over in his hands as though it were a fine fur. "Second, it doesn't belong to Stanley Merchant." Duke paused and watched Thumps' face. "You know who it does belong to?"

"Daniel Takashi."

"Oh, very good. Was that a guess or did you know?"

"It was a guess."

Duke put a finger through one of the bullet holes. "Something tells me you're not that good a guesser."

"Sheriff, does it make any sense for Stick to keep the jacket of a man he is supposed to have killed?"

"Like I said, it's an expensive jacket."

Thumps was suddenly tired. He was going to have to call Claire and tell her that her son had been shot. For all he knew, Stick might already be dead. "That's not the evidence Stick was talking about."

"Now how would you know that?"

"Because he was surprised to see the jacket."

Hockney motioned Thumps over to the Mustang. "You see anything else?"

The trunk of the car had the usual collection of junk—empty oil bottles, jumper cables, a tire iron, as well as the waders and the fishing pole—but nothing that had "clue" written on it.

"So, where's his big evidence?"

"He said it was here."

"And you believe him?" Duke motioned for his men to move the cars out of the alley. "I don't mind loyalty. And I don't even mind you snooping around. Who knows, you may find something we missed. But if you get in my way again ..." He winked and opened the door of his car. "Well, you fill in the cliché."

Thumps decided to take a run at it. "How did you know Stick was here?"

Duke let his face go blank. "Good police work."

"That's what we used to call anonymous tips, too."

"What makes you think we got an anonymous tip?"

172

"Then you're not going to arrest me?"

"Got enough bad guys already," said the sheriff. "But I wouldn't get too cheery. Andy says he's going to sue you."

The hospital looked bright with its lights on, almost festive, when Thumps pulled into the emergency entrance and parked his car in a stall that said Reserved MDs. He had called Claire from the house. There had been no time to sort out all the details. He simply told her that Stick had been injured and to meet him at the hospital. It would take her at least twenty minutes to get into town. By then, Thumps hoped he would have answers for the questions Claire was going to ask.

The first order of business was to find out if Stick was still alive.

The nurse at the desk wasn't terribly helpful. "He was just admitted. I don't have any other information."

"He was shot."

"Are you family?"

"Yes," said Thumps, knowing that the only people who were going to get any information were family members. "I'm his father."

People with children are generally willing to help other people with children. Evidently the nurse had several of her own because she got on the phone and within two minutes knew everything there was to know.

"He's in surgery."

"He's alive?"

"Yes," said the nurse. "Doctor Hoy is the surgeon."

"Is he any good?"

"She's excellent," said the nurse. "The cafeteria is still open, if you'd like to get some coffee."

"Maybe I'll just wait."

"He'll be fine," said the nurse, in a way that made Thumps sorry he had lied to her. "If I hear anything, I'll send someone to find you."

Anna had been a nurse. Thumps had met her one evening in the Mad River Hospital emergency room after a fight with a drunk had left him with a nasty knife wound on his shoulder. Anna had cleaned and dressed the wound, given him a tetanus shot, and told him to stay away from men with weapons. It was her quiet sense of humour that first attracted Thumps. And her green eyes.

Between the stitching and the needle, he found out that she was divorced with a daughter. The next day he went back to the hospital and asked her out. She said no.

"Can I call you next week?"

"It's not a good idea."

"I like the way you sew."

They started seeing each other. Slowly at first. Sometimes just the two of them, sometimes with Callie. They never talked about getting married or living together. Anna wanted her space. Space for herself. Space for Callie. It wasn't Thumps' choice. And he understood that it wasn't his decision to make.

He had been in San Diego at a forensics conference when their bodies were discovered on Clam Beach. Lying side by side in the sand. Officially they were number nine and number ten in the Obsidian Murders case. Thumps buried Anna and Callie. Then he resigned from the police force, packed his things, and headed north. Someplace away from the coast and the ocean and anything that reminded him of how miserably he had failed to protect the people he loved.

Somewhere on the road, between the numbing pain of losing everyone who mattered and suicide, he found Chinook.

The cafeteria was empty except for an old couple seated at a table by the coffee machine, staring at their hands. Thumps got a cup of coffee and a cup of green Jell-O and found a table at the far end of the room in the shadows.

The coffee was old and thick with that slightly burnt smell that coffee takes on when it's been boiled too long. Thumps was fond of green Jell-O, but while the squares in the cup moved and looked like Jell-O, the resemblance ended there. How could someone screw up Jell-O? Hot water and a refrigerator. That's all you needed. Thumps pushed the cup off to one side and went to work on the puzzle.

It had been a set-up. Someone had put Takashi's jacket in Stick's trunk and called the cops. The timing had been too good for anything else. No doubt Stick's evidence had vanished at the same time. But how did the killer know Stick was going to be at Thumps' house? Thumps doubted that anyone had been following Stick, which left only one possibility. Someone had watched his house. Someone had seen Stick arrive.

"They said I'd find you here."

Even at this hour of the night, in the harsh fluorescent lights of the cafeteria, Virginia Traynor looked elegant.

"You mind if I join you?"

"Why not?" said Thumps. "You like Jell-O?"

"You're probably wondering why I'm here."

Thumps shrugged. "You like hospitals at night."

"Are ex-policemen always so disingenuous?"

"Only when someone shoots at me."

"What?" Either the woman was surprised, or she was very good. "You were shot?"

"No," said Thumps. "Friend of mine."

"I'm sorry."

"Who are 'they?'"

"What?"

"The people who told you where to find me."

Traynor shook her head. "They said you might be at the hospital. The police, I mean. When I got to your house, there were several police officers there."

Thumps frowned.

"You were going to show me some of your photographs, Remember?" Traynor looked at her coffee. "I was in town tonight and thought I'd stop by."

Thumps waited.

"All right." Traynor pushed her hair to one side. "And I wanted to find out if you had made any progress on who killed Takashi."

"I thought you were only interested in 'why Takashi was murdered.'"

"It's the same question, don't you think?"

Thumps had to admit Traynor was right. Finding out why Takashi was killed would probably give them the killer in the same way that finding the killer would tell them why. The chicken and the egg. At this point, Thumps didn't care which came first.

"The sheriff thinks he has the man who killed Takashi."

"Your friend?"

"Stanley Merchant. Stick, to his friends. Nineteen. Passionate. A computer whiz. A general pain in the ass. Sound like a killer to you?"

Traynor smiled a sympathetic smile. "Sounds more like someone's child."

"Yeah," said Thumps, "that, too."

"You don't think he did it?"

"I know he didn't do it," said Thumps. "What I don't know is who did."

"Is there anything I can do?"

"Why? You don't know Stick." It was a cheap shot, and Thumps was sorry he had taken it.

Traynor didn't flinch. "Because I have a vested interest in finding out who did."

"All right," said Thumps. "Are you still at Shadow Ranch?"

"Yes," said Traynor. "At least for the time being."

"How about getting together tomorrow? Around noon."

"Just me?"

"Might as well make it a foursome."

"Elliot and George will be there." Traynor stood up. "You know something you're not telling."

Thumps gave the Jell-O one last shake. "Don't we all."

Actually Thumps knew nothing. As he watched Traynor walk down the corridor, he reminded himself that everything he knew for sure dead-ended with Stick. What he needed to find out was what Stick had discovered that had seemed so important. And from the look of things, that wasn't going to happen any time soon.

It took Claire just under half an hour to get the hospital. Thumps was waiting for her in the lobby.

"What happened?"

176

"Stick was shot."

Claire looked at Thumps' face, not wanting to ask the next question.

"No, so far as I know, he's not dead."

"Who?"

"The police."

Claire sat on the couch, her body stiff. "Were you there?"

Thumps had hoped Claire wouldn't ask that question. "Stick was at my house when I got home."

"You called the police?" There was rage in Claire's voice now.

"No," said Thumps quickly. "The police got an anonymous tip. Someone set him up."

"Oh, God."

"They found Takashi's leather jacket in the trunk of his Mustang. Hockney is convinced that Stick killed both Takashi and Floyd."

"Don't let him die." The rage was gone. There was nothing in Claire's voice now but desperation.

Dr. Hoy was a slender woman with close-cropped hair. Thumps tried to read her body language as she came down the hall, but all it told him was that she was exhausted.

"Mr. and Mrs. Merchant?"

Thumps nodded and hoped that Claire was too distraught to notice. "How is he?"

"He's in critical condition."

He could feel Claire tighten against him.

"The bullet fragmented badly. It took us a while to remove all the pieces."

"It hit bone?"

"No," said the doctor, "just tissue damage." But her mind seemed to be elsewhere.

Thumps tried to read her eyes. "But?"

"It was just odd," said the doctor. "The amount of damage. The bullet breaking up like that."

"Breaking up?"

"It split into several fragments."

Thumps could feel the first stirrings of real anger. No, he thought, it's not odd at all.

"When can I see him?" asked Claire.

"He's in recovery. You have to understand that he's sustained a tremendous amount of trauma." The doctor stopped there and left the rest of the prognosis hanging.

Claire turned pale. "Is he in a coma?"

"We don't know. His vital signs are good. He's young. We'll know more in forty-eight hours."

"Isn't that what they say on those television hospital shows?" said Thumps.

The doctor managed a tired smile. "Yes," she said. "I guess they do."

"Can I sit with him?"

Doctor Hoy nodded. "It can't hurt. Come on. I'll show you where he is."

Claire turned back to Thumps. "I have to see him."

"Go ahead," he said. "I have some business to take care of."

As soon as Claire and the doctor had disappeared, Thumps went back to the front desk. The same nurse was still there.

"How's your son?"

"Not too good," said Thumps.

"I'm so sorry."

"There was a policeman who was injured. His ankle, I think. He's a friend," Thumps added quickly."

"Oh, yes," said the nurse. "Officer Hopper. It was just a bad sprain. I'm afraid you've just missed him."

Not for long, thought Thumps as he pushed his way through the double doors and headed to his car. Not for long.

Nineteen

The lights were still on at the sheriff's office. Andy Hopper was sitting in a chair with his bad leg elevated, wrapped with a Tensor bandage, and packed in ice. Hockney was behind his desk sorting through files.

"Well, if it isn't the big chief," said Andy, grinning that nasty grin he had. "Hope you can afford a good lawyer."

Grin away, thought Thumps, as he crossed the room without breaking stride and kicked the chair out from under the deputy. It was Andy's lucky day. His face kept his brain from hitting the floor.

"Jesus!" Duke was out of his seat, but Thumps knew the sheriff was too slow to stop him. Andy wasn't. Thumps had surprised him, but the deputy recovered quickly, rolled over on his side, and went for his gun. Which was what Thumps was hoping he would do. Andy got the revolver clear of the holster just as Thumps stomped down on his hand. Thumps didn't enjoy inflicting pain any more than he enjoyed receiving it, but in Hopper's case, he was willing to make an exception.

"Goddammit, Thumps!" Duke was out from behind his desk now.

Thumps twisted the gun out of Andy's hand and jammed the barrel under the deputy's left ear.

"Whoa. Now hold on, Thumps," said the sheriff. "You don't want to do that."

"Shoot the sonofabitch," screamed Andy, whose hand was still pinned under Thumps' foot.

"Shut up, Andy!" yelled Duke. "Now Thumps, let's put the gun down." Thumps cocked the hammer. "Sheriff, I need a little clarification. If I were to shoot your deputy with this gun, what kind of a hole do you think it would make?"

"Thumps, you're not thinking straight."

"What kind of a hole?"

"Shoot him!"

"Thumps, I know you're upset, but it wasn't Andy's fault Stanley's getting hurt like that."

There was a telephone book on Andy's desk. It wasn't as thick as Thumps would have liked, but it would have to do. "Throw it on the floor!"

"What?"

"The phone book. Throw it on the floor!"

"Come on, Thumps, this is getting way out of hand."

"What's standard issue for your department, sheriff?"

"What?"

"Standard issue. Police standard issue."

"Thirty-eight," said Duke. "Look, I'm tossing the phone book on the floor. Okay? Let's just all calm down and stop talking crazy."

"Not guns," shouted Thumps. "Bullets. What kind of bullets?"

"What?"

Thumps lowered the muzzle of the gun and fired a single shot into the phone book. "What kind of hole?"

The sheriff didn't move for a moment. "You're not going to shoot me, are you, Thumps?"

"No," said Thumps, softly and he flipped the phone book over with his foot. "I'm not going to shoot anyone."

The hole in the front of the phone book was small and neat. But the back of the phone book was gone, as if it had been blown away. Thumps cracked the cylinder and let the last bullet drop into his hand. He looked at it for a minute and tossed it to Duke. "This standard issue?"

The bullet had an X cut into its soft lead nose. A dumdum round. A round designed to kill, to expand on contact and tear a man apart.

Duke turned the bullet over in his hand. "Sonofabitch."

Thumps took his foot off Andy's hand.

The deputy struggled to his feet. "It's a setup," he shouted. "I don't use dumdums."

Duke glared at Andy. "Who said anything about dumdums?"

"You hope I got a good lawyer?" Thumps set his feet in case Andy wanted to try for round two. "That boy dies and you'll be chin-deep in lawyers."

"Screw you!" Andy was rubbing his hand and trying to balance on one foot all at the same time.

"Shut up, Andy!" The sheriff looked at the bullet in his hand. "You wouldn't be threatening me, would you, Thumps?"

"Nope."

"This could disappear."

"I'll take my chances," said Thumps, and he tossed Andy's gun to the sheriff.

"You know," said Duke, "you're not making many friends."

"It's okay," said Thumps. "I have more than I need."

Duke nodded and glanced at Andy. "What do you expect me to do about him?"

"He's your dog," said Thumps. "He's not mine."

Thumps didn't get his heart rate back to normal until he got in his car. Charging into the sheriff's office like that had been a singularly stupid thing to do. The sheriff could have shot him. Or Thumps might not have been as fast as he thought he was, in which case Andy would have shot him. Andy might still shoot him, once his ankle healed and his hand stopped hurting. But Thumps didn't think so. Hopper was that special kind of bully who didn't like to play with anyone his own size. He'd already had his chance at the house. He wasn't going to try again. Not right away.

Thumps knew that he should have been arrested, at the very least. Threatening an officer. Assaulting an officer and causing bodily harm. Discharging a firearm in a reckless manner. Public mischief. Disturbing the peace. The choices were endless. But the sheriff wasn't going to do that. He had been blindsided by his deputy, and he didn't like it. If Thumps was any judge of character, Duke was probably more inclined to throw Andy in jail for impersonating an officer.

Not that throwing Andy anywhere was going to help.

Finding Takashi's jacket in Stick's car wasn't going to help either. If Stick was telling the truth, someone had planted it there. And if Stick was telling the truth about having something incriminating in his trunk, it was probably long gone. An added bonus for the killer. Frame the chief suspect and recover whatever evidence Stick had. But what the hell was it? What had Stick found that might point the investigation in a different direction? And how had the killer known what to look for? More to the point, when did the killer plant the jacket in Stick's trunk? It hadn't been there when Thumps checked the trunk at the trailhead. Someone could have followed Stick to his mother's house, but that was improbable. He hadn't been there long enough.

Which left the alley behind Thumps' house. It had to be that. The killer must have staked out Thumps' house on the chance that Stick would eventually show up there. The rest would have been easy. Plant the jacket. Get lucky and find the evidence at the same time. Call the sheriff and drop him a hint about where Stick could be found.

As Thumps turned the corner, it suddenly occurred to him that he had been following the wrong trail. He had spent most of his time trying to reconstruct what had happened to Takashi. Maybe he should have been following Stick.

Okay, Stick had gone to the complex on Saturday in time to find Takashi's body. He had moved the body to the condos, headed into the mountains, and stayed there Saturday night. He had showed up at his mother's house on Tuesday night and at Thumps' place on Wednesday night.

So where had he been the rest of the time? Where had he gone after he left the mountains? Where had he gone after he left his mother's place? He certainly hadn't been holed up in Thumps' basement for more than a few hours because there was still food left in the refrigerator. He had to eat. He had to sleep. He had to have a safe house. A place to work from, as he tried to play the hero.

Of course. The answer was so clear that Thumps couldn't believe he hadn't thought of it before now. Taking photographs might have sharpened his creative eye, but it had evidently dulled his analytic senses.

· · ·

Moses Blood was sitting on an old lawn chair taking in the early sun when Thumps pulled up in front of his trailer the next morning.

"Been expecting you," said Moses, and he poured a second cup of coffee from the stainless steel thermos.

"We have to talk."

"I'd like that."

"About Stick."

"Claire's boy."

"That night I came by. Was Stick here?"

"Oh, yes," said Moses. "He was staying in the Airstream."

"Why didn't you tell me?"

"You didn't ask."

Thumps cradled the coffee cup in his hands. "Stick's been shot."

Moses sat back in the chair and looked off at the sunrise.

"He's not dead, but he was hurt bad," said Thumps. "He told me he had evidence that would prove who killed Takashi."

"Ah," said Moses. "That must be the disk."

"Disk?"

"You know, one of those C Ds."

So, that's what Stick had found. A computer disk. Not that the answer was going to do any good, now. Thumps was almost afraid to ask the next question. "Did Stick leave the disk with you?"

"Nope," said Moses, "he took it with him."

Thumps leaned forward and put his face in his hands.

"You don't look too good," said Moses.

"I'm just tired," said Thumps.

"You going to help Stanley?"

"Not much I can do," said Thumps. "Without the disk, we don't have anything."

"Boy," said Moses, "good thing we made a copy."

It took a moment for Moses' words to register. "You have a copy?"

"Sure. They're easy to make if you have the right equipment." Moses stood up and headed for the maze of trailers behind his house. "People bring their old trailers by and leave them with me because they don't have the heart to kill them."

"What do you do with them?"

"Give them a place to live."

Thumps knew better than to argue with Moses. And he supposed that if he were a trailer, he'd like to be dropped off here rather than dumped into a junkyard and crushed into an aluminum brick.

Although Thumps tried to keep track of all the twists and turns, he suspected that he would have difficulty finding his way back. The farther they moved into the trailers, the more Moses began to look like a white rabbit and the more Thumps began to feel like Alice.

One of the trailers had a Radioactive Material sticker on its front door.

"Here we are," said Moses, taking out a set of keys.

"Radioactive?"

"It used to be one of those mobile X-ray stations," said Moses.

"No kidding."

"It's harmless now."

The outside of the trailer was ordinary enough. White aluminum with red trim.

But nothing prepared Thumps for what was inside.

"This is yours?"

"No," said Moses. "The band needed someplace to store their old computers."

The inside of the trailer was one long table of electronic equipment—computers, monitors, printers, scanners—twinkling and winking in the dark, all hooked together by a web of wires. More computers and computer parts were stacked against the far wall.

"That Stanley is pretty handy," said Moses.

"Stanley did this?"

"My grandmother could talk to animals." Moses pushed a button and one of the monitors flashed to life. "Stanley can talk to these machines."

"You know how to work this stuff?"

"Sure. Stanley showed me how." Moses pressed another button and a plastic tray slid out of one of the machines. "It's not hard once you under-stand how the Nephews think."

"The Nephews?"

Moses waved his hand over the computers. "They're just like little kids. They like to repeat everything you tell them."

Thumps shook his head. He could barely turn on a computer, and here was Moses Blood, one of the more traditional men on the reserve, sitting in front of a seventeen-inch monitor giving him lessons on computer protocol.

"Some people are suspicious of computers because we didn't have them in the good old days."

"Nobody went buffalo hunting with a laptop."

"That's right," said Moses. "But it's best to be up-to-date. Even in the good old days, the smartest Indians were the ones who were up-to-date."

"You said you made a copy of the disk."

Moses nodded and worked the mouse. The screen went blank for a second, and then came up all bright and cheery. "Here it comes."

Suddenly the screen was filled with long lines of numbers. Row after row of numbers. Ones and zeros.

"That's it?"

"That's it."

Thumps watched the numbers scroll up the screen, hoping that at some point he would see something that resembled words. "Nothing but numbers?"

"It's a program," said Moses. "You don't have to use words to write a program."

"Great."

"These machines are smart. You give them a bunch of numbers, and they understand what you want them to do."

"Do you know what kind of a program this is?"

"Nope," said Moses. "Stanley was talking things over with the computers, but he had to leave before they finished their conversation."

Thumps sat back and sighed.

"I can make you a copy if you like."

"Sure."

"We have some pretty good conversations about easy stuff like the weather and where to take a vacation. I can ask them how much it's going to cost me to fly to Calgary for the big powwow. And we can discuss the stock market." Moses worked the keyboard for a moment. "But I don't know their language well enough yet to ask them what this disk is trying to tell us."

Thumps watched while Moses burned a copy of the program,

marvelling at the skill with which the old man managed the keyboard. It was almost as if the computers in the room knew who he was, almost as if they liked him.

"Here you go." Moses handed Thumps a disk. "You tell Claire I hope her boy gets well soon."

Thumps had to give Stick credit. The computer system he and Moses had cobbled together from parts was impressive.

"Are you hooked up to the Internet?"

"You bet," said Moses. "We can go anywhere in the world. The other day I went to a really nice resort in Costa Rica."

"I don't need a vacation."

"Everybody needs a vacation."

"I need information."

"Sure," said Moses. "That's why they call it the information highway."

Thumps found a pen and a piece of paper. "See what you can find out about this company."

"Spy stuff," said Moses, looking at the paper. "Magnum PI does spy stuff. And you know what?"

"What?"

"He always gets his sidekick to do the computer work."

Moses closed and locked the door to the trailer, and the two men made their way back to where Thumps' car was parked.

"That's one of the good things about computers."

"What's that?"

Moses looked up at the sky. "They don't shoot people."

True enough, thought Thumps. Nonetheless, two men were dead, and a young man was lying in a hospital bed, and Thumps couldn't help but feel that he might be holding the reason for the murders in his hand.

Twenty

Thumps slapped his face and sang songs as he drove back into town. With only moderate success. It had been a very long night, and unless the tide turned in a hurry, it was going to be an even longer day. Outside of sleep, the only thing that was going to keep him awake and aware was food. And coffee. Lots of it.

Thumps turned the disk over in his hand and let the sun glint off the surface. The pessimist in him suspected that it contained nothing more than a word-processing program. Or an Internet something. Or a game.

Al's was full. Thumps leaned up against the wall along with the four other people waiting for a seat.

"Go home and go to bed." Al stood behind the counter with her hands on her hips.

"Morning."

"You look like hell."

"I'm hungry, too."

"Hear you made friends with Andy."

Thumps couldn't tell whether Al approved or disapproved. Not that it mattered.

"Heard about Stanley, too."

Maybe his luck was changing. The four people in front of him were waiting together for one of the two booths large enough to hold them, and Mike Decter, who ran the Shell station, was just leaving his seat at the counter. Thumps climbed on the stool, dropped his head into his hands, and waited for the coffee to arrive.

"The usual?"

"Please."

He wasn't sure he had the energy to lift the cup, so he sat slumped over and let the coffee fumes rise up and wash over his face.

"Looks more like depression than exhaustion."

"Could I get a little extra salsa?"

"Salsa isn't going to help depression."

Thumps looked out from under his hands and watched Al amble back to the grill. Maybe she was right. Maybe he was depressed. Claire had asked him to help find Stick, and he had helped get Stick shot. Sure, it wasn't really his fault, but depression wasn't a rational emotion—if it was an emotion at all.

The coffee was starting to work its magic, and Thumps could feel his eyes begin to focus. By the time the food arrived, most of his intuitive faculties were back on-line.

"You solve the case yet?"

"That's the sheriff's job."

"Can't take pictures all your life."

Thumps couldn't remember Al's breakfast ever tasting better. The hash browns were particularly delicious, crisp and buttery, as though Al had made them especially for him.

"You feeling better?"

"Much."

"So, you know who killed that Asian guy yet?"

"Nope."

"How about Floyd?"

"Don't know that either."

Al picked up the coffee cup and ran the rag across the counter. "Floyd was here, you know."

Thumps tried not to sound too interested. "Floyd's got good taste."

"Morning he died."

"Oh, yeah."

"He had a big stack of pancakes, full order of sausage, toast, and two large glasses of orange juice."

"He must have been hungry."

"He was always hungry. But that day he was happy, too." Al leaned a hip against the counter. "And there are only two things in the whole world that would make Floyd Small Elk happy."

Thumps didn't need Al to tell him what was at the top of Floyd's "happy" list. "What's the second thing?"

"More of the first," she said.

Thumps smiled. "He say where he was getting the money?"

"Not a word," said Al. "But the whole time he was working on the pancakes and the sausages, you could see him spending it."

That made sense. If Floyd's death was tied to Takashi's murder—and Thumps was willing to bet the ranch that it was—then there were only two reasons for the second killing. Either Floyd knew something, or he had been able to convince the murderer that he did. Floyd had tried to sell Thumps information on Takashi. There was no reason to believe that he hadn't offered it to the murderer as well.

But Thumps was sure that Floyd had not yet connected the dots when they had talked at the limo garage. Was it possible that Thumps had said something to Floyd that put him on the right track? Or had Floyd just figured things out on his own?

Two murders and a shooting, and the only leverage that Thumps had was a disk that no one could read. If he had a Plan B, now would be a good time to break it out.

When Thumps got to Shadow Ranch, Virginia Traynor and Elliot Beaumont were already waiting for him in the coffee shop.

"Mr. DreadfulWater." Beaumont stood up and stuck out his hand, as if he were playing the part of a banker in a romantic comedy. "Good to see you again."

Thumps took Beaumont's hand. It felt like a piece of polished marble. Thumps wondered what the man had to do to get his skin to feel like stone. "Sorry I'm late."

"You're not late," said Traynor, and she turned to Beaumont. "You did tell George about this meeting."

"Talked to him last night," said Beaumont.

Traynor signalled the server. "You hungry?"

Thumps shook his head. It would have been a travesty to eat anything while Al's breakfast was still entertaining his stomach.

"I was hoping to make use of Mr. Chan's computer expertise," he said.

Traynor was quick and direct. "What have you found?"

Thumps took the disk from his jacket and laid it on the table.

"A disk?" Beaumont picked it up and turned it over. "Where'd you get it?"

Thumps took a deep breath. It was time to run the bluff. "Actually, Stick found it. At Buffalo Mountain Resort."

"Stick?" Beaumont frowned.

"Stanley Merchant," said Thumps, watching Beaumont's face. "He's the one who found Takashi's body."

"But I thought a ... real estate woman found the body." Beaumont looked puzzled. If he was faking, he was doing a good job.

"Stanley was the leader of a group known as the Red Hawks. They were opposed to the casino."

Beaumont nodded as if he agreed with Thumps. "So this Stick killed Daniel."

"That isn't what you're telling us," said Traynor, "is it?"

The server came by with coffee. Thumps waited until she had left. "No. Stick didn't kill Takashi. Takashi was already dead. Stick just moved the body to the condo."

Beaumont settled back in his seat. "Do you know what's on the disk?"

Thumps took a deep breath. Here was the tricky part. Lie or tell the truth? "No," said Thumps, deciding on the truth. "Not yet."

"And you were hoping that George could tell you," said Traynor.

"Takashi was worried about the computer being sabotaged," said Beaumont. "Maybe this is it."

"No," said Thumps. "Stick didn't have a chance to do anything." There was nothing to do now but run the bluff all the way to the end. "I think this is what got Takashi killed."

Thumps thought he detected a nervous twitch pass Beaumont's lips.

Traynor put her napkin on the table and nodded. "Then we'd better talk with George."

Thumps picked up the disk. "Maybe I should just give this to the sheriff, and let him figure it out."

"Let's do both," said Traynor. "Give George a crack at it. If he can figure out what it is, it'll save the sheriff some work."

"But you did look at it." There was more than curiosity in Beaumont voice.

"Yes."

"And?"

"It didn't make any sense to me," said Thumps. "It was all ones and zeros."

"Then showing it to George isn't going to help," said Beaumont.

Traynor nodded. "Elliot's right. What you saw was machine language. Most programs are written in what is called source code, which consists of a series of text commands. However, once the program is written and tested, it's converted into a kind of numerical sequence called machine language. Machine language is impossible to read."

"Can't you translate machine language?"

"Yes. But you have to know in what program language the program was originally written. And even then it's difficult."

"But Chan could do it?"

"Any skilled computer programmer could do it," said Beaumont. "But Virginia's correct. You would have to know the source code language to have any hope of success."

"Of course, we may be chasing rabbits," said Traynor. "Daniel was programming the computer. The disk you have may be no more than a program that controls the odds on the slot machines or the sequencing of the security cameras or the text on the digital signs."

"Doesn't sound promising," said Thumps, turning the disk over in his hand.

"Let's talk to George anyway," said Traynor, sliding out of her seat and looking at her watch. "It can't hurt to ask."

The day had gone to clouds, and the air was cool enough to breathe. In the distance, against the mountains, Thumps could see the faint flash of lightning strikes, and he could feel the sky begin to stir. All around the resort, tourists would be searching for their umbrellas, but Thumps knew that there would be no rain. Just the illusion of rain. And a hot wind.

"How much do computer programmers make?" asked Thumps, as they walked up the path to the condos.

"It depends," said Traynor. "You thinking about changing jobs?"

"Actually," said Beaumont, "we try not to talk about salaries."

"That much?"

"No," said Traynor. "We don't talk about salaries because of the competition. The world of computer technology and technical services is a nasty place. If a company knew how much we were paying our top people, they'd try to buy them off."

"And if our top people knew what other folks made," said Beaumont, "they'd want to be paid at least as much."

"It's like sports," said Traynor. "You pay for your stars and try to keep the ball away from the other team."

Somehow Thumps couldn't picture Virginia in shorts and a jersey, running the court, splitting the defence, and floating to the hoop for a one-hand jam. She was more the private-box, big-screen-television, catered-food type. But that was the beauty of metaphors. They only existed in the imagination.

"So, who got paid more? Takashi or Chan?"

"I'm afraid that's confidential," said Beaumont.

"Doesn't matter to Takashi."

George Chan had the same kind of luxury townhouse that Daniel Takashi had had. All things considered, Thumps had to admit that he had probably made some questionable career choices.

Beaumont knocked on the door.

"What's a place like this rent for?"

"About three hundred," said Traynor. "You interested in another round of golf?"

There was no answer. "George. It's me, Elliot."

"When?'"

"Opening ceremonies for the resort are on Saturday. We're doing a full-scale test of the computer that day. Some time after that."

Thumps wasn't sure that watching a computer do anything would be exciting, but there was a bounce in Traynor's voice that resembled enthusiasm.

"George!" Beaumont knocked again, hard this time. And the door tipped open.

Thumps forgot about computers and high-priced hotel rooms and stepped in front of the man, pushing him back.

"Hey!"

Thumps quickly moved to one side, eased the door open all the way, and waited for his eyes to adjust. "George! It's Thumps DreadfulWater."

Beaumont moved impatiently behind him. "He probably went to the coffee shop and just missed us. I'll go back and get him."

"No," said Thumps. "He's not in the coffee shop."

Traynor stepped in against his shoulder. "What's wrong?"

"You two stay here."

"Bit melodramatic, don't you think?" said Beaumont. "I'm not sure George would want us going into his place."

George Chan wasn't going to mind anyone coming into his townhouse. Almost as soon as Thumps opened the door, he could smell the sharp stench of death. He took two quick steps into the room. George Chan was lying next to the sofa, his body splayed out on the floor, the side of his head blown away. On the floor beside him was a gun.

Beaumont froze. "My God!"

Thumps took one more step into the room, just to be sure. But there was no mistake. George's suit jacket had fallen open when the man hit the floor, and Thumps could see the label clearly. Brioni.

"Back out," said Thumps, taking out his handkerchief. "And don't touch anything."

"What are we supposed to do?"

"We call the sheriff," said Thumps, and he stepped out of the room into the sunlight, laid the handkerchief gently over the knob, and shut the door behind him.

Twenty-One

Hockney didn't waste any time getting to Shadow Ranch. Andy Hopper was not with him, and while Thumps was curious about the deputy, he wasn't willing to press his luck. So far he had been at the scene of three murders and a shooting. Sooner or later, Hockney was going to notice.

"You found Chan?"

"It was a group effort." Thumps looked at Traynor for support.

"That's right, sheriff," she said. "Elliot and Mr. DreadfulWater and I came here to talk to George."

"About what?"

"He was supposed to meet us in the coffee shop," said Elliot.

"Why?"

Duke was asking all the right questions, and Thumps guessed that the sheriff knew he wasn't getting any answers. No one had mentioned the disk. It was almost as if the three of them had each decided independently to leave that piece of information alone for the time being. Thumps knew what his reasons were. He wondered what reasons Traynor and Beaumont had decided on.

"You need me anymore?"

"Why? You got somewhere to go?"

"Want to stop off at the hospital and see Stick."

"You know, you got a real knack for this."

Thumps shrugged. The sheriff didn't know how right he was.

"Walk with me," said Duke.

The sheriff followed the stone path that ran above the swimming pool and vanished into the prairies. Thumps wasn't sure where Duke was going, but he knew there was no point in asking. The sheriff didn't stop until he got to the edge of the bluff overlooking the river.

"What do you suppose we found back in the room?"

He had a good idea, but the sheriff had earned the pleasure of explaining to Thumps what he already knew.

"Suicide note."

"No kidding?"

"On the guy's laptop." The sheriff pulled the brim of his hat over his eyes and looked down at his boots. "You know what it said?"

"No idea."

"I thought you might have looked when you were in the room."

"We didn't stay."

"But you saw the gun."

"Yeah."

"That was a nice surprise, too."

"Same calibre as the gun that killed Takashi and Floyd?"

"We did some checking," said Duke. "Chan didn't arrive with Beaumont and Traynor. He got here two days earlier. Did either of them mention that to you?"

No, Thumps thought, but Floyd had told him, if Thumps had been listening. That day at the garage. A couple more showed up, that's what Floyd had said. Beaumont and Traynor. Not Chan. Because Chan was already here.

"Looks like you've got it wrapped up."

"I'm the best." The sheriff looked at Thumps expectantly.

"You've got no argument with me," said Thumps.

"That's what the note said. 'I'm the best.' Now what do you suppose that means?"

"Professional jealousy?"

"People kill people for less."

"Works for me."

"You like it because it gets Stick off the hook." Duke rubbed his hands together. "How's he doing?"

"He's in a coma."

"Shit."

"So how do you figure Chan got in and out of the resort without Cooley seeing him?"

"There you go doing that dumb Indian routine again," said the sheriff.

"You think Chan was in the camper van?"

"Don't you? We did some checking and found that Takashi rented one of those camper vans every weekend. Evidently, he liked sightseeing. Anyway, he picks up the van, and he and Chan go to Buffalo Mountain. Chan hangs out in the back, so Cooley doesn't see him."

"It could work."

"I'm not asking why Stick was at the computer complex," said the sheriff, looking at Thumps, "but you're going to tell me, aren't you?"

"It's not important."

"Of course if I wanted to find out ..." Duke let the threat hang in the air.

Thumps didn't think the sheriff was looking for a reason to charge Stick with anything, but if Duke was still angry about what his deputy had done, making Stick partly responsible for being in a coma might help spread the guilt around.

"Lot of people on the reserve have problems with the casino. Maybe it was something like that."

Duke reached down and broke off a piece of brown prairie grass. "So, Chan kills Takashi because he's jealous of the man's success or because he wants his job. And to throw suspicion off him and shift it somewhere else, he paints 'Red Hawks' on the wall. Stick arrives, finds Takashi dead, sees the writing on the wall, and figures the frame right away. You can join in whenever you like."

"You're doing great."

"Screw you, DreadfulWater."

"No, I mean it."

"We found the paint roller in the dumpster in the garage, along with Takashi's wallet and the rags Stick used to wipe up the blood." Duke paused for a moment and picked at the corner of his eye. "Now why do you suppose Stick would take Takashi's wallet?"

"Guess you'll have to ask Stick."

"I figure he did it to buy time." Duke shoved his hands in his pockets.

"The one thing Chan didn't count on was Stick's showing up and ruining the frame."

"Sounds perfect."

"Except Chan has to get away without being seen."

"The camper van."

"Yeah," said the sheriff. "This is the part I like. Now, I'm not going to be the one to say they all look alike, but I'm betting that that's exactly what Chan was counting on. He trades jackets with Takashi, puts on Takashi's dark glasses and cap, and drives out the front gate. Cooley lets one Asian computer programmer in. He lets one Asian computer programmer out."

"And Cooley doesn't notice that it's not the same man?"

"Why should he? The people at the car rental office didn't."

"Chan returned the van?"

"Saturday afternoon," said Hockney. "Had to be him."

"And Stick hikes out of the resort?"

"Nothing to it. If you know the mountains."

Duke knew more than Thumps would have given him credit for. Maybe he had figured it all out.

"You think Chan was watching my place?"

"Why not? Soon as Stick shows up, Chan plants the jacket in Stick's car and calls us."

"And Floyd?"

"Somehow Floyd figured things out, and Chan had to kill him."

"I'm impressed," said Thumps.

"No, you're not," said Duke. "But you should be."

Thumps looked back toward Shadow Ranch. "What are you going to do now?"

"Retire to Hawaii," said the sheriff. "Assholes like Andy make this job harder than it needs to be."

Thumps waited in the coffee shop until the police were finished taking Traynor's and Beaumont's statements.

"Thank you for sticking around," said Traynor.

"Where's Elliot?'"

"In his room. He doesn't handle stress very well."

"Looks like he's in the wrong business."

"We normally don't shoot each other."

Thumps' stomach began growling, and he realized that, with all the excitement, he had missed lunch.

"Are you hungry?" Traynor signaled a waiter before Thumps had a chance to lie. "Steak sandwich sound good to you? My treat." She settled back in the chair. "Nasty little drama, wasn't it?"

"Did you know that Chan and Takashi hated each other?"

"We brought Daniel and George into the company at about the same time. Both men were talented. Daniel got the promotions."

"But Chan thought he should have got them?"

"Evidently."

"Why was Chan out here?"

"What do you mean?"

"Takashi was already here. He knew how to program and test the computer. Why did he need Chan?"

"Ah," said Traynor. "The sheriff may be satisfied, but you're not."

"Loose ends are always annoying."

"Daniel was worried about the Red Hawks. He thought they might try to do something to the computer system. George's specialty was computer security. He was a genius when it came to things like viruses and worms, anything that could crash a system. We sent him out as a precaution."

"The hired gun?"

"If you like. Why?"

"When did he arrive?"

"You'd have to ask Elliot," said Traynor, "but I think he got here the Thursday before Daniel was killed."

The steak sandwich arrived, and the conversation moved away from Buffalo Mountain and slipped into a string of pleasantries about golf and life in the west.

Thumps was finishing up the last of the French fries when Traynor's cellphone went off.

"That was Elliot."

"How's he feeling?"

"Better."

"You guys still staying for the grand opening?"

"Absolutely. Now that everything's cleared up, we might as well enjoy the rest of the trip. You wouldn't be interested in showing me around, would you?"

"What about Elliot?"

"He can find his own Indian."

There was a great deal about Traynor that reminded Thumps of Claire. A tough woman in a tough world. He wondered how she would have managed if her son had been shot.

"You don't seem very happy. Do you think the sheriff missed something?"

"Duke's pretty thorough."

"That sounds like a loose end."

Thumps could feel the disk riding in his pocket. "Why do you think Chan killed himself?"

Traynor shrugged. "He didn't want to get caught."

"No one knew he did it."

"You knew."

"No, I didn't. All I knew was that Stick didn't kill anyone."

"Maybe you were getting too close. Maybe George believed that it was just a matter of time before you or the sheriff put the pieces together."

Maybe, maybe, maybe. "Why not run?"

"George was proud." Traynor looked out the window. "He liked expensive things. Maybe he saw that world slipping away."

"He kills two people and then gets depressed?"

"People kill themselves for a lot less."

Thumps put his napkin on the table. "I better get back. I'm glad things worked out for you."

"Yes," said Traynor. "I guess they did."

Thumps took the disk out of his pocket and looked at it.

"What are you going to do with that?"

"Don't know," he said. "Should give it to Duke, but if I do, he's going to yell at me."

"Curious about what's on it?"

"Aren't you?"

"Very," said Traynor. "If you want, you can leave it with me and I'll get one of our guys back at our office to decipher it."

Thumps turned the disk over a couple of times in his hand. "Why didn't you tell the sheriff about the disk?"

"That was your call."

"Maybe I'll hang onto it for a while."

"Suit yourself." Traynor stood up and straightened her skirt. "What about golf?"

Thumps shook his head. "I'm probably going to be busy for the next couple of days."

"Pity," she said. "And just as I was beginning to enjoy the wide open spaces."

The wind was up. The cloud cover had been blown east, and the land was once again awash in sunlight. Some people lived for sunshine, wasted their vacations in places where there was nothing to do but lie in the sun. Even with all the warnings about the holes in the ozone and the damaging effects of sunlight and the real possibilities of skin cancer, humans continued to stampede to the sunny places in the world like a herd of lemmings looking for a cliff.

Thumps opened the door to the Volvo. It was a credit to Swedish engineering that the car hadn't melted by now. From the parking lot, he could see Sheriff Hockney's sport-utility and the police cruisers parked by the reception area. Duke would be putting the finishing touches on the case about now, closing the file, and moving on to the new crime of the week.

Hockney was right. All the pieces fit. Everything made sense. Chan had most certainly killed Takashi. The second cup of coffee had been for him. Chan had painted "Red Hawks" on the wall of the computer complex. Chan had killed Floyd. And Chan had planted the jacket in Stick's Mustang.

The only question that Thumps didn't have an answer for yet was who had killed Chan.

Twenty-Two

Of course, Thumps wasn't sure Chan hadn't killed himself, but the man's death made everything else much too neat. From what Thumps had seen of the room, it could well have been a suicide. Duke would check Chan's hand for powder residue. He'd look at the blood splatter patterns. He'd probably even consider the position of the gun. If Chan hadn't killed himself, someone went to a lot of trouble to make it look as though he had. And if Chan had been murdered, then whatever the killings had been about was still in play.

On the other hand, Thumps had nothing to offer to prove another murder. Duke had pieced the case together rather handily. And there was little that Thumps disagreed with. As soon as the jacket showed up in Stick's car, Thumps knew that Chan had to be involved. How else could someone get in and out of the resort with a vehicle and not raise Cooley's suspicions? As far as Cooley was concerned, his account of that morning was accurate. An Asian man in an Indian Motorcycle Company jacket, dark glasses, and a 49ers cap drove a camper van through the front gates, and an Asian man in an Indian Motorcycle Company jacket, dark glasses, and a 49ers cap drove the same vehicle out.

And while professional jealousy had something to recommend it as a motive, the timing made little sense. If Chan wanted to kill Takashi, why not do it in New Jersey, where murder was rumoured to be a demonstration sport and where the list of possible suspects would be endless? Why fly into a strange town, drive to a strange resort, kill someone, and then try to blame it on a small group of Indian activists? Of course, the killing could have been a spur-of-the-moment act. Takashi and Chan in the same room. Takashi says something that sets Chan off. Chan kills Takashi, panics, and sees the Red Hawks as his way out. But impulse killings are generally messy. Takashi had been killed neatly. So had Floyd.

For that matter, so had Chan.

When Thumps got back to the hospital, Moses Blood was sitting in the chair by the side of Stick's bed.

"You in charge?"

"You bet," said Moses.

"How is he?"

"He's keeping us guessing."

"Has he regained consciousness yet?"

"Nope," said Moses, "but I've been telling him jokes to keep his spirits up."

Stick had a tube in his arm and one that went up his nose. Thumps could barely look at the boy without wincing.

"I sent Claire to the cafeteria. She hasn't eaten all day."

"You okay here?"

"Sure," said Moses. "But you could bring back a doughnut."

"What kind do you want?"

"Something with chocolate on it. Those ones are Stanley's favourites."

Claire was sitting in a corner by herself, her hands wrapped around a cup of coffee.

"Moses thinks you're eating."

Claire didn't even try to smile.

"It looks as though they've caught Takashi's killer."

She nodded. "The sheriff called."

"He's dropping the charges against Stick."

"Bastards."

Thumps couldn't argue with that. While the sheriff had done his job reasonably well, letting someone like Andy Hopper carry a badge and a gun was a fundamental error in judgement, the kind of error that didn't make up for all the times you were right.

"He came to you for help." Claire's voice was low and controlled, but Thumps could hear the accusation.

"I didn't shoot him."

"He came to you for help."

"And I didn't tell him to sabotage the computer."

"He's a boy!"

Thumps had two options. He could play the bad guy and take the blame, or he could stand his ground. The smart move would have been to let Claire take out her anger and frustration on him. But it had been a long night and a long day, and while Stick did not deserve to be lying in a hospital bed, Thumps had little interest in protecting Claire from her son's mistakes.

"He may die."

"He's not going to die," said Thumps. "And there's no point in blaming yourself."

"I don't."

"Then don't blame me."

Claire pulled her shoulders up around her neck and stared at her coffee cup. There was no give in the woman.

"We have to talk," he said.

"There's nothing to talk about."

"This isn't about us. It's about the resort."

"I have to get back to Stick."

"Damn it, Claire, if you have to blame someone, blame Stick. No one told him to go to the complex. No one told him to move the body. And no one told him to run. Not you. Not me."

Claire's eyes flashed and she stood up. "Go to hell!" She brushed by him without looking back.

That went well, Thumps thought, as he sat at the table. All the bedside manners of a doctor. He couldn't blame Claire for being upset, but getting her more upset had not been the smart thing to do. He still had to talk to her, only now he was going to have to make amends before he could get any answers.

The special on the blackboard was meat loaf. Thumps got a serving of that, with potatoes and gravy, and a piece of pumpkin pie. He had seen a show on television where a doctor had done years of research to find out what kinds of smells men and women found attractive. One sex liked the smells of licorice allsorts and cucumbers, while the other preferred lavender and pumpkin pie. But Thumps couldn't remember which was which. He hoped that it was women who found pumpkin pie attractive. He was going to need all the help he could get.

When he got back to the room, Moses was gone. Claire was sitting by Stick's bed, pretending to read a magazine.

"Moses wanted some doughnuts." Thumps held the bag out as a peace offering. "I got you a sandwich."

Claire didn't even look at him.

"Moses wanted the chocolate kind." He waited to see whether she was going to let him in. "He said they were for Stick."

"Go away." Claire sounded tired now, defeated.

"We have to talk."

She leaned back in the chair and shut the magazine on her lap. "About what?"

"Genesis Data Systems."

Claire sagged back in the chair, as if the weight of the last week was crushing her. "What do you want to know?"

"How did Genesis get the contract?"

"What do you mean?"

"Did you contact them? Or did they contact you?"

"They contacted us."

"Did they put in a bid?"

"Everybody did."

"How many firms bid on the contract?"

"Four."

"And Genesis tendered the lowest bid."

"Yes," said Claire, who was showing signs of annoyance. "Where is this going?"

"How much lower?"

"That's confidential."

"Damn it, Claire."

"Quite a bit."

"And the rest of the bids were closer to each other?"

"More or less."

Thumps set the bag on the bedside table. "Give these to Stick when he wakes up."

"Where are you going?"

"To tie off some loose ends," he said. "I'm sorry about Stick. I didn't mean for this to happen."

"I know." There were tears in Claire's eyes now. All the fight was gone. There was nothing left but sorrow.

Sheriff Hockney was in his office talking on the phone. He looked up and motioned Thumps to a seat.

"Yeah," he said, rolling his eyes, "I want everything." And he shook his head as he slid the phone back on its cradle.

"Problems?"

"Nothing that a little common sense wouldn't cure." Duke leaned on the desk. "I thought we were done talking."

"Just thought I'd stop by and say hello."

"Bullshit. What do you want to know?"

"You'll tell me?"

"I didn't say that," said the sheriff. "Maybe I will, and maybe I won't."

Thumps was beginning to think that Duke actually enjoyed this give-and-take. "I was just wondering how many people heard the shot."

"You mean when Chan killed himself?"

"Thirty-eight makes a fair amount of noise."

"That it does." Duke shuffled a couple of files and rearranged them on the desk.

"You mean no one heard the shot?"

"We haven't talked to everyone."

"The people on either side of Chan?"

"Young couple on their honeymoon." Duke pinched his nose as if he was going to sneeze. "They were in bed."

"And they didn't hear anything?"

"They were busy. The people on the other side were on a tour."

Thumps had heard that sex dulled a person's sense of smell, but he hadn't heard that it dulled hearing. "Seems odd," he said.

"Who knows. Maybe they were heavy moaners." Duke was smiling now. "Maybe they had already passed out from exertion."

"Works for me." Thumps shifted his weight. "And I suppose you checked the ..."

"Yes, we checked the pillows on the bed and the cushions on the sofa."

"Nothing?"

"No bullet holes, if that's what you mean." Hockney wrinkled his nose. "But you should have seen the shit we found in the sofa."

Thumps thought about his own sofa.

"Tourists are real pigs."

"Thanks, sheriff."

"That's it?"

"Like I said. I was just curious."

"You think I missed something?"

Thumps shrugged. "Don't see how."

"Andy's on suspension," said Duke. "In case you were curious about that, too."

"First piece of good news I've had all day."

"DreadfulWater," said Duke, "do everybody a favour and go back to the photography."

Thumps left his car parked in front of the sheriff's office and walked the six blocks to the old land titles building. He was betting that Beth would be in the basement, and his luck held.

"Thought you didn't like hanging out in my kitchen."

"I don't."

"I should start giving you a finder's fee."

"Not guilty."

"So what is it this time?"

There was a body bag on one of the tables. Thumps didn't have to ask who was inside.

"Have you looked at Chan yet?"

"He just checked in."

"I need a favour."

"You always need a favour." Beth looked at Thumps as if she hoped to find a clue on his face. "This is supposed to be a suicide."

"I know."

Beth walked to the table and unzipped the bag. "Looks like a suicide.

Angle's right." She turned Chan's head to one side. "Sheriff is as paranoid as you. Did you know that?"

"What do you mean?"

"He ordered the deluxe autopsy with the trimmings." She shone a small light at the entry hole. "Hello."

"What'd you find?"

Beth picked up a pair of tweezers and began probing behind Chan's ear. Thumps could feel the waves of nausea begin to roll up out of the depths. "This is curious."

She rinsed the tweezers in a small glass dish.

"I don't see anything."

"That's because you're not a coroner."

Thumps leaned over and squinted at the dish. Now that he was looking closely, he could see a little piece of something floating in the water. Beth carefully transferred the piece to a glass slide and slid everything under her microscope.

"Take a look."

Looking at the piece under the microscope didn't help. It was larger now and looked vaguely like pink Swiss cheese, but Thumps still had no idea what it was.

"It's the blood that makes it pink."

"How about giving me some choices, so I can guess."

"Sure," said Beth. "An elephant or a nuclear reactor."

"Is there a third choice?"

"Foam rubber."

"Sonofabitch."

"My thought exactly. I guess I better call the sheriff."

"The grand opening for Buffalo Mountain is tomorrow. Tell Duke I'll meet him there."

"You know what, DreadfulWater?" Beth tucked Chan back in the bag and zipped it up. "For a photographer, you're not a half-bad cop."

Twenty-Three

Freeway was curled up in a tight ball on her blanket on top of the radiator, and she didn't even look up when Thumps opened the door. By all rights, he should have been tired, but, strangely enough, he was hungry. The meat loaf at the hospital had been a disappointment, thin and soggy, with a taste that vaguely reminded him of wet cereal and ketchup.

"You hungry?"

If Freeway was hungry, she wasn't going to admit it. And she certainly wasn't going to ask.

"Suit yourself."

The refrigerator was bare. There were skinless chicken thighs and a nice strip loin in the freezer, but it was late and Thumps was in no mood for anything that involved preparation. That left popcorn. He threw a bag into the microwave, set the timer for three minutes, fourteen seconds, turned on the television, and stretched out on the couch.

When he awoke, the popcorn was still in the microwave, the television was still chatting away, Freeway hadn't moved from her blanket, and the morning sun was streaming in the living room windows. Somehow, he had misplaced the night.

Thumps checked the clock. Nine-fifteen. The grand opening ceremonies at Buffalo Mountain Resort were due to begin at four o'clock. Six hours and a bit to try to sort everything out. But if he was right and if he was lucky, everything would come to him.

The knock at the front door startled him. Apart from Floyd showing up in his living room and Stick showing up in his darkroom, Thumps couldn't remember the last time he had a visitor who knocked.

Claire was on the front porch, and she didn't look any better than she had at the hospital.

"He's okay," she said, trying to smile.

"Stick?"

"He woke up this morning."

"Great."

"And he was hungry." Claire didn't even try to wipe away the tears.

"So, he's going to be fine."

"Could you hold me?"

It was a little awkward, standing on his porch, holding a crying woman, and Thumps would have preferred if Claire could have held off until she got inside the house. But he had learned years ago that crying women don't want to move and that trying to move them was always a mistake. Not until they stopped crying.

"I'm all right." Claire gently pushed away. "I always feel better after a cry."

Thumps was not sure exactly how that worked. How could crying make you feel better? Crying always made him feel miserable.

"You know what I wanted to do when the doctor told me Stanley was going to be okay?"

"Celebrate?"

"I wanted to spank him."

It was a good idea, but Thumps couldn't imagine Stick draped over his mother's lap. "Let me know if you need any help."

"I'm sorry about last night." Claire put her hand on Thumps' chest. "About what I said."

"You were upset."

"I thought he was going to die."

Thumps could still remember clearly how he had felt when they found Anna and Callie on the beach. Claire had nothing to apologize for.

She tried to straighten her hair with her hands. "The grand opening for Buffalo Mountain is today. I have to get ready."

Thumps watched Claire walk back to her car. Stick had been lucky. He would probably never know how lucky he was. Anna and Callie hadn't been that fortunate. They hadn't been lucky at all.

As Thumps closed the door, he noticed a faint but unpleasant odour. At first, he thought it was the cat litter or something going bad in the garbage. So he was mildly irritated to discover the source of the smell. Not that it was his fault. The last few days had been lived on the run without a chance to change his clothes, and his body had simply caught up with him. Belatedly, he hoped that Claire had been too upset to notice.

The shower was wet and mostly hot, and Thumps stood under the spray until the water ran cold. Freeway was waiting for him as he stepped onto the bath mat.

"It's all yours."

Freeway didn't have to be told twice. She hopped into the tub and began licking around the drain.

"I'm going to brush my teeth," he told the cat so she could plan her day. "Then I'm going to dress."

Thumps pulled a pair of dark slacks out of the closet. He hadn't worn them in a while, and there was a line of dust where they had hung over the clothes hanger. He found a grey dress shirt that might been white at some point and a red tie that didn't match anything in particular. Claire hadn't mentioned any dress code. Then again, she hadn't invited him, either.

He got his gun and shoulder holster from the lock box. He hadn't carried in a long time, and the gun felt awkward hanging below his armpit. He slipped two quick loads into his jacket pocket, just in case things got out of hand.

By the time he pulled into the Shell station and filled the Volvo, it was eleven-thirty. By the time he got to Moses Blood's place, it was just after noon.

Moses was waiting for him. "Stanley is going to be okay."

"I heard."

"It was those chocolate doughnuts that did it."

"You find anything yet?"

"Not much," said Moses. "Worrying about Stanley took up most of my free time."

"I'll take whatever you've got."

"Come on," said Moses. "I'll show you."

Having been to the computer trailer the other night, Thumps half expected that he would be able to find his way back. But walking through the maze was even more confusing in the daylight. When they finally got to the door with the warning sign, Thumps had no clue where he was or how he had got there.

Moses eased himself into the chair in front of the large monitor. "Okay. Here we go."

For the next hour, Thumps watched the screen as Moses brought up everything he had found on Genesis Data Systems. Most of it was the sort of business garbage that Ora Mae had found. Year-end reports, business prospectuses, production goals, and earning potentials.

"Can we find out who owns Genesis?"

Moses began working his way through a series of newspaper articles and web sites. "Here it is," he said at last.

"And?"

"Another corporation."

"What?"

"Stanley told me that that's how everybody does business these days. They make up swell corporations so no one can find them."

"It's shell corporations."

"That's what we should have done when that Columbus guy showed up."

Genesis Data Systems was owned by a corporation called Laurent Industries, which was owned by another corporation called National Associates. National Associates was based in the Cayman Islands.

"Can you tell who owns National Associates?"

"Nope."

"What about the other casinos that Genesis Data Systems does business with?"

"Stanley says I have the magic touch." Moses worked the keyboard. "He says computers tell me things that they won't tell anyone else."

"Stick knows a lot about computers."

"Animals are the same way." Moses hit a key, and the information moving across the screen slowed down.

"Wait a minute."

Moses hit another key and the information on the screen came to a stop.

"That can't be right."

"Computers don't lie," said Moses. "Unless people tell them to lie."

"That's a list of their clients?"

"That's what it says."

"I'll be damned."

"Have you figured everything out?"

Thumps pushed back from the computers and ran several scenarios through his head until he found the one he liked best.

Then he turned to Moses. "Close enough."

"I guess it doesn't go away, even if you want it to." Moses was grinning as if he had just heard a good joke.

"What?"

"Feeling responsible."

It was four-thirty before Thumps got to the main gates of Buffalo Mountain Resort. Cooley was standing outside the guard shack looking positively regal. His uniform was clean and pressed, his shoes were polished, and his hair was loose so it could cascade down his back.

"You know what this is?" Cooley wiggled a clipboard in front of Thumps' face.

"Beats me."

"It's a list of important people. And if your name's not on the list, I'm not supposed to let you in." Cooley ran his finger down the list. "And, your name's not on the list."

"I have to get in."

Cooley stuck his head close to the window. "Hell, you're not even dressed for this party."

"Tuxedos?"

"Penguins all the way down." Cooley's face softened. "I'm sorry about Stick."

"He's going to be okay."

"No, I mean about thinking he killed Floyd."

"Why don't you stop off at the hospital and say hello."

Cooley thought about that for a moment. "Naw," he said. "Those places give me the creeps."

The opening ceremony was at the casino. The parking lot wasn't full, but there were more cars than Thumps had expected. Including a television van. Cooley had been right. Dress was formal.

Ora Mae and Beth caught him first.

"Honey," said Ora Mae, "you look like a pair of tennis shoes at a wedding."

"I didn't know it was formal."

"I think you look fine," said Beth.

"Yeah, he does," said Ora Mae, shaking her head, "if he's going to a barbecue."

"Have you seen Claire?"

Ora Mae reached out and straightened Thumps' collar. "So, what are you going to do now?"

"Maybe you should think about working as a private detective," said Beth. "You know, Kate Fansler, V.I. Warshawski, Jane Lawless."

" 'Course, you'd have to get up in the morning," said Ora Mae.

Thumps smiled. "Next time you find a body, call someone else."

Archie caught up with him next.

"Thumps! What a party!"

"Have you seen Claire?"

Archie turned and looked across the crowd. "Sure. She was here with her boyfriend."

"Boyfriend?"

"First it's Claire. Then it's Beth." Archie shrugged. "What did you expect?"

"Claire doesn't have a boyfriend."

"Guess what?"

"And Beth is not my girlfriend."

"I just got a first edition of Louis Owens' *Dark River*. Very hard to find." Archie ran his hand along the lapels of his tuxedo. "How do I look?"

"You look great."

"You want my advice?" said Archie. "Roses. And stop fooling around." Archie gestured off to the left. "I'll bet he bought her roses."

Claire was standing at the far side of the room with Sterling hanging onto her elbow as if she were a life raft. The man couldn't be drowning. This was his environment. A room full of rich and important people who might just be in the market for a little something in real estate.

Out of the corner of his eye, Thumps spotted Elliot Beaumont standing against the wall. Beaumont didn't look happy. He seemed nervous, his eyes constantly in motion, as though he were trying to find someone.

Decisions, decisions. Okay, Thumps said to himself, Claire first and then Beaumont.

"Thumps!" Sterling looked ready to explode with good cheer. Claire mouthed a silent, thank you.

"Hello, Sterling. Am I too late to get one of the condos?"

It was a mean thing to say, but Thumps was still a little tired and a little grumpy.

"They're a great investment," said Sterling as he shifted into sales mode. "We've had a lot of interest. They won't last long."

"Excuse us, Sterling," said Claire, not wanting to let the man get up a full head of steam. "Thumps and I have to discuss a business matter."

Sterling was not happy about losing his flotation device, and Claire had to peel his fingers off her arm.

"Thank you," she said, when they had cleared Sterling's range of hearing.

"What business do we have?"

"Rescuing me from Sterling," said Claire. "And what are you doing here?"

"I need your help."

She looked at him. "Am I going to like it?"

Thumps shook his head. "Chan didn't kill himself."

Claire took in a deep breath of air and held it.

"He was murdered. There was foam rubber in the wound. Someone used a pillow or a cushion to muffle the gunshot."

Claire turned away for a moment and when she turned back, Thumps could see her eyes. He wasn't sure whether he was looking at simple anger or rage. Just so long as Claire remembered that he was one of the good guys.

"What do you need?"

"Today's itinerary."

"The reception. A couple of speeches. A tour of the condos."

"Any gambling?"

"One bank of slots is up and running."

"What about the computer?"

"What about it?"

"Is there anything scheduled?"

Claire paused for a moment. "A full test of the system. They want to be sure everything works."

"I want to be there," said Thumps. "Can you arrange it?"

"What's wrong?"

"Maybe nothing." Thumps could feel Claire's eyes tearing strips of skin off the back of his neck. "Maybe something dangerous."

"Just knowing you is dangerous," said Claire.

"Who's conducting the test?" Claire looked over the crowd, but Thumps already knew who she was looking for. "Elliot Beaumont?"

"Yes."

"Anyone come with Beaumont?"

"I don't think so."

Thumps scanned the crowd one more time. "When's the test?"

Claire glanced at her watch. "Right about now."

"The sheriff's on his way. When he gets here, tell him where he can find me."

"I'm coming with you."

"No, you're not. Look, if I'm wrong, I'm going to look like an ass. If I'm right, there could be trouble. Either way, I don't want you there."

"Then you better come up with better reason than that."

"Stick."

"Stanley?"

"He's too young and arrogant to be left on his own."

Claire took a deep breath and let it out slowly. "Damn you, Dreadful-Water. I don't want you getting hurt, either."

"Photographers are a dime a dozen."

The computer complex was cool and dark. Elliot Beaumont was seated at the console by himself.

"How's it going, Elliot?"

Thumps' voice in the deep silence of the room caught Beaumont by surprise.

"God, you startled me."

"Sorry. Claire asked me to come by and monitor the test."

"Help yourself," said Beaumont. "But there's nothing much to see."

Thumps watched the screen as it went through some sort of routine. "What are you doing?"

Beaumont turned back to the screens. "Checking the transfer sequences for the casino and adjusting the sweep of the security cameras at the condos. Here, have a look." He pressed a couple of keys and over a dozen monitors lit up. "Stairwells, hallways, garage, everything safe and secure."

"Too bad they weren't working when Takashi was killed." Thumps leaned over Beaumont's shoulder. "What's a transfer sequence?"

"Actually it's the heart of our system. Do you know much about electronic banking?"

"Debit cards?"

"In a manner of speaking, yes. You see, nobody works with cash anymore. What I mean is, cash still exists, but most of it is moved electronically through large banks."

"Transfer sequences."

"Exactly. The money from the casino is deposited in one bank and then the funds are moved electronically wherever they need to go. To pay vendors. To pay employees."

"And the computer controls those transfers."

"Of course."

"Show me."

Beaumont's fingers danced across the keys. That's why the man's hands were so smooth, Thumps thought. The only work he did was with his fingertips.

"Every day at five o'clock, the computer deposits the day's receipts and, at the same time, makes the necessary transfers."

Thumps tried to keep the sarcasm out of his voice. "Why do you need a computer to do that?"

"It's complicated."

"Why not just take the money down to the bank?"

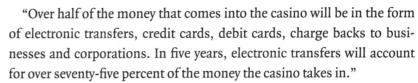

"Over half of the money that comes into the casino will be in the form of electronic transfers, credit cards, debit cards, charge backs to businesses and corporations. In five years, electronic transfers will account for over seventy-five percent of the money the casino takes in."

The time in the right-hand corner of the monitor said 4:59. "So, at five o'clock, the casino's money begins moving."

"In a manner of speaking," said Beaumont. "The transfers are actually drawn against the credit that the customer has at the bank. Let's say that the casino made a gross profit of a hundred thousand. That same day, that amount of money would be credited to the casino's account, and at the same time, the computer would generate the necessary transfers."

"What about the actual money?"

"That has to be deposited within twenty-four hours."

"Who keeps track of where the money goes?"

Beaumont looked amused. "Why the computer, of course." Suddenly the big monitor came to life and began rolling figures across the screen. "Here we go."

As Thumps watched, the computer ran through a series of numbers.

"Those are expenses," said Beaumont. "And those are profits."

"How can you have profits when the place isn't even open?"

"They're projected profits," said Beaumont. "We put in some numbers just to see how the system would function under actual working conditions."

The phone on the desk rang. In the quiet of the computer room, it sounded like a fire alarm going off. Beaumont cradled the phone against his shoulder.

"Yes?" he said, continuing to work the keyboard with one hand. "Yes, it's fine ... Perfect ... Mr. DreadfulWater is here ... To watch the test."

Beaumont handed Thumps the phone.

It was Traynor.

"Hi," she said, with an airiness that made Thumps think of palm trees and white sand beaches.

"Thought you were coming out for the grand opening."

"Elliot can manage on his own," said Traynor. "It's too nice a day to be indoors. Why don't you join me?"

"Where are you?"

"Headed for the golf course."

"I don't think I can."

"Six o'clock tee time. In case you change your mind," said Traynor. "Give me back to Elliot."

Thumps waited while Beaumont and Traynor finished their conversation.

"One of the perks of being the boss," said Beaumont as he hung up the phone. "If I were you, I'd go play golf."

"Who came up with the idea for the system?"

"The STS?"

"Yes."

"Daniel. He was a genius when it came to stuff like this."

"What about Chan?"

"George helped. But it was Daniel's project all the way."

Thumps took the disk out of his pocket and dropped it next to Beaumont. "So who killed Chan? You or Traynor?"

Beaumont turned in the chair. "What are you talking about?"

"Chan didn't commit suicide. He was murdered." Thumps wasn't sure what the man would do. Deny, bluff, run, attack. "It's about what's on this disk, isn't it?"

Beaumont leaned back in the chair. "Is this a joke?"

"It's no joke, Mr. Beaumont." Sheriff Duke Hockney was standing in the doorway with his gun drawn. "We found the cushion that was used to muffle the shot."

"Where?"

"In Mr. Beaumont's townhouse."

Thumps glanced at Beaumont. It was hard to tell whether the man was amused or annoyed.

"The sofas in Mr. Chan's condo and in Mr. Beaumont's are exactly the same. We didn't catch that the first time through."

Beaumont wasn't amused. "Bullshit! You've got nothing on me."

"You wouldn't believe how many times I've heard that one." Hockney brought his gun to eye level. "Put your hands on the table in front of you. You're under arrest for murder."

"This is ridiculous!" said Beaumont, working himself into a rage. "I don't have time for this!"

"You have the right to remain silent ..."

Thumps would have guessed that Elliot Beaumont was generally stiff and unemotional, but the man standing in front of him and waving his hands around was anything but that.

"You have the right to an attorney ..."

"And just what do you expect me to do with this?" Beaumont spread his arms and gestured toward the security camera screens and the computer monitor. "Just look at all this!"

Thumps wouldn't have believed the man could move that fast, but in the split second that the sheriff took his eyes off Beaumont to look at the monitors, Beaumont came off the table with a gun in his hand.

"Duke!"

The first shot hit the sheriff in the shoulder and knocked him down. With no lost motion, Beaumont swung back and found Thumps.

"Looks like we get to play cowboys and Indians again."

"You can't get away."

"Want to bet?" Beaumont reached down and picked up the sheriff's gun. "I shoot you with the sheriff's gun, and I shoot the sheriff with this gun and leave it on your body."

"No one is going to believe that."

"Probably not. But by then, none of us will care."

"I'll care." Cooley Small Elk stepped out of the shadows of the room, his rifle levelled at Beaumont. Beaumont blinked, but kept his gun pointed at Thumps' head.

"I'll shoot your friend," said Beaumont.

"He's not a good friend." Cooley shrugged. "Why, just the other day, he lied to me."

Thumps could see Beaumont thinking, calculating the odds. "Give it up, Elliot."

"All right," said Elliot. "Just don't shoot."

"Throw the gun away," said Cooley.

Beaumont let the gun swing from his finger by the trigger guard. Then he slowly turned the gun, butt first, and held it out for Cooley.

Cooley shook his head. "Don't do it."

But Beaumont was already committed. Even before he realized that Cooley hadn't lowered his rifle, Beaumont snapped the gun around with a twist of his wrist into a firing position.

The explosion from Cooley's rifle was deafening. Elliot grunted once and pitched backwards into the main monitor.

"You believe that?" said Cooley. "Everybody knows that move."

"Maybe he doesn't watch enough television." Thumps hurried to the sheriff's side.

"Jesus, that hurts." Duke lay sprawled against the wall. His left arm was hanging down as though it was broken.

"Lie still. I'll get an ambulance."

"Is he dead?" asked the sheriff.

Cooley walked over and poked Beaumont with his rifle. The man moaned softly, but didn't move.

"Nope," said Cooley. "He's still ticking."

"So, DreadfulWater, how come he didn't shoot you?" said Duke.

"He was too busy shooting you."

Hockney tried to shift his weight. "I suppose you figure you saved my life."

"No. Cooley did that," said Thumps. "Shut up and hold this against the wound."

"How'd you know it was Beaumont?"

"It was a guess."

Duke took a deep breath and grimaced. "You know, you're kind of a good-news, bad-news guy."

"You're not blaming me for getting shot?"

"That's the bad news."

"The fact that you're old and slow isn't my fault."

"You have any idea how much paperwork a cop has to do when he shoots someone?"

"You didn't shoot anyone."

"Yeah," said Duke, trying to smile through the pain. "That's the good news."

Cooley was standing beside Beaumont, making sure the man didn't get any more bad ideas.

"Thanks," said Thumps.

"I was only kidding about you not being a friend."

"I know."

"You know what?" said Cooley. "I like playing cowboys and Indians."

"Looks like you kicked a little cowboy butt."

"You got your camera?" said Cooley, a big smile on his face. "Maybe you can get a picture of me standing over the cowboy. My girlfriend would like that."

Now that, thought Thumps, was the best idea he had heard all week.

Twenty-Four

Thumps was sure that being shot was not high on Hockney's list of things to do, but being shot during a grand opening of luxury condominiums turned out to be a blessing. Excluding Beth, of the two-hundred-odd guests who were lounging in the casino looking wealthy, seven turned out to be doctors. Before the ambulance had even left the city limits of Chinook, three were attending the sheriff, who was not badly wounded, and four were looking after Beaumont, who was still alive.

Cooley, who had done most of the shooting, was standing off to one side, talking to guests and getting his picture taken.

Claire, who had not been shot, wasn't any happier than the sheriff. "Since I asked you to help, three people have been murdered, two people have been shot, and my son is in the hospital."

"Two people murdered," corrected Thumps. "Takashi was already dead."

The computer complex itself was now crowded with the curious, straining to see what a crime scene looked like. The tour had evidently been cancelled or at least postponed because Sterling Noseworthy, who should have been herding the rich through the condos, was instead standing by the door, unsure whether to come in or stay out. The man was on the verge of quivering, but there was no way to tell whether it was from fear or excitement.

"I have to go back into town," said Thumps.

"What about this?" said Claire, as if the mess was his fault.

"And you have company."

Claire didn't turn around. She searched Thumps' face, trying to catch a reflection off his eyes. "Don't leave me with Sterling."

"It's okay. He appears to have lost his raison d'être," said Thumps, pleased that he could still remember some of his university French.

"Shouldn't you be taking pictures?"

Beth was kneeling next to Duke, checking his wound. The sheriff was looking better now. His colour was back, and he was beginning to sound like his grumpy old self. "DreadfulWater," he said, trying to find a comfortable position against the wall, "you look remarkably spic and span."

"Remember." Thumps said with a smile. "I didn't get shot."

Beth shook her head. "I hope you boys are done having fun for the day."

Duke turned his head and gritted his teeth. "Beaumont going to live?"

"Maybe," said Beth. "If I leave you two alone, will you promise to be good?"

Duke watched Beth as she moved into the crowd of doctors standing around Beaumont. "Now there is a woman who could kick both our butts."

"I need a favour."

The sheriff looked as though he wanted to laugh. "You get me shot and now you want a favour?"

"I saved your life."

"Thought you said Cooley saved my life."

"We're related."

"Get out of here," said Duke. "Before I arrest you."

"For what?"

"Practice."

The ride back to town was exhilarating, partly because Thumps had the windows rolled down and partly because he kept his foot on the accelerator. He did slow down as he slipped into Chinook and out the other side, but as soon as he hit the edge of the city and open road again, he leaned into the Volvo and pushed it well over the speed limit.

And he didn't slow down until he hit the turnoff for Shadow Ranch.

• • •

The parking lot in front of the golf club was nearly empty. The rich, Thumps thought uncharitably, probably preferred to play in the morning so that the evening activities of dining and drinking wouldn't be interrupted or delayed. He parked his car in a reserved space next to the clubhouse. No one tows cars out of a golf course parking lot where the wealthy play. Not even twenty-year-old Volvos.

The man behind the desk was older than Thumps, which was a pleasant change from all the vacant and scrubbed faces he had had to endure on his other visits to Shadow Ranch.

"You must be DreadfulWater."

"Guilty."

"Ms. Traynor said you might show up."

"She tee off already?"

"About twenty minutes ago." The man turned and looked out the window. "She asked me to set up a cart for you, in case you showed up. You can probably catch her on number three."

Clouds were piling up against the mountains. The wind had shifted, and there was the smell of rain in the air. Thumps sat in the cart and considered the tables on the patio overlooking the eighteenth green. It had been a long day, and what he really wanted to do was find a comfortable spot, order a ham and brie sandwich with a Caesar salad, a large glass of lemonade, and a piece of cherry pie, and wait for Traynor to finish her round.

That's what a photographer would do.

Traynor was waiting for him on the fourth tee.

"Glad you could make it."

"The party was too exciting for me."

"Elliot didn't come with you?"

Beaumont wasn't going anywhere for a very long time. If he lived at all. The doctors had not been unanimous about his survival. He had lost a great deal of blood. The bullet had shattered a rib and punctured a lung.

"No," said Thumps. "He had some loose ends to tie up."

"I understand the computer system is working well."

"You're asking the wrong person."

"But I'm playing golf with the right person," said Traynor. "Why don't you take honours. I have to make a quick call."

Thumps fished a ball out of the bag and set it in the grass on a tee. The fairway in front of him was wide and rolling, with a fringe of trees on either side. The sun was behind him and low, and the shadows stretched down the fairway as if they were trying to reach the safety of the green in the distance.

His ball found one of the two fairway bunkers on the right. Traynor had walked off the tee with the phone to her ear. He wondered whether she was trying to reach Beaumont. He planned to tell her what had happened, but not yet, not until he had had a chance to unwind and enjoy the game.

"Sorry about that." Traynor took her driver out, set the ball in position, and drove it straight down the fairway. "Let's be sociable and take the one cart."

"Okay."

"They can pick the other one up later. So," she said, looking down the fairway, "where did you go?"

The shot out of the sand trap went right, and Thumps was left with a short chip out of heavy rough. Traynor's second shot found the green.

"I don't suppose you want to put a little money on each hole."

"I can't even afford to play here."

"It's the computer age," said Traynor. "How about we play for information?"

"Sure."

"Person who wins the hole gets to ask a question."

"About anything?"

"Why not?" said Traynor. "Neither of us could be that exciting."

Thumps' third shot was a delicate piece of work that wound up six feet from the hole. Traynor almost dropped her putt and tapped in for a par.

"If you miss this putt," she said, "I get first blood."

Thumps lined the putt up, stroked it clean, and watched it slide into the hole and lip out.

"Nice par," he said as they drove to the fifth tee. "What do you want to know?"

"The Obsidian Murders. Did you ever catch the killer?"

"No."

Traynor smiled. "'No' won't do."

"We found some physical evidence, and there were all sorts of theories about the placement of the bodies, but nothing ever fit."

"And then the killings stopped?"

"Yes. The killings stopped."

"And you left the police force shortly after that."

"I thought you only got one question," said Thumps.

"It is only one question," said Traynor. "Was the little girl your child?"

Thumps could feel his face turning to stone. This wasn't a game he wanted to play.

"If I'm being too personal," said Traynor, "just tell me."

"You're being too personal."

Traynor hooked her drive to the left edge of the fairway. Thumps hit a better drive and kept the ball on the short grass.

"Her name was Callie. She wasn't my daughter. I was friends with her mother."

"How long?"

"Three years."

"That's a long time."

Yes, Thumps thought to himself, three years was a lifetime.

He won the hole, dropping a twenty-five-foot putt. When they got to the sixth tee, Traynor held up her arms in surrender.

"Your turn to skin me alive."

"I don't know enough about you to do that."

Traynor's face softened. "I suspect you do. Did I thank you for saving my company?"

"I didn't save anything."

"Sure you did. I mean, it was messy, but it wasn't as bad as it could have been."

"It was worse." Thumps teed his ball up and turned to Traynor. "Where were you born?"

"Sacramento, California. I'm thirty-eight. But I don't look it."

"No, you don't."

"Is that really the question you wanted to ask?"

"Sacramento's a nice place."

The next two holes were played even. When they got to the ninth green, they were both lying two.

Traynor leaned on her putter and looked back toward the clubhouse. It was off in the distance, and all you could see was the roof and part of the parking lot. "Did you know that we are at the farthest point of the course? From here, if you walked quickly, it would take you fifteen minutes to get to the clubhouse."

"How about by golf cart?"

"Five minutes. More if you stayed on the cart path."

"Long course."

"And the ninth green is the largest green." Traynor marked her ball. "It's sixty feet by forty feet."

"Looks like you're away."

"Yes," said Traynor, "it certainly does."

Virginia's putt was a thirty-five footer, with a nasty right-to-left break. Thumps watched as she lined it up and stroked the ball into the centre of the hole.

Thumps' putt wasn't even close.

"My turn for another question."

"Fire away."

Traynor walked over to Thumps, touched his face, and kissed him. It wasn't the way Claire kissed him. This one was sad and tasted like regret.

"So," she said. "When did you figure everything out?"

"After Chan was killed."

"But you suspected earlier on."

"Too many things didn't make sense."

"Like what?"

"Friend of mine looked you up on the Internet."

"And?"

"It was odd that a computer company which works almost exclusively for large banks and investment houses was setting up a casino computer system for a small tribe in the middle of nowhere. And doing it for less than the going rate."

"We have a social conscience."

"Genesis Data Systems has never been in the casino business."

"Banking's a gamble."

Thumps shook his head. "You needed a test site. Somewhere to test a particular system without drawing any attention. The sequence transfers. That's it, isn't it?"

"Sounds like a 'B' movie." Traynor was smiling and playing with her hair, as if she had just been paid a compliment. "And what do you suppose these ... sequence transfers do?"

"They transfer money. From one bank to another."

"Very good."

"But yours does something else, doesn't it?"

"Does it?" She was enjoying herself.

Thumps slid his putter back in the bag. "The only reason for banks to exist is money. My guess is that your program, your sequence transfers, is going to allow you to help yourself to that money."

"An intriguing guess."

"But bank security is good. This is a one-shot deal, isn't it? And before you could risk triggering the system, you had to test it somewhere quiet and out of the way, in case it didn't work exactly as it was designed."

Traynor took off her glove, leaned her putter against the cart, and opened a pouch on her bag. "Takashi's death wasn't particularly quiet."

"Maybe Takashi found out about the system. Maybe he was in on it and wanted a bigger share. You want to tell me?"

"You don't need my help."

"I'd bet on his wanting a larger share. Chan kills Takashi and then has to kill Floyd when Floyd gets too close."

In the distance, Thumps could hear the sound of sirens.

Traynor half turned to look back at the clubhouse. "Is that the cavalry?"

"Sheriff sort of owed me a favour."

"Elliot?"

"He tried to kill the sheriff and me."

"Ah," said Traynor. "And that's why he's not able to join us."

"He's not dead. I expect he'll fill in the rest of the blanks."

"Blanks?"

"For instance, which banks are involved. How much you expected to make. Stuff like that."

"But you're not interested in that."

"To some degree," said Thumps. "But what I'm really curious about is who killed Chan. You or Beaumont?"

"Sorry," said Traynor. "You didn't win the hole."

She was still smiling, but now she also had a gun. And it was pointed at Thumps' chest.

"I'd like that disk, please."

"Why?"

"A souvenir, if you like."

Thumps looked back at the clubhouse.

"They won't get here in time," said Traynor. "Right now, they're trying to decide what to do. The club won't let them bring their cars on the course. It will be at least fifteen minutes before they organize themselves in golf carts. Another five before they get here."

"Are you going to shoot me?" It was a stupid question. Thumps was quite sure that Traynor would shoot him if she felt like it.

"It's not part of my immediate plans."

He took the disk from his pocket and tossed it to her. "You going to make a run for it in a golf cart?"

Traynor laughed and pulled her hair out of her eyes. "A golf-cart chase through the woods. Intriguing, but not very practical."

"Then it looks as though you're going to get caught."

"That's what I like about you, Thumps. Ever the pessimist." She turned the cart off and took the key. "Ah, sounds like my ride is here."

Off in the distance, Thumps heard the faint hum of an engine. At first he thought that the club had let the police bring their cars onto the course. But as the sound came closer, he realized that it was coming from the wrong direction. It was coming from the forest.

"It's around a hundred million," said Traynor. "And you're already too late to stop it."

The helicopter came sliding over the tops of the trees like an airborne shark. The downdraft caught Thumps and knocked him off balance. Virginia waited at the edge of the green, while the helicopter landed and a door was opened.

"I still want to see some of your photographs," she shouted as she climbed into the helicopter.

"Stop by next time you're in town," shouted Thumps, but he was sure she couldn't hear him over the thump, thump, thump of the rotor.

Traynor had been right. The police cars were still parked at the clubhouse and there was no sign of the law, mounted on golf carts, galloping down the hill to the rescue.

Thumps watched the helicopter rise into the evening air and head south. He watched it until it disappeared. Then he took out his putter and practised the putt he had missed until the police arrived.

Twenty-Five

Thumps spent the next three hours in the Shadow Ranch clubhouse explaining the plot to the police until they got it straight. A call had gone out within thirty minutes of Virginia's escape, but Thumps doubted that anyone was going to find the helicopter in time to keep her from going where she wanted to go. More than likely, she had timed everything so that she would be out of the sky by the time the police were airborne.

"We may want to talk to you some more," one of the deputies told him.

"Sure."

"So, don't leave town."

Thumps would have liked to have finished the back nine, but it was almost dark now, and he wanted to get to the hospital before visiting hours were over.

"You need me anymore?"

"You're sure she was headed south?"

Thumps could have said she was headed west or north or east with the same chance of being right. Once Traynor was out of sight, she could have changed directions at will. Thumps guessed the phone call that she had made on the golf course was to bring the helicopter in. Had she realized she was in jeopardy as soon as he showed up? That must have been it. And then she had played six holes of golf while she waited for her ride to arrive.

For the sake of law enforcement, Thumps told himself, it was probably a good thing that most of the criminals in the world were men.

. . .

Stick was sitting up watching television. Claire was reading a magazine. If it hadn't been a hospital room, the whole scene would have looked domestic.

"Hey, Thumps," said Stick. "Mom says you shot some dude."

"Cooley shot him."

"Mom's kind of pissed that you got me shot."

"I didn't get you shot."

"I told her that, but she's still mad."

Claire didn't look up from her magazine. "When you two are done, let me know."

"How you feeling?"

"It hurts like hell," said Stick. "I may sue that bastard."

Claire put the magazine down. "Sheriff Hockney is just down the hall. He wants you to stop in when you get the chance."

"He probably wants to bawl me out for not catching Traynor."

"I can't believe she was behind the murders," said Claire.

"Anybody buy any of the condos?"

"You won't believe it," said Stick. "Ora Mae sold fifteen of the expensive ones."

"Before or after the shootout?"

Stick's face lit up with a big grin. "After," he said.

"It's not all good news," said Claire. "Now we have to find another computer firm. It's going to set the project back at least two months."

"Hell," said Stick, "that's not bad news."

"What did she want?" asked Claire. "Why did she choose this reserve?"

"I'll explain everything when we have more time."

"You mean like late at night?" said Stick. "Like in bed?"

Problematic though it was, Thumps liked Stick better on death's doorstep. Thumps looked at Claire. "How much longer does he have to stay in the hospital?"

"At least four days."

"What are you doing tomorrow night?"

"Hey," said Stick. "Knock it off."

"Nothing," said Claire. "Nothing at all."

"What are you doing right now?"

Claire smiled. "Why?"

"We could practise for tomorrow night."

"You guys are sick," said Stick, and he turned up the volume on the television.

Duke was lying in bed, but he wasn't asleep. "Hey," he said. "Hear you've been causing trouble again."

"That seems to be his calling in life," said Claire.

"How come you let her get away?"

"She had a gun."

"So did Beaumont."

"Thanks for sending the backup."

"For all the good it did," said the sheriff. "How the hell did you know it was Traynor?"

"Beaumont might not have been the sharpest needle in the haystack, but he wasn't stupid enough to leave the cushion that was used to muffle the gunshot in his townhouse."

"Man," said the sheriff, "that is one cold woman."

No, Thumps thought to himself, just smart.

"By the way," said Hockney, "you making a living from your photography yet?"

"Hand over fist," said Thumps.

"'Cause if you get tired of staring at mountains and rivers, there may be a deputy's job open."

"My darkroom's safer."

"Suit yourself," said the sheriff. "I hear Clarence Fellows is looking for a new position, too."

The cafeteria was closed, and the coffee machine in the hall was broken. The perfect end to the perfect week. Thumps and Claire walked outside and let the cool night air wash over them.

"I know where we can get coffee," said Thumps.

"When did you learn to boil water?"

"I'm a good cook."

"Let's stick with coffee," said Claire.

Overhead, the sky was black and bright. And for a moment, in spite of his best efforts, he was on that beach in California where Anna and Callie had been found, lying in sand and starlight.

"You okay?"

"Yeah."

Thumps looked up at the night canopy one last time. Somewhere under those stars, Virginia Traynor was winging her way to a fortune in stolen money. And somewhere a serial killer was walking the beaches of a distant coast, looking for his next victim.

"You think Traynor will get away with it?"

"Maybe."

And somewhere under those same stars, Thumps DreadfulWater would be waiting.